**Praise for Heather Blake's
Wishcraft Mystery Series**

It Takes a Witch

"Heather Blake has created an enchanting and thoroughly likable slueth."
—*New York Times* bestselling author Denise Swanson

"Sparkling dialogue, colorful characters, and a clever plot!" —Casey Daniels, author of *Wild, Wild Death*

"Blake successfully blends crime, magic, romance, and self-discovery in her lively debut.... Fans of paranormal cozies will look forward to the sequel."
—*Publishers Weekly*

"Wow! Ms. Blake has taken the paranormal mystery to a whole new fun yet intriguing level. . . . This story is . . . mysterious, whimsical, delightful. . . . Heather Blake makes it *work*!" —Once Upon a Romance

"Heather Blake has created a wonderful new spin on witches in Salem that is both lighthearted and serious. An all-around wonderful read." —The Hive

"Heather Blake casts a spell on her audience."
—The Mystery Gazette

"A good quick, breezy read."
—Pagan Newswire Collective

Also by Heather Blake

It Takes a Witch

A Witch Before Dying

A WISHCRAFT MYSTERY

HEATHER BLAKE

AN OBSIDIAN MYSTERY

OBSIDIAN
Published by New American Library, a division of
Penguin Group (USA) Inc., 375 Hudson Street,
New York, New York 10014, USA
Penguin Group (Canada), 90 Eglinton Avenue East, Suite 700, Toronto,
Ontario M4P 2Y3, Canada (a division of Pearson Penguin Canada Inc.)
Penguin Books Ltd., 80 Strand, London WC2R 0RL, England
Penguin Ireland, 25 St. Stephen's Green, Dublin 2,
Ireland (a division of Penguin Books Ltd.)
Penguin Group (Australia), 250 Camberwell Road, Camberwell, Victoria 3124,
Australia (a division of Pearson Australia Group Pty. Ltd.)
Penguin Books India Pvt. Ltd., 11 Community Centre, Panchsheel Park,
New Delhi - 110 017, India
Penguin Group (NZ), 67 Apollo Drive, Rosedale, Auckland 0632,
New Zealand (a division of Pearson New Zealand Ltd.)
Penguin Books (South Africa) (Pty.) Ltd., 24 Sturdee Avenue,
Rosebank, Johannesburg 2196, South Africa

Penguin Books Ltd., Registered Offices:
80 Strand, London WC2R 0RL, England

First published by Obsidian, an imprint of New American Library,
a division of Penguin Group (USA) Inc.

First Printing, August 2012
10 9 8 7 6 5 4 3 2 1

PUBLISHER'S NOTE
This is a work of fiction. Names, characters, places, and incidents either are the
product of the author's imagination or are used fictitiously, and any resemblance
to actual persons, living or dead, business establishments, events, or locales is
entirely coincidental.
  The publisher does not have any control over and does not assume any responsibility for author or third-party Web sites or their content.

ALWAYS LEARNING   PEARSON

For my family, who brings the magic to my life.
With much love.

ACKNOWLEDGMENTS

Every one of my books has come about with the help of many. A big thank-you to my agent, Jessica Faust; my editor, Sandy Harding; everyone at Obsidian and the Penguin Group, from copy editors to marketing; and to my very talented cover artist, Bella Pilar.

In my books, every once in a while I exert a bit of fictional license, and for those of you familiar with Massachusetts law enforcement, you'll see exactly where I did in this series. In Massachusetts, only a couple of cities have homicides investigated by local police—in all other areas, those cases are handled by the state police. The presence of the state police in this book doesn't quite work for my fictional little village, so I took a few creative liberties with how crimes are investigated.

I also want to thank some of my readers for their creativity. On Facebook, I put out a call for naming the fictional rock and mineral show in this book. I had so much fun choosing options. I ended up choosing Merry Lu Pasley's entry for the Roving Stones, but I also included options from Kris Fletcher (Hot Rocks) and Nikki Bonanni (Gold Diggers and Natural Elements). Without a doubt, I have the best readers in the world.

I'm very grateful to my friend, the wonderful Lori Gondelman, book blogger and reviewer extraordinaire, for everything she does to support me and my writing. From reading early drafts to book tours to giveaways and online promotion—I can't thank you enough. If you haven't checked out Lori's blog, you should: www.loris readingcorner.com.

Last but not least, I need to thank Shelley, Cathy, Hilda, Tonya, and Sharon. Couldn't do this without all of you. Lots of love.

Chapter One

"It's going to be a horrible job, Darcy."

Elodie Keaton's voice was loud, clear, and completely distraught. If I'd known what was ahead for me, I would have listened to that warning. But unfortunately, that morning I was too distracted to heed anything as I met with Elodie, As You Wish's newest client, at her shop, the Charmory.

I was so enchanted by my surroundings, it was easy to say, "I'm sure the job's not that bad."

I'm not much of a glitzy-glam person, but even I was charmed inside the Charmory as I stood in the midst of bright, shiny, sparkling, colorful bliss. Everywhere I looked there were gems of various cuts and hues. In fanciful glass cases, handcrafted loose beads waited to be strung into custom bracelets and necklaces. Displays held vintage jewelry including pendants, charms, talismans, and amulets. Whimsical cases contained tableaus of stunning natural stones and minerals of various sizes, shapes, and colors. Like a magpie, I wanted to pick everything up and bring it home.

As You Wish, my aunt Ve's personal concierge service, had received a phone call from Elodie this morning, wanting to hire the company to help clean out a cluttered house. My sister, Harper, was no longer an

employee and Aunt Ve was currently bedridden with a
summer flu, so tackling this job fell to me. And as I was
desperate to escape Ve's germs, I'd volunteered to walk
over to Elodie's shop right away to talk with her about
the details.

It was a short walk. The Charmory was just a block
away from As You Wish, where I worked and lived with
Ve. Both businesses were located in the Enchanted Village, a themed neighborhood of Salem, Massachusetts.
The village was a tourist hotspot for those who came to
see for themselves if the village slogan of "Where Magic
Lives" was true.

It was, not that mortals knew it. The Enchanted Village offered a safe haven to hundreds of witches, or as
we called ourselves, Crafters. Here we hid in plain sight
among the mortals with whom we lived and worked.

There were many types of Crafters, such as Curecrafters (healing witches), Vaporcrafters (who had the ability
to vaporize in thin air), Cloakcrafters (master clothiers),
and even several like me; my sister, Harper; and Aunt Ve:
Wishcrafters, witches who could grant wishes using a
special spell.

And, as I'd come to find out, Elodie was a Wishcrafter,
too.

Well, partly. Elodie was technically a Cross-Crafter (a
Crafter hybrid). Elodie's wish-granting abilities, inherited from her father, were practically nonexistent. Her
predominant Craft was Geocrafting—her mother's Craft.
Rarely were a Cross-Crafter's abilities split equally—
one gift was always stronger than the other.

Everywhere I looked inside the shop, a bauble or
glitzy trinket caught my eye. Elodie's Geocrafting skills
with clay, gemstones, rocks, and minerals were obvious.
Tiny price tags hung from ribbons. Some of the merchandise was quite affordable, and some was out-of-this-
world expensive. Undoubtedly there was something in

this store that would appeal to everyone—tourist, villager, mortal, or Crafter.

A frown pulled on the corners of Elodie's mouth. "Not bad?" She echoed my words. "No, Darcy, not *bad*. It's *worse*. Much, much worse."

Her tone was starting to make me nervous. "How much worse?"

Short and thin with shoulder-length curly blond hair, a long narrow face, wide-set blue eyes, and a shy but somewhat sad smile, Elodie was younger than me. I placed her to be more my sister Harper's age—early to mid-twenties. Fairly young to own her own shop—just like Harper, who'd recently taken over Spellbound Books. Tapping the countertop that separated us with short fingernails painted a sparkly blue, she said, "Have you ever seen that TV show about people who hoard?"

I had seen it. And immediately afterward started cleaning and throwing clutter away. "This is your house you're talking about?" She didn't look the type to live in squalor.

Crystals hung in the big bay window overlooking the village green, and every time the sun peeked out from behind fluffy white clouds, rainbows streaked across the room, spilling color on the already vibrant collection of goods in the shop.

"No," she said. "Well, maybe." Then she looked at me, her eyes pained. "I don't know."

"If it's your house?" Seemed like a fairly straightforward question.

"Technically, it belongs to my mother, Patrice, as does this shop, but I've been taking care of both." Her forehead wrinkled slightly and her voice dropped. "Mom's been missing for a year and a half, and there's just not enough money to keep up payments on both places. I'm going to have to sell her house."

I didn't know much about Patrice Keaton's disappearance. Only what Aunt Ve, in her feverish state this morning, had told me: Patrice had vanished without a trace.

"Can you do that?" I asked.

"As her trustee, I can. I don't want to, but I can't see any other option. I don't have enough savings to pay her bills and mine."

I had many questions, mostly about her mother and the circumstances surrounding her disappearance, but I didn't think now was the right time to ask them. "Are you living there, in your mother's house?"

She shuddered and dragged a finger along the glass countertop, leaving behind a smudgy streak. "No. It's really not livable. My fiancé, Connor, and I live here—upstairs."

Village shops were either side-by-side shared storefronts or detached homes that doubled as businesses. As You Wish was in a gorgeous Victorian on a large corner lot at the west end of the square. The Charmory was also a Victorian. Though it was much smaller than Ve's place, it had a similar footprint. On the first floor was a front parlor, a wide hallway leading to a private office space, and a small powder room. In the back of the house would be a big kitchen and family room. Upstairs, there were probably only two bedrooms (instead of Ve's three)—plenty of room for two people.

I noticed Elodie wore only a modest diamond engagement ring—surprising, since I thought a Geocrafter would have an outrageous stone. And now that I was looking, I saw that she didn't wear any other jewelry. Not even a dainty pair of earrings. I wasn't a big jewelry-wearer either, but if I was surrounded by all these crystals and beads every day, I'd be tempted.

"In order to sell Mom's house," she was saying, "it needs to be cleaned out. Really cleaned out. I can't hire just anyone. Mom didn't collect just junk. She also collected treasures. Her house is full of them, mixed in between twenty-year-old newspapers, cardboard boxes filled with flea market finds, and even some wedding presents that were never opened."

A feeling of dread took root in my stomach. "When was her wedding?"

"Nineteen eighty-five."

I gulped. What was I in for?

Elodie's mention of a wedding suddenly reminded me of my aunt Ve, who'd recently become engaged to potential husband number five, Sylar Dewitt. After two months, I still wasn't sure how I felt about the upcoming nuptials, mostly because I didn't have a good feeling about it. The wedding was this coming Sunday. And unfortunately, Ve had come down with a nasty virus. One that had terrible timing—as there was no wedding planner and she was the one in charge of the preparations for the ceremony and reception. Preparations that now fell on me to complete since Sylar was too busy running his optometry office . . . and the whole village (he was the village council chairman). First up for me as Darcy Merriweather, wedding planner, was a menu tasting later today. Then I had to try and figure out why there was a surprising lack of RSVPs coming in.

"My dad tried to keep her collecting in check," Elodie said. "But after he died, my mother's hoarding escalated. I was talking to Mrs. Pennywhistle the other day, when she was in here shopping, and she gave you the highest of recommendations. I need someone I can trust. Someone who's not going to find an uncut gem amid the trash and stick it in a pocket."

Mrs. Pennywhistle, or as most everyone called her, Mrs. P, was the village's geriatric spitfire. I'd helped her clean out her late granddaughter's apartment a couple of months ago. Since then Mrs. P had become like family.

"Can I trust you?" Elodie asked me.

For some strange reason I had a feeling she was asking about something beyond nicking a few trinkets. It made me nervous, which immediately gave me second thoughts about saying, "Absolutely."

"Then you'll take on this task?" Her hands gripped the edge of the counter, and her blue gaze fixed upon me. She stared, unblinking.

Suddenly she seemed anxious, and a little bit desperate. Which made me *really* nervous. Was there something she wasn't telling me?

Traces of panic lined her eyes. "Darcy?"

Cleaning a hoarder's house sounded like a nightmare, but I had little choice. "As You Wish's motto is that no request is too big or too small and no job impossible. I'll do it."

I didn't break my word ever. So now that I had given it, I was all in on this job, for better or worse.

She smiled her sad smile and tucked a blond curl behind her ear. "You might come to regret that motto, especially after seeing the house."

I gazed at her. "Are you *trying* to scare me?"

"Just giving you fair warning."

I ignored the growing pit in my stomach and tried to keep the conversation light. "You do know we charge by the hour, right?"

She laughed. "You'll earn every penny, Darcy. Every penny."

Chapter Two

I left the shop with a promise to meet with Elodie at Patrice's house later that afternoon for a quick look-see. I had to gauge for myself what I was getting into so I could plan ahead. I was a planner—I couldn't help myself.

For August, it was a relatively mild day, not too hot or humid. A slight breeze rustled the colorful awnings above village storefronts. It was almost noon, and the shops were already full of tourists. Adding to the usual hustle and bustle were the Roving Stones. The popular traveling rock and mineral fair was camped on the village green for the week. Multiple matching crimson tents dotted the landscape, flaps raised to show off gems, fossils, minerals, rocks, and hand-crafted jewelry. It looked a little bit like a flea market setup to me, but the Roving Stones certainly didn't sell their wares at flea market prices. I had bought a gorgeous—but pricey— pair of obsidian earrings from a vendor to give to Harper for Christmas.

If she knew, she'd surely tease me about buying Christmas presents in August. But in my opinion, the earlier I started shopping, the better. Harper, on the other hand, preferred the mad dash of buying everything on Christmas Eve. Not because she was a procrastinator, but because she loved the thrill of a whirlwind shopping trip. Since I'd been her mother figure from the day she was born (which, sadly, was also the day our mother died), sometimes I questioned where I'd gone wrong raising her. I wasn't at all sure where Harper had gotten her adventuresome nature—it surely wasn't from me, though sometimes I wished I was a little more spontaneous. Considering I couldn't grant my own wishes (a pesky Wishcraft Law), I was trying my best to make the change on my own. It wasn't happening easily.

I spotted my friend and fellow Wishcrafter Starla Sullivan in the crowd on the green, her blond ponytail swaying as she snapped pictures. Owner of Hocus-Pocus Photography, she padded her bottom line by selling candid snapshots of village visitors. She had her dog, Twink, with her, a little bichon frise that Evan, Starla's twin brother, liked to call the Beast. The dog hopped more than walked, and lapped up the attention of the tourists who *ooh*ed and *aah*ed over him.

Walking quickly, I turned my attention to my next destination—the Sorcerer's Stove, a local family restaurant. I had a noontime appointment for a final taste test of Aunt Ve's wedding menu, and I was running late.

The restaurant anchored the north end of the square, and its architecture was a village favorite. With its multi-gabled and steep-pitched rooflines covered in faux thatching, diamond-paned windows, stone facing, central chimney, and board-and-batten door, it really looked as though a sorcerer lived there. Fitting, since the people who dined on Foodcrafter Jonathan Wilkens's food often claimed, appropriately, that he was a culinary wizard. His talent of combining casual dining and gourmet foods had once made his restaurant a hotspot.

Ve had told me that the Stove had fallen on some hard times over the last couple of years. She didn't go into details but said there had been a rodent problem and several outbreaks of food poisoning, including one as recent as last week.

When I questioned why on earth Ve would use them to cater the wedding, she smiled. "I believe in second chances, Darcy dear. Don't you?"

I did, but food poisoning? I wasn't sure it was a risk I would take and told Ve so. "We Crafters have to support one another. I have faith in Jonathan. This is but a mere bump in his road."

I was going to have to trust her on this one.

Something smelled wonderful as I neared, and it helped assuage my doubts. Food that smelled so good couldn't possibly give me food poisoning. Or at least that's what I told myself so I'd actually eat the tasting menu.

When I pulled open the door, I saw that the restaurant was almost empty. The delicious, savory scents hadn't enticed tourists or villagers to come inside. It was lunchtime, and the restaurant should have been packed. It was sad to see both large dining rooms full of empty chairs. I gave my name to the hostess and told her why I was there.

While I waited in the small vestibule near the front door, I read the "local notices" bulletin board. Tacked to the board was a flyer about the Roving Stones Fair. I wondered if Elodie, as a Geocrafter, was involved in the show somehow. Seemed like a great place to buy some stock for her shop—and to market her merchandise.

Then my sights landed on a notice from the Sorcerer's Stove that they were holding a series of cooking classes, twice a week for six weeks. I checked the dates. The first lesson started tomorrow night and was touted as a culinary boot camp, designed to turn even those who had trouble boiling water into gourmet chefs.

"Are you interested in signing up for the class, Darcy?"

I turned and found the Stove's owner, Jonathan Wilkens, standing behind me. He was tall and thin, with silver-streaked hair and slightly cloudy brown eyes. He gave me a peck on the cheek and added, "There are a few openings left."

It seemed like fate. I'd always wanted to take cooking classes. But the timing of these particular classes wasn't great. I was busy at As You Wish and with Ve's upcoming wedding. Plus I was helping Harper with the bookshop and redecorating her new apartment. Then there was the whole food poisoning thing.

But hadn't I just been thinking about spontaneity? Because it was hard to say no to fate, I said, "Sign me up." I'd make it work. The classes were at night, so they had the added perk of distracting me from the fact that I was going home to an empty bed. My divorce had been finalized over two years ago, but certain things persisted in reminding me that I was single. Like that queen-sized Serta.

My thoughts suddenly shifted to single dad Nick Sawyer, whom I'd met shortly after moving to the village. There was something happening between us, but it was happening slowly. Which was okay with me. The last thing I wanted was another broken heart.

"Wonderful!" Jonathan enthused.

The wrinkles around his eyes multiplied as he smiled, but I noticed that he looked tired, wan. His thinness now seemed more like gauntness. I hoped he wasn't coming down with the same flu as Ve.

"Now, what's this about your aunt?" he asked. "She called and told me to expect you in her place."

I explained about the flu and finished with, "I'm sure she'll be just fine by this weekend." I knew she would. She was expecting a house call today from Cherise Goodwin, an old friend who also happened to be a Cure-crafter, a healing witch.

"Bad timing," Jonathan said as he led me slowly through the restaurant.

As we walked, I spotted Vincent Paxton across the room, eating alone at a corner table. A few months ago, he'd been a murder suspect. Now he was the owner of Lotions and Potions. He was also a Seeker—a mortal who wanted to become a Crafter. He was fixated with the Craft, wanting to learn anything and everything. I was fully aware that his level of obsession could be dangerous. How far would he go to uncover our secrets? How much, I wondered, did he already know?

After all that had happened with that murder case, I wasn't sure if we were friends or foes. But as he caught my gaze, he tentatively raised his hand in a friendly wave.

Caught off guard, I hesitated slightly before returning the wave. He smiled as if relieved and went back to his burger.

I almost walked into a table, wondering what I had just done. Did I want to be friends with a Seeker? Wasn't that just asking for trouble? I hurried to catch up to Jonathan as he clumsily wended his way through the maze of tables—I was glad I wasn't the only one who lacked grace. The silver in his hair glistened under hanging lanterns, and I placed him somewhere in his early sixties.

I saw village lawyer Marcus Debrowski sitting alone at the bar as Jonathan pulled out a chair for me at a little table tucked into a corner reserved for tastings. Marcus smiled when he saw me and hopped off his stool to come say hello.

"Will you be joining Darcy for the tasting?" Jonathan asked him after shaking hands. "There's plenty."

Marcus lifted an eyebrow and looked at me. "Will I?"

Smiling, I said, "You will."

Jonathan said, "Zoey will be out in a moment with your starters."

Zoey Wilkens had been Jonathan's executive chef—

and wife—for almost two years now. There were mum-
blings in the village that she'd been granted the executive
chef title only because she'd married Jonathan, but I'd
tasted her food. She was a talented chef in her own right.

As Marcus sat, he said, "What are we tasting?"

Marcus was a Lawcrafter, and in his late twenties was
already the best lawyer in the village. He had represented Ve's fiancé, Sylar, a couple of months ago when
Sylar had been accused of murder. Thankfully, he'd been
cleared of that crime.

The scents in the air had my stomach rumbling. Sau-
téing garlic and onions, something else that hinted of
spice. "Ve's wedding menu. I'm glad you're here, especially since I don't like fish, and half of Ve's menu is
seafood."

With Marcus's dark brown hair, inquisitive light green
eyes, and slim build, he looked a lot like your average
lawyer next door. He was buttoned-up, slicked back,
smooth, and suave. He gave me a mock-serious smile.
"So you're using me?"

"Definitely."

"I'm okay with that. Seafood is my favorite." He took
off his suit coat and placed his napkin in his lap. "How
come Ve's not testing her own menu?"

I explained about the flu.

"Bad timing," he said.

I smiled. The statement seemed to be a general con-
sensus.

He sipped from a multifaceted water goblet and said,
"Will Ve and Sylar postpone the wedding until she's
well?"

"They're trying not to. Cherise Goodwin is coming by
today to see Ve."

"Ah," he said, understanding immediately. "Under
Cherise's care, Ve will be on her feet in no time."

We were dancing around the fact that Cherise was a

Crafter. The Craft wasn't something we often talked about aloud. Too dangerous. If a mortal overheard, we would be in danger of losing our powers. Not that there was anyone around, but a Crafter could never be too careful.

"Did you send in your RSVP for the wedding?" I asked. "Because if not, I'm tasked to track you down and find out if you're coming. Ve's orders."

He laughed and put his hands in the air in surrender. "Sent mine in last week."

I wondered if he was bringing a date. He'd had his sights set on Harper for the past couple of months, but she wasn't showing much interest. For shame. He was a nice guy. And exactly what she needed in her life. Her last boyfriend, a state policeman, had fizzled before a relationship even began when he revealed that he'd never read *To Kill a Mockingbird*. There wasn't a worse sin in Harper's mind. She was currently single and looking, and I wished she would look Marcus's way.

Unfortunately, again, I couldn't grant my own wishes.

Zoey burst through the swinging doors next to us and set down a platter covered in appetizers.

I'd been taken aback the first time I met her. Only because of her age. She was mid-twenties at most, which was quite a big gap between her and Jonathan. She had a wonderful smile, and although she wasn't what most would consider conventionally pretty, I particularly liked her dozens of freckles, her blue-gray eyes, and her short, sassy light blond hairstyle. Her hooked nose and strong chin gave her face character, uniqueness. She pointed to the pear tartlet and said, "I hope you enjoy this one in particular. You'll be learning how to make it tomorrow night." She then rushed back through the swinging door, an energetic whirlwind in a white chef's coat.

Marcus raised his eyebrows at me. "You signed up for the cooking class, too?"

"I couldn't resist," I said, trying not to think of my mile-long to-do list and how I really didn't have the time to spare. Especially not if Patrice Keaton's house was as bad as Elodie was making it out to be.

"What do you know about the disappearance of Patrice Keaton?" I asked Marcus as I filled my plate with appetizers.

I was trying not to think about salmonella, E. coli, or Listeria when a stuffed apricot slipped from Marcus's fingers and landed with a splat on the table. His face had gone as pale as the crème fraîche on the salmon cucumber cups. "Where'd you hear that name?" he said softly, looking around as if afraid to be overheard.

I dropped my voice, too, just because he was making me so nervous. "Her daughter, Elodie, hired As You Wish to clean out Patrice's house. She's planning on selling it."

Letting out a deep breath, he said, "You may want to turn down the job."

What was with all the warnings? "What am I missing? What happened to Patrice?"

He looked around. "Stop saying her name!"

"You're freaking me out!" I could barely eat the tomato, bacon, and cheese crostini I was holding.

"You should be freaked."

"Why? What happened to her?"

"No one knows," he said.

"You're not telling me everything," I accused. "Spill it."

Again, he glanced around and lowered his voice. "Mortal version or Crafter?"

"Either. Both."

Leaning toward me, he motioned for me to meet him halfway. I bent my head in, and my dark hair fell forward onto the table. I swept it back before it touched the food.

"Mortal version is that the last anyone saw of her, she'd been here, at the Stove. She had a fight with her date and left, never to be seen again. Her purse was found at her house, along with her keys and cell phone. She simply vanished."

"Who was her boyfriend?"

He sighed. "Andreus Woodshall."

"I don't know him."

"Be glad."

It felt like part of the crostini had wedged in my throat. "Was he questioned?"

"Of course, but there was no evidence of any crime. It's hard to charge someone without evidence."

I put the crostini down. Between this news and the food poisoning worries, my stomach was rolling. "And the other version of what happened to her?" The Crafter version.

His light eyes held dark foreboding. "That the Anicula amulet led to her demise."

"The Anicula amulet?"

His Adam's apple bobbed. "It is a powerful, highly sought-after amulet that grants its owner—mortal or Crafter—unlimited wishes. It's kind of like Aladdin's lamp, only better, because there are no stipulations other than it is to be used for good, not evil."

Do no harm. It was the Crafting way of life.

"Rumor is that she had abused the powers of the amulet and was punished for it."

"Abused how?"

"Wishing harm," he said.

"On who?" I asked.

"I don't know. Rumors don't come with a deposition."

I frowned at him. "Did the rumors offer any speculation on the kind of harm?"

"No. It had to have been bad, though, as the Anicula

doesn't have many stipulations. You can pretty much wish for anything, even matters of love, life, and death."

I whispered, "Really?" Those things weren't possible for me, as a Wishcrafter. Some things were out of our hands. All Wishcrafters had to abide by certain laws and rules, the Wishcraft Laws, including the biggies of never revealing our power to mortals; not interfering with life and death; and the fact that we can't grant our own wishes—or the wishes of other Wishcrafters. Broken rules meant harsh consequences. I'd already been called before the Craft's Elder (who governed all the Craft laws) twice and reprimanded for infractions. I was hoping to stay on her good side for a while.

I used to be able to grant other Crafters' wishes immediately. But after the situation a few months ago where my powers had been somewhat abused by another Crafter, the Elder had created an amendment to the Wishcraft Law stating that no wishes would be granted to another Crafter without approval from the Elder.

Since the amendment, I'd yet to experience a wish from another Crafter, but the Elder had informed all Wishcrafters that she would somehow (magically, I assumed) hear the wish as it was made and either approve it immediately or summon the Crafter to discuss the wish at hand in more detail.

Marcus nodded solemnly. "Which is why the Anicula is the amulet coveted by Wishcrafters most of all."

I tipped my head. "I don't understand. Why Wishcrafters specifically?"

"Darcy, using the Anicula is the only way Wishcrafters can grant their own wishes."

I let that sink in—the gift, the potential repercussions.

Marcus said, "If the Anicula's owner is not pure of heart, or abuses the power"—he glanced around— "the owner becomes cursed."

It took me a second to get his meaning. "So you think an amulet is the reason behind Patrice's disappearance? What do you think happened to her exactly? I mean"—I poked a crab puff—"where is she?"

Beads of sweat formed along his hairline. "If you ask me, Darcy, she's as good as dead."

Chapter Three

Patrice Keaton's house stood at the end of Incantation Circle, near the Enchanted Trail, a path that circled around the village and twined through the Enchanted Woods. The house was a small Cape Cod with clapboard trim, its blue paint slightly faded, the window boxes full of blooming flowers, the lawn and landscape lovingly tended.

It didn't look like the house of someone who'd been missing for eighteen months.

I'd come by to see if Elodie's warnings held any weight, but as I looked around I had my doubts. The knot in my stomach loosened, unraveled. This job wasn't going to be so bad after all. The only hint that something might be off with this charming little house was the drawn drapes. What, exactly, lurked behind them? Was she really an extreme hoarder? Or had Elodie been exaggerating?

I'd have to wait to see, as Elodie hadn't arrived yet. I'd walked over to Patrice's with my dog, Miss Demeanor, better known as Missy. She was the product of a dog-snatching, one that had landed my sister, Harper, in lockup and charged with a misdemeanor herself. The judge had let her off easy since her actions had helped reveal illegal activity by the pet shop owners and uncovered the operations of a horrible puppy mill—which had been Harper's intent all along. When all was said and done (and fines paid), Missy had been ours to keep.

Missy was a Schnoodle, half mini schnauzer, half teacup poodle. She was quite small, even for being less than a year old. Her light gray and white curly coat was freshly trimmed and her dark eyes gleamed as she barked at an orange tabby that streaked by.

I glanced at my watch. Elodie was late. I strolled with Missy around the house and noticed that all the curtains had been pulled tight. An air-conditioner hummed loudly, and a white picket fence separated the yard from its only neighbor. The trees in the woods rustled in the breeze, their leaves a brilliant green against the blue sky. Squirrels scampered and birds flitted from branch to branch. It was a peaceful yard, a nature lover's retreat, and I felt myself relaxing even more.

A small deck extended from the back door, leading to a tidy flower garden and shed designed to match the house. The shed door was ajar, and I couldn't help but peek inside.

Hinges creaked loudly as I pulled the door fully open. Disbelieving, I kept blinking, hoping the image before me would change. It didn't. The entire space, except for a spot right near the door, was crammed with boxes. Floor to ceiling. Not so much as a dandelion fluff could fit between the cracks. Missy backed away from the door, using her leash to tug me along, toward the front of the house.

Goose bumps rose along my arms as we walked, and that knot was back, tight, twisting my stomach.

Was the house filled with that kind of clutter?

Standing on my tiptoes, I tried peeking through a side window, but the shade had been pulled all the way down. Someone didn't want people looking inside. If the interior looked anything like the shed, I could understand why.

When we reached the front yard, I was surprised to see a bright yellow village police car in the driveway.

And even more surprised to see who was leaning against its hood.

Nick Sawyer.

Missy started dancing, jigging back and forth. She yapped happily until I let her go, and she bounded over to Nick.

He bent down to rub under her chin, but she pulled away as though looking for someone else.

"Sorry, Mimi's not with me today," he said to the dog.

Mimi was Nick's twelve-year-old daughter, and Missy had taken an extreme liking to both of them.

Me too. Maybe a little too much. After my divorce, I'd sworn off men, but Nick had certainly dented the armor around my heart.

Confused, I looked at him and then at the yellow four-door MINI Cooper. "I thought you turned down the job offer?"

After the murder that occurred two months ago, it had become obvious that the village police force needed a complete overhaul. The police chief had been forced to retire and Sylar Dewitt, the village council chairman (or as Harper liked to call him, the grand hoo-ha), had offered Nick, a security expert and a former Rhode Island state trooper, the job.

"Sylar is persistent. He finally made me an offer I couldn't refuse. That"—he smiled—"and Mimi insisted."

I knew he'd had some concerns about taking the job and how it would affect his daughter. As a state trooper, he'd once been shot in the line of duty and his former wife, Melina, had demanded he quit his job in fear of him losing his life.

The sad irony of that situation didn't escape me. Not long after he retired from the state police, the two separated and divorced. Then she fell terminally ill with cancer and eventually passed away.

Missy suddenly growled low in her throat, nipped at his ankle, and then backed away from Nick. His eyebrows drew downward as he watched her saunter over to sniff at the front bushes. "What's wrong with her?"

"I don't know." It wasn't like her to be aggressive toward—or to walk away from—Nick. "We saw a cat earlier—maybe it's hiding in the shrubs. Or she didn't like your decision to join the police force." I wasn't too sure how I was feeling about it, either. "Mimi's not scared?" I asked. Because suddenly, as I looked at the gun at his hip and imagined it being used against him, I was terrified.

"I suspect she is. A little. But she said she knew how much I wanted to do it. She did give me a stern lecture on being careful, and then admitted it was hard to be too afraid when I was driving a tiny bright yellow car."

She had a point. The cars had also been part of the village police force overhaul. Nick was driving a yellow and black MINI Cooper emblazoned with the Enchanted Village logo (complete with the silhouette of a witch on a broomstick) that had been retrofit into a police car, complete with internal computer system and safety partition between the front and back seats. Sylar had deemed the new cars "tourist friendly." He believed the old, traditional police cruisers hurt the village's image by imbuing fear among visitors. The new cars proclaimed that there was no need for tourists to think any big bad wolves lived in the village. Though, as I had found out the hard way, sometimes they did.

But Sylar was right about the MINI Coopers being tourist friendly. No one was going to be fearful when they saw one monitoring the streets. And it was also his idea to buy four MINI Coopers in varying cuddly colors—

yellow, light blue, purple, pink. But the thought of hunky Nick behind the wheel of one made me smile. Big.

"What's so funny?" he asked.

I rocked on my heels and tried to tame my smile. "Nothing."

Sylar, as the grand hoo-ha, also believed starchy police uniforms were off-putting. Instead, the village police dress code consisted of khakis and either a short-sleeved polo shirt or a traditional button-down. Nick wore the former, and a shiny badge was clipped to his belt. I approved of Sylar's decision, though I wouldn't have minded seeing Nick in a real uniform.

There had been some talk in the village about the new changes and people taking them seriously. After all, a colorful MINI Cooper and casual-Friday clothing didn't exactly garner respect. But I wasn't worried about that. One look at Nick and people would know who was in charge. Especially when he wasn't pleased. Like right now.

A scowl deepened the lines around his mouth—and I had the feeling he knew what I was thinking about him and that car, which made me want to smile wider.

Nick was only thirty-five, but he had a weathered, lived-a-hard-life look about him. Maybe because when he was a state trooper, he'd been wounded in the line of duty. Maybe because when Melina got sick with pancreatic cancer he'd moved back in with her to help with her care. Maybe because he'd had to watch her die.

He'd become a single dad, the sole caretaker of his daughter, and the keeper of her biggest secret. Mimi was a Crafter, a Wishcrafter (her mom had been one), but Nick hadn't known which Craft until a couple of months ago.

I'd been working with Mimi since then—giving her Wishcraft lessons. I wasn't the most knowledgeable teacher (I was still learning the Craft myself), but we were doing pretty well.

"You aren't going to give up your woodworking, are

you?" He made beautiful handcrafted pieces for the village's souvenir shops and also for some of the finer furniture stores. It wasn't just a hobby of his, but something he was truly passionate about. It was his craft, his magic, even though he had no magical powers—just immense talent. He was once a mortal, but when he married Melina and she decided to tell him about the Craft (and by doing so, lost her magical abilities), by Craft law they both became Halfcrafters. Half mortal, half Crafter. A Halfcrafter had no powers, but was privy to all Craft history, laws, and bylaws in order to help parent any Craft children, because kids born to a Crafter and a mortal would have full Craft powers.

However, it's up to the child's parents whether to share the Craft secret with their kids. In my case, my mother and father had kept my and Harper's abilities a secret, and it wasn't until after my father died and Aunt Ve paid us a visit that we learned of our heritage. In Mimi's case, Nick and Melina had told her of the Craft, but she hadn't truly learned the extent of her gift until a few months ago.

"I can do both."

"Good." My gaze lingered on his strong hands, and I resisted the urge to reach out and hold one.

A beat passed. Two. Finally, I said, "What are you doing here, anyway?" Patrice Keaton lived on a cul-de-sac, so I knew he wasn't just passing by on patrol.

His brown eyes crinkled at the corners and the breeze ruffled his dark hair. "There was a report of suspicious activity at this address. I should have known you'd be involved. Ever since you moved here, where you go, trouble follows."

"Hardly," I protested. Though he had a point. I'd only lived in the Enchanted Village for a few months and had already been involved in a murder case and several break-ins, and identified a pickpocket. It had been fairly quiet in my world the last few weeks, however, and I wanted nothing more than to keep it that way.

He asked, "So what are you doing here? Besides acting suspiciously?"

I watched as Missy toddled over to a tall arborvitae and started sniffing for all she was worth. I wasn't worried about her wandering off. With Nick near, she wouldn't go far. "As You Wish was hired by Elodie Keaton to clean up her mom's house." I glanced over my shoulder at the house, then checked my watch. "I was supposed to meet Elodie here more than fifteen minutes ago, but it looks as though I may have been stood up."

His eyes glinted in the sun as he said, "I can't imagine anyone would stand you up."

My heartbeat kicked up a notch. "It wouldn't be the first time."

My flirting skills were seriously rusty. Luckily, I was saved from another of his flirtatious comments when a car pulled up in front of the house. I'd seen the man who came toward us around the village but hadn't met him and didn't know who he was.

He held out a hand to Nick and said, "Good to see you, Nick." He then glanced at me and said, "You must be Darcy. Elodie was caught up at the shop and sent me over. I'm Connor Merrick. Elodie's fiancé." He glanced at the Bumblebeemobile. "Is there a problem?"

Nick folded his arms across his chest. "Someone called in suspicious activity."

Connor rolled his eyes. He was a big, beefy, teddy bear kind of guy. The type that probably played linebacker on the football team but really longed to do theater instead. Light curly brown hair, wide smile, long-lashed MoonPie eyes. "My mom?"

Nick smiled. "Might have been."

Missy came and sat at my feet. "Your mom was the one who called?"

Connor's chubby cheeks reddened as he pointed at a charming two-story house across the street. "She lives right there and always has an eye on what's happening in the neighborhood. I bet she's around here some-where—she's never one to watch what's going on from afar. Mom, come out wherever you are!" he singsonged.

Not just theater but *musical* theater. He had a nice, soothing voice, baritone bordering on tenor. The village theater needed to sign him up.

Glancing around, I felt as though I was six years old, playing hide-and-seek. I held in the urge to shout, "Olly olly oxen free," and bit my lip instead.

A woman stepped out from behind the arborvitae, brushing her hands over her arms as if dusting them off. "Hello. Hello there!" She smiled and acted as though she were greeting guests.

Well. That certainly explained Missy's fascination with that shrub. I looked down at her. She looked up in-nocently at me and quirked an ear.

Some watchdog she was. Someone hiding in the bushes and not so much as a warning bark. Not so much as a whine.

Lassie would be ashamed.

I looked at the woman and saw a leaf in her hair. How long had she been watching us? It was creepy, to say the least, but the woman herself wasn't the least bit frighten-ing. Maybe late-forties, she was a tiny thing with big, brown buglike eyes, a blunt-cut blond bob, and eye-glasses that dangled from a chain around her neck. She wore Bermuda shorts, loafers, and a pink twinset. Just your average lurking-in-the-bushes schoolmarm.

"I'm sorry for the fuss," she was saying, "but I saw the young lady casing the joint."

Casing the joint?

"Mom," Connor said, "you have to stop watching *Law & Order*."

"It's a highly informative show," she said, coming up to us. She gave Connor's cheek a pat, tucked some of his hair behind his ear, and *tsk*ed as she said, "You're overdue for a haircut."

"Mom." Connor sighed.

"What are you doing here, sweetheart?" she asked, ignoring his embarrassment.

I had a feeling she did that a lot.

"I'm meeting Darcy. Mom, this is Darcy Merriweather. She works at As You Wish, and Elodie hired her to clean out Mrs. Keaton's house. Darcy, this is my mother, Yvonne Merrick."

As we shook hands, I had the feeling she was still sizing me up as a potential burglar. Little did she know the experience I already had with breaking and entering. No need to bring that up now—or explain that it had been done to help a friend.

"You must be Ve's niece," Yvonne said. "I've heard a lot about you, and it's nice to finally meet you." She pivoted to face Connor. "What's this about cleaning up Patrice's house? Why hadn't I heard about this before now?"

Connor dodged the question by saying to me, "Do you want to see inside the house?"

I was trying to keep up with what was going on. Connor was acting as though his mother popped out of shrubbery all the time.

I eyed her. Did she?

"Darcy?" Connor asked.

"Yes," I said. It was, after all, why I was there. "I'd like to see it."

Yvonne grabbed on to Connor's forearm. "This isn't a good idea. Patrice wouldn't want anyone in her house."

"Patrice isn't here, Mom," Connor said.

Yvonne blanched and took a step back. "I don't like this. Does your father know about this?"

Again, he dodged. "It's Elodie's decision." Connor headed up the front steps with Missy at his heels. He pulled a key out of his pocket, poised to stick it in the lock; then he turned to face us, a frown on his face. "The lock is broken."

Nick came alert. "Newly broken?"

"It was fine last night when I came by to water the flowers," Connor said.

"Not again," Yvonne muttered.

"Does this happen a lot?" I asked her. "Someone breaking in?"

"Every few months," she said.

Missy barked as Nick stepped forward, going from easygoing to on-the-job in the blink of an eye. "Stay here," he said to us.

He pushed open the door and went inside. From where I stood, I could see only beyond the front door. What I saw had my dread rising. It was a messier version of the shed. I hadn't thought that was possible.

A long minute later, Nick emerged. He ran a hand down his face. "No one's in there now."

"Did they ransack the place? Steal anything?" Yvonne asked, clutching the chain that held her glasses. She swung it back and forth like a pendulum.

Nick looked at her blankly. "Honestly, I can't tell. There's so much stuff. . . ."

"I'll look around," Connor said, heading in. "I know the inventory pretty well."

"I'm coming, too," Yvonne said, hot on his heels.

Nick made his way to the Bumblebee. "I have to make some calls."

I was left standing there on the lawn alone. It took me a second to realize that Missy had gone into the house. What else to do but follow?

A blast of cool air greeted me as I tentatively stepped over the threshold. It had to be around sixty degrees inside the house. Yvonne and Missy stood just inside the doorway, in what I assumed was the living room. It was hard to tell. Boxes and bags and clothes and trash and *stuff* were piled at various heights all around us, looking a lot like a mountainous garbage range. A snaking shoulder-width path had been raked through the clutter and led to the dining room. I was suddenly claustrophobic.

A stale smell permeated the air—the scent of an unused space. Of must, of dust. Almost like an attic that hadn't been aired out in decades. I gaped in wonder.

Yvonne and I stood sideways, hip to hip, on the narrow path. She patted my arm. "It takes some getting used to."

Some? That was the understatement of the century.

Connor came back into the room, raking a hand through his shaggy hair. "Same as always. Nothing's missing."

I didn't know how he was so certain. "With the burglaries before, nothing was taken?"

"Nothing obvious, anyway," Connor said.

Again, I was reminded of big bad wolves.

The room felt like it was closing in on me. To keep from hyperventilating, I focused on a wall covered in shadowboxes. A diploma and tassel in one. A 5K race bib and ribbon in another. A baby-themed box held a card with baby footprints on it, a silver rattle, and a tiny knit hat. Another had a Girl Scout sash with dozens of badges.

I recognized the wall for what it was—a Wishcrafter's "photo" gallery. Wishcrafters were visible on film only as white starbursts—so there could never be any photos of us. Even though Elodie was only part Wishcrafter, she would have the same problem. This wall represented Elodie's childhood, from birth to high school graduation. It was a sweet way to keep the memories alive, and I hated seeing the thick layer of dust on each box.

I glanced around and was having trouble taking in the

amount of *stuff*. It would take days just to clear this room alone—maybe longer, since I had to go through each individual box and bag looking for treasures. The kitchen space didn't look much better. Had Elodie grown up like this? To what degree had her father been able to keep the hoarding in check while he was alive?

Nick came back inside. "Find anything missing?"

Connor shook his head. "No."

I shivered. "Why is it so cold in here?"

Connor said, "The air-conditioning is broken. Only runs at one temp, and we can't afford to get it fixed."

I glanced at it. It was one of those enormous seventies-era thermostats. The little plastic piece you pushed to adjust the temperature was gone. "Why not shut it off?" I asked. It seemed like a reasonable question.

"Elodie wouldn't hear of it. Some of the things in here need to be temperature controlled. Artwork and stuff."

Looking at the walls, I inventoried the art in the room. Beside the shadowboxes, there were several hanging tapestries, a couple of oil paintings, and a wall of antique portraits.

I was feeling light-headed as Yvonne said, "Patrice would hate this. People in her home, the police involved. Elodie should never have hired anyone to clean this place out. What if Patrice comes home and finds all her things gone?"

None of us said anything. I was touched and humbled that Yvonne still held faith that Patrice would be back.

Yvonne shuddered. "I just wish we knew where Patrice was."

Nick's gaze shifted to me. He knew that I, as a Wishcrafter, was obligated to grant the wish.

I turned under the pretense of examining the extent of the clutter behind me (which was monumental) and mouthed the wishing spell under my breath. "Wish I might, wish I may, grant this wish without delay."

"We may never know, Mom," Connor said.

Missy suddenly barked as the orange tabby we'd seen outside earlier streaked into the house. Missy chased after her, dodging through our legs as the tabby dove on top of the piles of clutter. Missy found an opening in the mess and went under.

I had a bad feeling. That feeling escalated into a vibration. The mountains were starting to crumble. I held out my hands to brace myself.

"Watch out!" Nick yelled, pulling me back toward him.

One of the piles wobbled in slow motion, swaying left. Swaying right. I felt the thudding of Nick's heart against my back as the mountain gave one final lurch and toppled. An avalanche of clutter crashed down around us. Dust plumed like a mushroom cloud.

Nick held me tightly (I didn't mind that part so much) while the dust settled. When the floor stopped shaking, I glanced around. Connor and Yvonne stood unscathed on the other side of the room. My heart beat in my throat as I looked for Missy, and I could feel my pulse pounding in my ears. If something happened to her . . . I couldn't even think about it. I had to find her.

I coughed at dust lingering in the air and frantically started moving boxes. "Missy!" I called out.

Nick helped me look, lifting some of the heavier objects. "Missy!" he echoed.

I heard a bark and breathed in relief when, after moving a box aside, I found Missy sitting atop some rubble next to a vintage leather suitcase. She was whimpering. At first I thought she was injured, but then I saw *it.*

A mummified hand was sticking out of the suitcase.

"Is that . . . ," I whispered to Nick, unable to finish my sentence. My vocal cords had frozen in sheer terror.

He stepped forward and carefully undid the suitcase straps. Slowly, he lifted its top, then lowered it again. He looked at us, his face ashen, and said, "There's a body in there."

Yvonne started screaming.

My hand went to my mouth as I tried to absorb this shock, knowing *I* had done this. Granting Yvonne's wish had led to this discovery.

Patrice Keaton had been found.

Chapter Four

I was sitting in a rattan rocker on Yvonne's front porch, watching police officers mill about the crime scene.

The crime scene.

I could hardly believe I was involved in another murder case.

And I had no doubt it was murder. Suicidal people didn't contort themselves into suitcases, secure the straps, then cover themselves with tons of clutter.

I shuddered at the memory of that corpse as Yvonne handed me a glass of water and then sat in the matching chair next to me. Her hand shook as it held her glass. Water sloshed over the rim, but she didn't seem to notice.

Missy sat at the edge of the walkway, her head turning back and forth as she took in all that was going on. Nick had told us to wait at Yvonne's house until the scene was under control and our statements could be taken.

He currently stood in the doorway of Patrice's house, talking to someone from the medical examiner's office. I was hoping he'd share some details with me later—Harper was going to have tons of questions, and if I didn't have the answers she was going to nag until I did.

I watched Nick carefully, feeling a pang of empathy. Nothing like trial by fire. This was the first week of his new job—everyone was going to be watching to see how he handled this case. Watching to see if he could find a killer. He was going to be under a lot of pressure.

Connor and Elodie were somewhere inside Patrice's house. Elodie had been oddly quiet about the discovery. Not so much as a tear when Connor had broken the news.

Maybe she's in shock, I reasoned.

I knew I was.

Neighbors gathered beyond the orange cones that had been set up to block off the street. Several brightly hued MINI Coopers, a van from the medical examiner's office, a fire engine, and an ambulance lined both sides of the road.

News that a body had been found would spread fast.

I bit the inside of my cheek and thought about that mummified hand. It looked like it had been reaching out . . . grasping for something. Someone.

Was it possible that Patrice had been alive when put in that suitcase? How long had she tried to escape? How long had she been buried alive in her own house?

I shuddered again and couldn't help but wonder why someone hadn't made a wish to find Patrice long ago. Not Elodie—that was impossible because she was a Wishcrafter. But why not someone else? It made me consider whether the people closest to Patrice hadn't really wanted her found before now—or if they simply hadn't considered the possibility that a Wishcrafter could have helped locate Patrice.

"This is more shocking than any episode of *Law & Order*," Yvonne mumbled. A breeze stirred a hanging fern. "Even the one where Claire Kincaid dies. And that was up there."

The technician from the medical examiner's office took something out of the back of his van. My stomach rolled at the sight of the empty body bag. I tore my gaze from the tech as he went into Patrice's house. I forced myself to focus on Yvonne. "Had you known Patrice long?"

"Almost my whole life." She rocked slowly. "We went to high school together, got married around the same time, right after graduation, bought houses across from each other, had babies the same year."

I wondered at what she *didn't* say. No mention of being friends. I pressed for clarification. "You were the best of friends, then?"

I didn't know why I was being so pushy. Maybe I'd been hanging out with forensics-happy Harper too long. Maybe the last murder investigation I was mixed up in had whetted my appetite for solving crimes.

I wasn't sure. All I knew was that I had the sudden hunger to find out who killed Patrice. And why. No one deserved to die the way she had, stuffed in that suitcase, reaching out for help.

Help I couldn't give her then, but I could possibly give her now by assisting Nick in figuring out who had killed her. Which would also help Nick . . . and I liked that thought very much.

Yvonne must have noticed her hands were shaking because she suddenly gripped her glass so tight I was afraid it might shatter. "We were close once. Not so much by the time she disappeared . . ." Her voice trailed off. Softly she said, "By the time she died. Do you think she's been in there the whole time she was missing?"

The question had gone through my head, too. "I'm not sure." The autopsy would probably be able to provide the answer.

Two more police officers went into the house. Rocking faster, Yvonne watched them and said, "Patrice would hate her house being trampled through."

"Why?" I asked. It wasn't the first time Yvonne had said so.

"In public, she was very outgoing and friendly, but in

reality, she was a very private person. Because of that, very few people were allowed into her home."

"Not because of the clutter?"

"Patrice called it her treasure, and wasn't embarrassed by it at all. However, she'd hate the thought of people touching things, moving stuff around." She slowed to take a sip of water. "Patrice was very particular. It might look like chaos to us in there, but she knew where everything was. Down to every last mineral she ever collected."

"Who was allowed in her house?" I asked, again pushing for some answers.

In my head I'd already started a suspect list. As of right now, there was no one on it. Harper, undoubtedly, would laugh if she knew I hadn't come up with a single possible perpetrator.

Thankfully, Yvonne was a talker and didn't mind my nosiness. "Well, Elodie, of course. Connor. Me. My husband, Roger." Her voice dropped when she said her husband's name, and she picked at the loose rattan on the arm of her chair. "Roger kind of took over the man-of-the-house duties when Patrice's husband, Geer, died. Fixed the broken gutter, helped plant the vegetable garden, that kind of thing."

Yvonne jumped onto my suspect list. There was a melancholy in her voice that told me she suspected Roger did more than just help around Patrice's house.

Had he cheated on her with Patrice?

Was that why Patrice and Yvonne had stopped being friends?

"If only we hadn't let Patrice leave the Sorcerer's Stove alone that night," Yvonne said.

Stunned, I rocked faster. "You were at the Stove with her the night she disappeared?" Neither Ve nor Marcus had mentioned that little fact.

Missy loped up the steps and jumped onto my lap. I petted her head as she sniffed Yvonne's arm.

Her rocker came to a stop. Yvonne stretched out her legs and nodded. "A double date. Me and Roger and Patrice and Mr. Macabre."

For a second I thought I heard her wrong. "Mr. Macabre?"

Yvonne smiled mischievously. "My pet name for Andreus Woodshall. He's a Charmcrafter, and one of the most popular vendors with the Roving Stones. Every time the fair was in town, Andreus wooed Patrice. But he was only interested in her for one thing."

"Sex?" I asked in a whisper.

"Worse," Yvonne said.

Worse? What kind of marriage did she and Roger have?

"All Mr. Macabre wanted was the Anicula."

Missy barked, one short yap. I rubbed her ears and realized what Yvonne was saying. Charmcrafters. The Anicula . . . She knew about the witchcraft in the village.

There was no way to tell at first sight if someone was a Crafter. The only ways of knowing were from word spread among Crafters about who was who, or if their powers were revealed through the double twitch of the left eye—a sure sign a spell had been cast. And since revealing powers to a mortal, even accidentally, could cause Crafters to lose their powers forever . . . people didn't tend to talk about it openly.

She must have heard through the Craft grapevine that I was a Wishcrafter. Which meant that Yvonne had to be some sort of Crafter, too.

"I can see your thoughts spinning," Yvonne said, eyeing me carefully. "We're Halfcrafters. My husband, Roger, used to be a Geocrafter before he married little ol' mortal me. I'm president of the neighborhood association of Halfcrafters as well."

She'd taken quite a risk in telling me. The punishment

for a Halfcrafter who revealed anything about the Craft to a mortal was to be turned into a frog.

When a Crafter married a mortal, in accordance with Craft Law he or she had two options. One was to reveal the Craft to the spouse. In that case, the Crafter forfeited his or her powers (the Craft really frowned upon such unions) and became a Halfcrafter (the loss of powers essentially turned a Crafter into a mortal). My mind automatically filled in the blanks. In this case, Connor had to be a full-fledged Geocrafter like his father had been since his mother once had been fully mortal.

The other option was, of course, to keep the Craft a secret from a spouse, thus leading a difficult life of lies and magical subterfuge, but retaining the ability to perform magic. The clueless spouse in that instance did not become a Halfcrafter, and held no knowledge of the Craft at all.

Within the Craft community, Halfcrafters were still treated as Crafters. They still had to attend Craft meetings (and apparently held their own), had to answer to the Elder, and were held to Craft laws. And when the marriage ended for whatever reason (death, divorce), the Crafter could petition the Elder to have powers restored. That request wasn't always granted, however.

The Craft-mortal marriage laws were a bit harsh, in my opinion. But I supposed there was a reason why our heritage had been able to thrive without exposure all these centuries.

I was still trying to process the fact that there was a neighborhood association of Halfcrafters—and wondering if Nick was part of it—when I spotted, across the street, a stretcher being brought into the house from the ME's van. Elodie and Connor still hadn't come out. And now Nick was nowhere to be seen.

"I've said too much, haven't I?" Yvonne said, putting

her hand on my arm. "It's just that sometimes I get carried away. Plus, the shock of seeing that hand . . . I tend to babble when I'm stressed. Am I babbling?"

Missy barked.

I agreed.

Yvonne sighed as if she had already known the answer. "I should be more distraught, I know. And I am. Deep down. I'll miss Patrice—our old friendship at least—but I think . . . I think I knew this day would eventually come. Patrice never would have left Elodie willingly. I can't say she always had Elodie's best interests at heart, but she wouldn't have walked away on her own."

There was so much to ask, I was having trouble figuring out what to say first. "She didn't have Elodie's best interests at heart?"

Yvonne waved a hand in dismissal. "It was nothing."

It was something. I could tell by her tone. I could also tell by the purse of her lips that she wasn't going to say more about that subject, so I forged ahead. "Why did Patrice leave the Stove alone the night she went missing?"

Yvonne tucked a strand of blond hair behind her ear and fussed with her glasses as she said, "Patrice and Andreus had a big fight at dinner. I think she was finally realizing that he was only after the Anicula. She accused him of stealing it."

Andreus went on my suspect list, too. I felt a little smug—I was getting pretty good at this investigating thing. "Stealing it? It was missing?"

"That's what Patrice wanted us to believe."

"But was it true?"

"I don't know. I always suspected she accused him because she wanted him to think she didn't have it anymore. It was a challenge. Was he with her because he liked her? Or was he using her?"

Stolen. Was it possible?

"Did she use the Anicula a lot?" I wondered aloud.

A passing cloud threw shadows across Yvonne's face. Her eyebrows dipped, her mouth tightened. "No. Patrice used the Anicula only sparingly. On her own terms."

Her voice was tight with anger, and I studied her carefully. There was something really important in the statement she'd made, but I didn't know what it was. I could only feel it. Feel her anger. Feel her hurt. I shifted, uncomfortable with the weight of her emotion.

"I didn't hear the whole of their argument," Yvonne said. "They took it outside. Next thing I knew, Andreus came back in to pay the bill and said that Patrice had gone home."

It was less than a five-minute walk from here to the Stove, so I felt safe in assuming that she'd made it home before something happened to her.

"Do you think Andreus had anything to do with it?" I gestured across the street.

"Honestly, I don't know. It's possible, I guess. He'd do just about anything to get his hand on the Anicula." She sighed. "This is just horrible."

"Yvonne!" someone shouted. A burly bear of a man barreled through the crowd and jogged up the sidewalk. "I came as soon as I heard the news."

He was out of breath and starting to wheeze. Everywhere I looked on him there was hair. A wild mane on his head, a grizzly beard, tufts sticking out of the neck and cuffs of his button-down shirt. I could only imagine what his legs looked like and was somewhat grateful he was wearing pants and not shorts. He pulled Yvonne into an engulfing hug.

"It was horrible, Roger." She was stiff in his arms, clearly uncomfortable, and soon wriggled her way out of his furry grasp.

Roger Merrick. Yvonne's husband and Connor's father. I could see where Connor inherited his size. Roger was a big, big man. His eyes, a grayish green, shifted to me. Caution and wariness hardened his gaze, giving me a sudden case of the heebies.

"Who are you?" he asked.

"This is Darcy Merriweather, Roger. She's Ve Devany's niece. Elodie hired As You Wish to clean out Patrice's house." She explained how we'd found the body.

Roger snarled. His eyeteeth were long and pointed. I gathered up Missy, who had been busy sniffing the man's leg, and wished Nick would hurry up and take my statement so I could get out of here.

"This is all his fault," Roger growled.

His? His whose? Andreus Woodshall's?

"For Pete's sake," Yvonne said, hands on hips. "Not this again."

"You know it's true," he insisted.

She leveled him with a hard stare. "No, I don't."

"You're not being sensible." Beefy arms folded across his chest.

I almost laughed. Yvonne, not sensible? I'd known her for only a couple of hours, yet I knew there was no one *more* sensible.

"And you're holding on to inappropriate jealousy," she snapped.

Zing! Her words hit their mark as Roger huffed, his spine stiffening in anger. His hair bristled. All of it. "Nonsense. Whatever happened to Patrice is his fault, plain and simple."

I was desperately trying to follow along. There was a whole history here I was missing. My curiosity was killing me, and I had to know who they were referring to. "Whose fault?" I asked, sharpening my mental pencil, ready to add another suspect to my list.

Roger turned hard eyes on me and blinked as though he'd forgotten who I was.

"Whose fault?" I repeated softly.

Red-faced, he growled again. "Jonathan Wilkens, of course."

"Jonathan Wilkens, culinary wizard from the Sorcerer's Stove?" I asked, thinking of the tasting I had just come from. Roger had to be mistaken.

He lifted a stern wooly eyebrow. "No, I mean Jonathan Wilkens, Patrice's killer."

Chapter Five

"Some witches have all the luck!" Harper cried when she opened the door to let me and Missy in.

The news of Patrice's murder had obviously reached her. "I wouldn't call the death of a woman lucky." I brushed past her gleaming, eager eyes. Missy bounded in behind me.

It was good to be here, away from Ve's germs (she had been sleeping when I stopped home) and away from the bad juju on Incantation Circle.

Roger's remarks were still ringing in my head. Jonathan Wilkens a killer? I just couldn't believe it.

As soon as he'd said so, Yvonne had taken him to task for accusing the chef with no proof. All Roger would say in his defense was, "You know his actions killed her even if he wasn't the one behind her physical death."

I'd tried my best to wheedle more information out of them, but they had clammed up. Not long after, Nick had sent an officer over to take my statement and release me. I'd never been happier.

Now, at the bottom of Harper's stairwell, I listened for the click of the security door—the one that led into the alley behind the bookshop—before climbing the narrow, nondescript steps up to the open door of her new apartment. I was learning that one couldn't be too careful, even in an enchanted little village.

Maybe *especially* in an enchanted little village.

Upstairs, Starla Sullivan and Mimi Sawyer, Nick's daughter, were hard at work painting a wall a vibrant blue. I smiled. Harper had always been good at delegating.

Missy immediately made a dash for Mimi. Mimi dripped paint into the dog's fur as she bent down to allow her chin to be licked to death, but neither seemed to notice. The mutual affection was obvious.

It wasn't hard to see why. Both were completely lovable. Twelve-year-old Mimi had become like another little sister to me. (One that wasn't nearly as annoying as my own.)

Starla, as always, looked like a thirty-year-old version of a perky cheerleader. High blond ponytail. Bright blue eyes. Open, friendly, somewhat naive face. Only a huge paint splotch on the front of her pink T-shirt detracted from her flawlessness.

Harper pushed a paintbrush into my hands. She was seven years younger than me, but I was more a mom to her than an older sister. I'd practically raised her on my own since our mom died shortly after Harper was born prematurely, both events the result of a tragic car accident. Our father, unfortunately, had sunk into a deep depression after the loss and never quite pulled himself out of it. He'd passed away last year.

I thought I'd done a fairly decent job of bringing Harper up right, but then again, I was prone to overlooking her mischievous streak, her penchant for finding trouble, and her ability to stick her nose into other people's business.

The judgment of "fairly decent" was obviously a matter of opinion.

"Way to be a downer, Ms. Serious-Pants," Harper said. "We've been waiting for the details of the crime scene. Start at the beginning. Don't leave anything out."

There was that phrase again. Crime scene. I kicked off
my shoes and looked from face to face. Starla and Mimi
were as excited as Harper. Ghouls, the lot of them.

I wasn't sure what to say or where to start. In the past,
I would have glossed over the whole situation. Tried to
downplay the fact that someone had stuffed a woman
into a suitcase and left her to die (as if that were possible
to downplay!). But now . . . Harper's enthusiasm for
criminal investigations had definitely worn off on me as
I started to tell them what had happened.

The painting party was forgotten as the three sank
onto the sheet-covered sofa. Eyes widened—especially
at the part with the hand sticking out of the suitcase.

Starla shook her head, interrupting. "Poor Elodie.
That girl has been through so much in the past two years.
First her mom goes missing; then she had to cancel her
big wedding; now you're saying she's broke and has to
sell her mom's house. . . . And"—she let out a whooshing
breath—"Patrice was inside the house all along?"

I kept an eye on Mimi, who was curled in the corner
of the couch, cuddling with Missy. Were some of these
details too much for her? She didn't appear to be both-
ered. In fact, she looked like a younger version of
Harper—intent on absorbing every little detail.

I was sitting on the floor—Harper didn't have many
furnishings yet. "Wait a sec. Elodie canceled her wedding? I'm confused. Aren't she and Connor engaged?"

Starla waved a paint roller as she talked. "They've
been engaged forever, since college. They were supposed
to have this big fairy-tale wedding about two years ago.
Elodie had hired me to do the photographs, and she
gushed and gushed about how lavish the wedding was
going to be. Huge guest list, the best of the best. Then it
all kind of fell apart. She had a big fight with her mom.
The dress shop ordered the wrong gown. Her venue
closed. The caterer quit. The deejay went to jail. A few

months later, Elodie and Patrice made up and Elodie managed to set another date, but then Patrice went missing."

"Elodie had a fight with Patrice?" I asked. "About what?"

Starla shrugged. "I'm not sure. She never said. But it was a doozy—they didn't talk for months."

"I can't imagine being that mad at my mom," Mimi said. She, I noticed, had put away her paintbrush and now held her mother's diary. She'd been carrying it around with her everywhere lately. The cover was made of white leather, weathered with age. Mimi's mother had died a couple of years ago, and it was through her diary that Mimi started learning about her Craft. The book was chock-full of Craft tidbits, which was both dangerous and incredibly resourceful.

Dangerous because if the book fell into the wrong hands, the spells within could be used with nefarious intent. Resourceful because Melina had been an accomplished Crafter before she forfeited her powers to marry Nick, a mortal. I hadn't read the diary, but from what Mimi had shared with me, the book was practically a how-to on practicing the Craft.

"Unfortunately, it happens," Starla said, sounding like she was talking from experience. "For a while Elodie kept hoping her mother would show up one day with a crazy story of where she'd been. But the days turned into weeks, into months. The big wedding was coming up and a decision had to be made. Elodie ended up canceling it, and as far as I know, it hasn't been rescheduled."

It sounded as if a big chunk of Elodie's life had been on hold since her mother went missing. I couldn't imagine living that way. Always wondering. Never knowing. It had to have been terrible.

And now . . . now her mother was never coming back. She would never be at her daughter's wedding.

It was something Harper, Mimi, and I could relate to.

When I married my ex-husband, Troy, my mother's absence had been keenly felt at my wedding, an ache that didn't quite go away the whole day long. I tried to put myself in Elodie's shoes as she planned her own wedding, not knowing where her mother was. I'd have postponed, too. Indefinitely.

Unfortunately, my marriage had fallen apart. Now I was thirty years old, divorced, and living with my aunt. But—and this was a big one—I'd never been happier. I loved living in the Enchanted Village. I adored Aunt Ve. And the villagers and my new friends.

I stood up and headed for the paint can. Mimi said, "How's Aunt Ve today? Any better?"

A thread of happiness wove through me. Ve insisted that Mimi call her "Aunt Ve." I liked how much a part of my family Nick's daughter had become. "She didn't look much better when I stopped in at home before coming here."

"Wasn't Cherise supposed to stop by today?" Harper asked.

"I thought so. I didn't hear otherwise. Maybe she didn't make it over?"

"I saw her going inside," Mimi said, "when I was visiting Archie."

Archie was our neighbor, the Elder's majordomo, a former London theater actor, and . . . a macaw. He was a familiar—a Crafter spirit residing inside an animal's form. He was also funny, conceited, and a whiz at movie trivia.

"Does it take a while for Cherise's spell to work?" Starla asked.

"I'm not sure. I guess time will tell. I'll check on Ve again when I get home."

"Well," Starla said airily, "I have some news. I met someone new."

"Who?" Long, dark curls pulled back in a ponytail bounced as Mimi jumped up. "Is he cute?"

"The cutest." Starla smiled. "He's a vendor with the Roving Stones. I met him on the village green today, and he asked me out to dinner. I counter offered with meeting for coffee tomorrow morning. I mean, dinner is too personal for a first date, isn't it?"

"Definitely a second or third date," Harper agreed.

"Why?" Mimi asked, soaking in the conversation.

"Coffee," Harper explained, "will give you enough time to figure out if you want to see him again. Kind of a quickie date. Dinner is a commitment. Dressing up. Lots of talking. It should be reserved for when you already like the person enough to want to get to know them better."

Mimi nodded as if she were taking mental notes. I wasn't sure taking them from Harper was the wisest, but I was staying out of this conversation. No need to go there tonight.

But the mention of the Roving Stones reminded me of Patrice's boyfriend, who also was a vendor with the show. "Starla, do you know Andreus Woodshall, by any chance?"

She shuddered dramatically, making a squished-up face.

Laughing, I said, "I take that as a yes?"

"How do *you* know him?" Starla asked, her blue eyes concerned.

Harper interrupted. "Him who? Who is he?"

Mimi dipped her roller in the paint tray. "I think he's kind of nice."

We stared at her.

"What?" she asked, shrugging. "He is. He lets me touch all the geodes and answers all my questions."

Of which I was sure there were many.

"Who?" Harper demanded.

"Andreus Woodshall," Starla said patiently. "He's the director of the Roving Stones. A Charmcrafter. He's . . . Well, have you seen *Dracula*? The one with Bela Lugosi?"

Who hadn't? We all nodded.

"He kind of looks like that. Except his teeth aren't as pointy, and in the wrong light he's scarier looking." She rolled a rectangle of blue onto the wall.

Scarier looking than Dracula? Was she kidding?

"But," Starla said, picking a stray piece of her blond hair from the roller, "in the right light he's kind of handsome. It's very disconcerting, one minute him looking like Dracula, the next looking all suave and debonair."

"Dracula? Really?" Harper asked, clearly intrigued. "Is he a vampire?"

"Nooooo." Starla continued to bathe the wall in blue. So far, only one wall was completed. I had a feeling it was going to be a long night if we kept painting at this rate.

"You don't have to sound like it's a crazy thought," Harper said. "After all, *we're* witches."

"She has a point," Mimi said pragmatically. "But Mr. Woodshall goes out in the daylight. That rules him out as a vampire."

I couldn't believe we were having this conversation. Six months ago I was out of work and living in Ohio. When my dad died last year, not only did I lose my father, but my job as well, as I had worked for him at his dentist's office since I was eighteen. Then Aunt Ve paid Harper and me a visit, and I'd gone from unemployed office manager to having a job at As You Wish. Oh yeah, and I was a witch.

And now I was a witch seriously considering whether there was a vampire in the neighborhood. I almost wanted to laugh at the absurdity as I dipped my paintbrush into the blue and went to work along the base-board, explaining why I'd asked about Andreus in the first place. "Yvonne Merrick calls him Mr. Macabre. He was Patrice's date the night she went missing."

"No," Starla gasped.

I nodded. "Yep. Yvonne and Roger had a double date with Patrice and Andreus." I filled them in on the fight and Roger's claim that Jonathan Wilkens had something to do with Patrice's death. I left out the part where he accused him of killing her. I also held back on explaining about the Anicula until I could find out more about it.

"Roger's crazy," Starla said. "Jonathan? No way."

"Did he even know Patrice?" Because I'd only moved to the village recently, I didn't know a lot of its history.

"They dated for a while, but I don't recall that it was anything serious. Jonathan was a bit of a playboy before he met Zoey."

It was an interesting fact I stored away. Jonathan and Patrice, dating. Was that why Roger hated the man? Was that what Yvonne meant by "inappropriate jealousy"?

I was debating how I was going to get the answers to these questions and had just settled on asking Pepe, a mouse familiar who lived and worked at Bewitching Boutique, when Harper's buzzer rang. Someone was downstairs in the alley.

"I'll get it!" Mimi said.

"Make sure you check and see who it is first!" I called after her, fighting the urge to go after her and make sure she did. I was a nurturer at heart—I couldn't help myself. I glanced at Harper. She was grown now and needed me more as a sister than a mother figure, so I was trying to break my mother-hen habit and not transfer those feelings onto Mimi. It was turning out to be a harder task than I thought.

I was more than a little surprised when Nick Sawyer came into the apartment. His eyes brightened just a bit when he spotted me. My stomach went gushy.

Harper nudged me with her toe. I swore I heard her murmur, "Some witches have all the luck," before she said, "Hi, Nick! Come to get Mimi already?"

He was still wearing his Enchanted Village security uniform. I had to admit I liked it. Khaki pants, a tight knit shirt that hugged all the right muscles. I could get used to looking at those muscles every day.

Missy growled a little. For whatever reason, she was displeased with him. It would pass soon—of that I had no doubt. She adored Nick.

"Early-morning swimming lessons," he said. "If Mimi stays up too late she'll be impossible to wake up."

"It's true," Mimi said with no trace of self-consciousness.

Pretty soon Mimi would be back in school full-time, and I realized with a pang that I would miss having her around so much.

"Get much done?" he asked, taking in the space.

"More gossiping than painting," Starla said. "Patrice's murder is quite a shock."

"Any leads?" Harper asked him hopefully.

"Not yet," he said. His brown eyes lingered on me. I felt a blush rising.

The radio clipped to his belt crackled and someone said, "Nick? You there?" To us, Nick said, "We haven't worked out codes yet." He pressed a button. "Yes?"

The excited voice said, "Suspect spotted on Gossamer Court moving west toward the woods."

"I'm on my way," Nick answered. To us, he said, "Is it possible that Mimi stay a little longer?"

"Sure," Harper said. "What's going on? What suspect? The murder suspect?"

Nick smiled at her rapid-fire questions and shook his head. Looking resigned, he said, "You'll find out soon enough, I suppose." He took a deep breath. "There have been a couple of reports of a Peeping Tom over the last two days and one possible burglary."

"Possible?" I said, suddenly very alert. "Wouldn't they know for sure?"

"It appears as though the house was entered but nothing was taken."

"Just like at Patrice's house last night?" I asked.

He shifted his weight, lightened his tone. "Probably a couple of teenagers playing pranks."

His suddenly relaxed attitude was contradicted by the serious look in his eye. Clearly he didn't believe what he was saying. He was trying not to worry us.

Which worried me quite a bit.

Just how many big bad wolves were on the loose in this idyllic little village?

Chapter Six

Keeping an eye out for anyone lurking in the shadows, Missy and I made our way home later that night. Harper's place was almost directly across from As You Wish; they were separated from each other by the village green. It was a short five-minute walk, but for some reason tonight it felt as though it were taking longer than usual.

Missy led the way as old-fashioned gas-style streetlamps and lanterns hanging from the trees lit the pathways, spilling plenty of light to guide our way. Ordinarily, I wouldn't think twice about my safety, but tonight I had Peeping Toms and murderers on my mind. It was close to ten o'clock, and I was glad Missy was with me—she was no bigger than a bit, but she had a keen sense of hearing. She'd know if someone was sneaking up behind me and warn me. At least that's what I told myself so I wouldn't break into hives.

Then I remembered how she'd let Yvonne Merrick eavesdrop from behind the tree without making a peep.

Suddenly, I was itchy.

It didn't help that the green was occupied by a dozen Roving Stones tents, all closed up for the night. Loose tent flaps slapped against their poles, echoing ominously in the dark.

With visions of fangs coming at me from out of nowhere, I kicked up my pace, my gaze on my destination. As You Wish was well lit, the windows filled with a soothing yellow glow. Ve's bedroom light was on, and I hoped she was awake. I was eager to find out exactly what had happened with Cherise Goodwin.

The tent flaps continued to *thwap* ominously, a car horn honked across the square, and I swore I could hear someone walking behind me. But every time I turned, no one was there. Missy was beginning to get agitated, too, growling low in her throat. Goose bumps rose on my arms. To be on the safe side, I scooped up the dog and broke into a jog.

Actually, it was a dead run, and I hoped no one saw me. For one, I wasn't a graceful sprinter, elbows and legs flying out in every direction. For another, it would be hard to explain how paranoid I was being. Starla's talk of Dracula on top of a killer and a Peeping Tom on the loose had truly spooked me. All I wanted was to get home as fast as I could. Tucked into bed with the covers over my head sounded even better.

As You Wish was a glorious Victorian, a complete charmer with its fancy trimmings, sloping rooflines, and magical-looking turret. In the daylight, its fanciful paint job really stood out as something special. With its purples, whites, and blues, the house often had tourists using it as a backdrop for vacation photos.

I'd just crossed the street and was sprinting for the gate leading to the house's back door when the shadowy figure of a man came stumbling off the Enchanted Trail, hurdled over the back fence behind the house, got caught on a picket, and ended up falling through the shrubs. He lay sprawled, unmoving, five feet in front of me.

Missy barked and wriggled until I couldn't hold on to her anymore. I set her down and she immediately ran to the prone form. I followed and dropped down on the ground. "Evan!" I cried.

Evan Sullivan, Starla's twin brother, groaned and rolled over. A huge red knot was forming on his head. "Darcy?"

I heard flapping and was relieved when Archie came in for a landing. In addition to being a scarlet macaw, he was one of the village's familiars. By day, he entertained the tourists passing by his cage in the yard. By night, he was the Elder's right-hand man. Bird. Whatever. Technically, he'd been dead for over a hundred years, but his spirit lived on in the macaw form—which was an appropriate choice considering how much he enjoyed hearing himself talk. Once upon a time, he was a London theater actor, and his favorite game to play with me was Name That Movie Quote. We'd spent many hours passing time trying to stump each other.

"'Whatever happens tonight, I will never, ever, ever speak a word of it,'" he quoted.

"Now is not the time for movie trivia," I said, slapping Evan's face, trying to get him to focus.

"Now, now," Archie said in a clipped tone. He sounded a lot like a British James Earl Jones. "If you don't know the answer, you just have to say so."

I didn't want to admit I had no idea what movie that line was from.

"*The Hangover*," Archie supplied. There was a smug lilt to his voice.

I glanced at him. "You've seen *The Hangover*?"

"You haven't?"

"Doesn't seem like your standard fare," I said.

"I'm full of surprises," he said, ruffling his feathers to shoo Missy away from licking him. "As are you, apparently. What did you do to poor Evan?" The white rings around his eyes practically glowed in the dark.

So caught up in the image of Archie watching such a

guy flick, I'd momentarily forgotten about Evan. Most days, I could find him at the Gingerbread Shack, his bakery. With his clean-cut ginger-blond hair and sparkly blue eyes, he was adorable. But not my type. Nor was I his type—he was gay. We bonded over mini cupcakes and how handsome we both thought Nick Sawyer was.

Over the past few months, Evan had become one of my closest friends. My stomach was in knots, seeing him this way. "Are you okay to move?"

Missy ran circles around us, but she wasn't barking. In fact, she looked like she wanted to play.

Evan struggled to sit up. He moaned and held his head. "What happened?"

"I was going to ask you the same thing," I said.

He winced as his fingers palpated a giant goose egg rising above his temple. "I - I'd been visiting Vc," he said. "She wanted some last-minute changes to her wedding cake, so I came over with some options."

"And they were so bad she bopped you on the head?" Archie asked.

Evan made a sour face at the bird.

I examined the knot on Evan's head. It looked painful. "Go on," I said.

"When I was leaving, I thought I saw someone hiding in the woods, watching your house."

I stiffened. "The Peeper Creeper?" I asked.

"The who?" Evan said.

"The neighborhood Peeping Tom," I said. "There have been a couple of sightings tonight."

"I'm not sure. When I called out, the person took off. I gave chase, but the next thing I knew I was coming to on the ground in the woods. Whoever it was must have knocked me out somehow."

Archie whistled low.

Evan gazed at me. "That's not the worst of it."

"No?" I said. "Because being attacked in the woods is pretty bad."

"Darcy." Evan took my hand. "I think the person had been waiting for you to come home."

Missy growled.

Panic fluttered in my stomach. I made an instant decision. "Come on," I said, tugging Evan to his feet. "It's probably going to be a long night, so let's go inside and make you comfy. Then we're calling the police."

Ten minutes later, as I poured hot water into Evan's teacup, I said, "You can't know for sure the person was lying in wait for *me*."

I was doing my best not to be freaked out. A village police officer was in the woods, sweeping the area with a flashlight, looking for any evidence. I had high hopes that Evan was mistaken, and that, in fact, no one had been watching the house at all.

That he'd imagined a confrontation.

That his huge goose egg was a figment of my over-active imagination.

Closing my eyes, I wished it and everything. When I opened them again, Evan was still sitting across the kitchen island, solemnly stirring sugar into his tea with one hand and holding an ice pack to his head with the other.

Damn it. I loathed my inability to grant my own wishes and suddenly completely understood the Anicula's appeal.

"You're right, Darcy," Evan said. "The person could have been lying in wait for Ve."

"Dear heavens!" Ve exclaimed. She was wrapped in a chenille robe, her long coppery hair pulled up in a twist. Dark circles drooped under her eyes and her cheeks were aflame with fever.

I didn't understand why Cherise Goodwin's spell

hadn't cured her. When I'd asked Ve, she'd had no answers, either. It was very strange.

Ve pressed her hands to her chest. "Who would want to hurt *me*?"

Openmouthed, I stared at her. "Are you implying that someone would want to hurt *me*?"

She sniffled and dabbed at her red nose with a wadded tissue. "Of course not, dear. But of the two of us, however . . . *I* wasn't the one who stumbled across a dead body today."

Great. She had to go and bring that up. I'd been happily in denial about finding Patrice Keaton's body, and now all those queasy feelings were back.

Evan brightened, his blue eyes wide, his color high. "Do you think Patrice's killer is after Darcy?"

"Could be, my boy, could be," Ve said, patting his hand.

"Hello!" I cried. "I'm standing right here."

Missy had curled up in her dog bed by the back door and was watching us with drowsy eyes. Tilda, Ve's Himalayan, eyed us warily from the top of the steps on the upper landing. It was late, and she wasn't pleased that her beauty sleep had been disturbed.

Archie had flown home. He lived next door with Terry Goodwin, who happened to be the ex-husband of both Cherise Goodwin . . . and Ve. To hear Ve tell it, the man had spent the last ten years living next door to her, trying to win her back. I'd yet to see him express any devotion. I'd never even met him as he was a bit of a recluse.

"It only makes sense, dear." Ve sneezed. "However, I am sorry if it upsets you."

Evan wrinkled his nose and patted her hand. "Sometimes it hurts to speak the truth." He glanced at me. "And to hear it."

"Why would the killer come after me?" I viciously dunked my tea bag. "I don't know anything."

Evan said, "Ooh, maybe the killer thinks you do!"

Ve perked up. "That's true. In my opinion, killers are very paranoid."

I stared at her. She was serious.

"You two are impossible." Cranky, I sipped my tea.

Evan rolled his eyes and adjusted his ice pack.

"You poor boy," Ve soothed. "Do you need more ice?"

"This one's still good." He held up the bag and looked at me with puppy dog eyes. "See, you can't be angry with me, Darcy. I'm injured."

He was right. I couldn't stay mad at him. Especially since that knock on the head could have been really bad if he wasn't so hardheaded.

"And thanks to me, we now know someone's out to get you," he added, ruining any sympathy I had for him. "We can be proactive. Take appropriate steps to protect you."

I eyed the stairs. I just wanted to go to bed. "No one is out to get me." I willed myself to believe it.

There was a knock at the back door, and I went to answer it. A village police officer stood on the back step. Not Nick, unfortunately. Even more unfortunate was that the woman standing there was stunning. Glorious blond wavy hair, brilliant blue eyes, generous smile. Her hot-pink MINI Cooper was parked at the curb. I tried not to be jealous that Nick would now be working closely with her.

"Darcy Merriweather?" she asked.

"That's me," I said. "Come in. Did you find anything?" *Please say no. Please say no.*

"Glinda Hansel!" Ve exclaimed. "Is that you?"

"Ms. Devany, how're you?" Glinda broke into a wide toothpaste-ad smile.

Glinda? Her name was really Glinda? Like the Glinda the Good Witch from *The Wizard of Oz?*

"I'm fine, just fine," Ve said.

My aunt was obviously lying. She was sick. Really sick. I was going to call Cherise in the morning to find out why her curing spell hadn't worked.

"You're working late," Ve added.

"New kid on the force," Glinda said. "I have the night shift for a while."

"Tough hours," Ve sympathized. "How's your mother?" Ve asked tightly, as if she was doing it only because it was proper etiquette.

"Oh, you know," Glinda said. "Feisty as ever. She's looking forward to your wedding."

Ve said, "I was a little surprised she agreed to come, considering, well, you know."

I looked between the two of them. What? What did Glinda know?

"I know," Glinda said. "But she doesn't want to miss Sylar's big day."

Not Ve's big day. *Sylar's* big day. I was dying of curiosity. Evan, too. He looked at me with eyebrows raised in question.

Ve smiled—a little too brightly to be genuine. "Dorothy's a good friend to him."

Dorothy Hansel. I'd have to get the scoop from the biggest village gossip aside from my aunt—Archie.

"Now, what's that you got there in your hand?" Ve asked.

Wooden curlicues filled a small plastic evidence bag.

"Wood shavings." Glinda's tone was suddenly serious. "Fresh shavings."

"Oh?" Ve asked.

My stomach was starting to hurt.

Glinda said, "I'm afraid Evan was quite correct in his assessment, Ms. Merriweather."

"What do you mean?" I asked.

"Someone sat watching this place long enough to whittle some wood." Something flashed in her eyes and her lips thinned. "My guess," she added, "is that it's probably that Peeping Tom who's been prowling around. Best to keep an eye out. I'll make a report. Lock up tight tonight. Windows and doors. I'll do a full sweep around the house before I go."

I saw her out, still unbelieving. Someone had been watching the house? Why?

When I went back to the kitchen, I was greeted with grim faces. "We don't know that someone was watching *our* house," I said. Someone had to be the voice of reason among us. "Maybe they were watching Terry next door."

Even I didn't believe what I was saying.

"Darcy, you're missing the bigger issue," Evan said.

"What's that?" I yawned. It had been an exhausting day.

He fidgeted. "Whoever was waiting for you had a knife."

Chapter Seven

Around midnight, I found myself strangely wide awake. Sleep just wasn't happening, so I gave up trying. Down the hall, I slowly cracked open Ve's bedroom door. Hallway light spilled across her bed, revealing her tucked in snugly. She was sound asleep thanks to some over-the-counter medicine that had knocked her out cold. Tilda, Ve's Himalayan, tipped up her head and looked at me curiously.

"It's okay," I whispered to the cat. "Just checking on Ve."

Tilda flicked an ear, then set her head back into the crook of Ve's leg.

As Ve snored lightly, I dodged the tissues that littered the floor and made my way over to the bed. I replaced Ve's tea mug with a glass of water and took a second to feel her forehead. It was still hot.

Whatever illness she had, she had it bad.

I tiptoed out of the room, leaving the door slightly ajar so Tilda could get out if she had to.

The back stairs creaked as I headed for the kitchen. Missy was zonked out in her doggy bed by the mudroom door. She didn't even flinch as I passed by to put the mug in the sink. I did some dishes, wiped the counters, and was contemplating a bag of popcorn and a late movie when I heard a light tapping at the mudroom door.

Missy's head shot up, and she growled low in her throat.

"Shh," I said, wondering who on earth it could be. "You'll wake up Ve."

Actually, I was pretty sure a Mack truck crashing through the front door wouldn't wake Ve, but I didn't want to take any chances.

I looked at Missy. "Who do you think it is?"

Surely the Peeper Creeper wouldn't knock.

Missy stumbled out of bed, wobbled in her sleepiness, and rushed to the door. Her tail wagged, and I took that as a good sign that whoever was on the other side meant me no harm.

Another knock sounded, this one a little louder. The porch light was on, and when I moved the curtain to peek out, I was more than a little surprised by who was standing there.

"I didn't wake you, did I?" Elodie asked as I opened the door. "I saw the light on. . . ."

"Not at all," I reassured her. "Come in. Come in. Are you okay?"

Mentally, I shook my head. Stupid question. Of course she wasn't okay. Her mother was dead. Murdered.

She smiled wanly. "I'm doing all right."

I motioned for her to have a seat at the counter. "Would you like something to drink? Coffee? Tea? Are you hungry?"

"Tea would be nice. I don't have much of an appetite right now."

I completely understood. After my mom died, I probably didn't eat a full meal for months.

As I put the kettle on, I stole a glance at her while she played with Tilda, who'd come downstairs.

Elodie's blue eyes had lost some luster, her blond curls were a tangled mess, and she looked tired. So tired. Why, I wondered, was she here? At midnight? I didn't feel like I could come out and ask straight off. She'd get there in her own time.

"I think," she said, stroking Tilda, "that I expected this would be the outcome. I kind of knew all along that she wasn't . . ." She shook her head. "That she wasn't here anymore. I felt it. Does that make sense?"

I nodded as I set out two mugs, two tea bags, a sugar spoon, and the creamer. "I've heard of that kind of thing before."

She looked relieved that I didn't think she was crazy.

"So, I'm probably better off than most would be in this situation," she said. "I already went through my grieving period when she first went missing. But finding her like that . . . it's a bit of a shock."

A bit—an understatement.

"To know that she'd probably been there all along is just eating at me." Her gaze flicked up to me. "The police think the broken air-conditioning is why she"—she gulped—"mummified. It was the perfect temperature, plus being under all that stuff . . . That's why we never smelled anything."

I couldn't believe she could talk about this so openly.

Tilda nudged Elodie's chin with the top of her head. I'd never seen the cat so cuddly. Could she possibly sense Elodie's inner turmoil and be trying to console her?

I eyed her. I had my doubts. Tilda was all about Tilda.

The kettle began to hiss and whistle low. I pulled it off the heat before it became too loud and poured hot water into the mugs. I dunked the tea bags and pushed a mug her way. *Why is she here?*

Drawing in a deep breath, she inhaled the steam from her mug and said, "Do you know about the Anicula?" She held my gaze. Suddenly, she looked older than her twenty-four years.

"Just found out about it today."

She scratched under Tilda's ears, and I could hear purring. "People are bound to talk about it since Mom's been found. You should have heard all the gossip when she went missing. The rumors." She sipped from her mug, dunked her bag, added more sugar, and sipped some more.

"About?" I asked, being blatantly nosy.

"About how my mother had brought on whatever happened to her. That she misused the Anicula. That she was cursed."

"Any truth to that?"

Her eyebrows snapped downward. "Not possible. My mother respected the Anicula too much. It's very powerful. Life-changing," she whispered. Her gaze flicked to me. "I think whoever killed my mother wanted the Anicula."

"Who knew about it?" I asked.

"Just about every Crafter who knows my family. Some mortals, not a lot."

"Mortals know about the Anicula? It's not limited to the Craft?"

She shook her head. "The powers given to charms, talismans, and amulets are created for everyone, mortals and Crafters alike, to use. However, Crafters usually keep the really special charms to themselves."

"I had no idea," I said.

"But here's the real kicker. My mother didn't even have the Anicula when she disappeared. Someone had stolen it six months before."

Yvonne's theory that Patrice had made up that story ran through my head. "Are you sure it was really stolen?"

Elodie sighed. "You've been talking to Yvonne."

Guilty, I nodded.

"There are a lot of people who thought my mother was lying about the Anicula being stolen, but she wasn't. Someone broke in and stole it. Took it right off her neck when she was sleeping."

It didn't sound likely—who slept that deeply? But then I thought about Ve upstairs and the Mack truck and realized it was entirely possible.

Elodie gripped her mug. "Darcy, I want to hire you, through As You Wish, to find my mother's killer."

I could feel my mouth drop open. "I, ah—" Our motto of no job too big or too small might just prove impossible after all. "We're not private investigators, Elodie. I would need a license for that."

She stood up, still holding Tilda. "It doesn't have to be a formal investigation. I just want you to ask a few questions. Snoop around. Everyone in the village knows you played a big role in finding Alexandra Shively's murderer a couple of months ago. I just want you to do the same for my mom." Setting Tilda on the floor, Elodie stretched and headed for the door.

I wanted to ask her about the fight she'd had with her mother, but before I could, she said, "You'll start as soon as possible?"

What could I do but accept? I nodded.

"Thank you," she said softly. "I'm counting on you, Darcy, to help me find out what happened to my mom." After a brief second, she said, "She would have liked you."

I couldn't believe what I'd gotten myself into. I followed her into the mudroom, where she pulled open the door, stepped out, then abruptly turned around.

"Oh, and, Darcy? If you're really all that concerned about having proper licensing to snoop around, you might want to see Marcus Debrowski. He can probably help you out."

Help me ... *magically*. It was something to think about.

Chapter Eight

I barely slept at all and woke up early the next morning with a lot on my mind. Dawn was slipping under my window shade, and now that it was light out and I felt relatively safe from any big bad wolves lurking out there, I unlocked the window and lifted the sash a few inches.

I slipped on my glasses and glanced out over the village green, blinking when I saw a man standing under the birch tree across the street, near Mrs. Pennywhistle's bench (her favorite sunning spot). His silhouette was in shadow, but he was tall with dark hair. From this distance—I squinted—he looked a little bit like Vincent Paxton, former murder suspect, owner of Lotions and Potions, and Seeker. When I'd waved to him in the Sorcerer's Stove yesterday, I'd never expected him to stake out my house.

But . . . I squinted harder. I couldn't tell if it was him or not. The man was too far away.

Whoever he was, he appeared to be watching the house. The Peeper Creeper?

I shivered, and after rubbing my eyes, I looked again. No one was there.

Whoever it was had moved on. Or maybe he'd been a figment of my overactive imagination.

I was being paranoid, that was all. It was understandable after what had happened last night with the person in the woods.

As a gentle breeze stirred the white curtains, I flopped back onto my bed. I watched the sheers flutter as I breathed in deeply and picked up the hint of sea salt in the air. The Enchanted Village wasn't too far from Salem's coastline, but I'd yet to spend a day at the beach—something I needed to change before the weather turned too cool.

I'd adapted to the salty scent almost immediately. It's a strong, distinct smell, one that Harper had instantly disliked, but I found it oddly comforting.

Now, months after moving here, we had both become accustomed to the scent. Harper didn't even notice it anymore, and I eagerly sought the quiet moments when I could really focus on it. Like now.

Reaching over, I lifted the window sash just a bit higher, leaned back on my pillows, and breathed in. Tilda tiptoed her way up the empty side of the bed, acting as nonchalant as a prissy Himalayan can. Which wasn't much.

I held out my fingers to her. She ignored them. Instead, she oh-so-casually stretched, flattened herself on the mattress, and elongated her body against the side of mine. Then she oh-so-casually batted my stomach with her paw. I dutifully scratched her chin. Tilda wanted affection only on her terms. I knew better than to go against her wishes. Hairballs hacked onto my comforter were a common occurrence when Tilda was displeased.

I glanced around for Missy and found her on the fluffy dog bed on the floor. Curled into a tight ball, she was sound asleep, her breathing rhythmic and heavy.

Missy had changed so much in the short time since we moved from Ohio to the village, almost as though she'd gone from puppy to dog during the trip. In Ohio, she'd been feisty, a bit hard to control, and never at a loss for a shoe to chew. Here, all that had changed. She was still energetic, but her frenetic personality had morphed into one that was more mature. At first I thought something was wrong with her and almost made an appointment with a vet. Then I came to my senses. She was just about the perfect dog now. Except for her bouts of being an escape artist. She had the uncanny ability to break out from any enclosure. It had become somewhat of a game over the past couple of months, sort of a canine hide-and-seek.

I sat up in bed, pulled my hair into a sloppy knot, and reached for the notebook I'd been jotting in before I went to sleep. I intermittently scratched Tilda while reading over my notes . . . notes on Patrice Keaton's murder.

Heaven help me, I was going to investigate this murder.

Harper was going to be beside herself.

I supposed I could have turned down Elodie's request, despite As You Wish's motto. After all, solving a crime was a far cry from what we normally did for clients. But I didn't because (and I blame this completely on Harper), with the last murder investigation, my inner Nancy Drew had emerged. I liked being in the thick of things, nosing around and asking questions. Taking this job allowed me to do that more openly.

I focused on my notebook. I'd written:

Who was Patrice?

I tried to figure out how old she was and recalled that Elodie had said her mother had wedding presents from 1985, and Yvonne had mentioned that she and Patrice both got married and had babies right after graduating high school. . . . I did some mental math. If she were still alive, she'd be in her mid-forties. So young still.

Why would someone want to kill her?

Despite what Elodie believed about the Anicula,

there might be other motives for her death. I just had to figure out what they were.

- *The Anicula (Mr. Macabre)*
- *Greed*
- *Love (Jonathan??? Mr. Macabre?)*
- *Jealousy (Roger, Yvonne)*

I had to admit, I wasn't very good at investigating yet. First things first. I needed to learn more about Patrice. And the Anicula.

A rooster crowed loudly beneath my window. Smiling, I looked out. Archie was sitting on the porch roof. Displacing Tilda (she hissed, hopped off the bed, and ran for the door—a sure sign I'd pay for my actions later), I opened the window all the way and leaned out.

"We saw your window open," Archie said in a stage whisper. "And thought you'd be awake."

If I weren't, his crowing assured I would be. It had been loud enough to wake the dead.

On Archie's back, Pepe clung to bright red feathers. "*Bonjour, ma chère!*"

"*Bonjour,*" I said cheerfully. Pepe was one of my favorite people—even if he was a mouse. "Do I want to know why the two of you are out so early?"

Archie puffed his chest. "Morning rounds." He flew up to the window ledge and then into my room. He landed on the bed—his red, blue, and yellow feathers a vibrant contrast to my white comforter. Pepe hopped off his back and gave me a slight bow.

He wasn't your average mouse. Slightly chubby, he wore a red vest with three small gold buttons, round glasses perched on his tiny nose, and his whiskers were manipulated into a Dali mustache. He'd been a familiar for over two hundred years, and had been with Godfrey Baleaux's family almost as long. Godfrey owned the

Bewitching Boutique and also happened to be my aunt's third ex-husband (whom she often referred to as a rat-toad bottom dweller).

Pepe lived at the boutique and was one of the best clothing designers and tailors around. He was also the town's historian, something I desperately needed right now. I hoped he could help me fill in some of the missing pieces in Patrice's case.

Missy lifted her sleepy head and thumped her tail when she spotted our guests. She leapt onto the bed in one motion and daintily licked Pepe's face. I pulled her back onto my lap and rubbed her ears.

"Morning rounds?" I asked. "What kind of rounds?"

Archie stiffened, slipping into his role as the Elder's majordomo. "The Elder is concerned about the security in the village and has issued a task force to regain order."

I couldn't help my smile. "And you two are the whole task force?"

"Your humor is unappreciated." Archie preened. "Pepe and I are more than capable of holding down this fort, so to speak."

Ah yes, I could see it now. Archie could peck the person while Pepe chomped an ankle.

"But alas," Pepe said mournfully, "we do not act alone. There are others at the watch. We will prevail in finding this—what did you so eloquently refer to him as last night, *ma chère*?"

I must have looked confused because Archie supplied the answer. "The 'Peeper Creeper,' I believe it was."

The Peeper Creeper. The Peeping Tom. Was he the one in the woods last night? Or had it been, as Evan so kindly surmised, Patrice's killer? I pushed the thoughts aside. "Does the Elder think the Peeper is a Seeker?"

A Seeker was a mortal who wanted to become a Crafter—a virtual impossibility since the Craft was hereditary. There were ways to be adopted into the Craft family—though marriage, for example—but powers were never included in those unions. So if a Seeker married a Crafter just so they could *practice* magic, he or she was going to be sadly out of luck.

However, there were ways for mortals to achieve powers. Certain spells could produce magical results—and as it turned out, amulets and charms, as well.

"Unknown," Archie said, "but we cannot be too careful. Did the village police discover anything last night? We need to report back to the Elder."

Ah, the real reason for this visit. I explained about the wood shavings.

"Interesting." Archie flapped his wings.

"What's this?" Pepe squinted through his glasses at my notebook.

"Just some notes on Patrice Keaton's murder."

Archie *tsk*ed. "Horrible business, that."

"Did you know her?" I asked him.

"Of course," he said. "I know everyone."

Missy had gone slack in my lap, her head resting on my leg. She hadn't fallen back to sleep, but I could tell she wasn't quite ready to wake up.

"Of course you do." I smiled to appease his ego. "Can either of you tell me anything about her?"

"Like what?" Archie asked.

Pepe was still eyeing the notebook page, as if he was memorizing what I'd written.

"For one, what did she look like?" The only mental image I had of her was of a mummified hand. I'd do just about anything to get that picture out of my head.

Archie held his wing to his forehead in a faux swoon. "A beauty in the vein of Susan Hayward."

"*Non.*" Pepe shook his head.

Archie gave him a beady evil eye. "What do you mean, *non*?"

"Ingrid Bergman. A classic beauty." He kissed the tips of his paws. "*Oui, oui.*"

"No, no, no," Archie cried.

"Shh!" I said in case Ve was still sleeping. "I get the picture. She was a classic beauty." For the sake of my sanity, I conjured up an image of an older Elodie, a woman who kept up with her looks. This really didn't jibe with the mess Patrice's house was in, but for the sake of keeping peace, it would do.

"She was quiet," Pepe said.

"Very private," added Archie.

Glancing at my notes, I said, "Is it true Patrice dated Jonathan Wilkens?"

"They dated for approximately nine months," Archie said.

"Do you know why they broke up?" I asked.

"Jonathan fell in love with someone else," Pepe said, holding his paw to his heart.

"Zoey?" I asked.

Pepe nodded. "Love at first sight. It's so romantic, no?"

"Hogwash is more like it," Archie answered.

"You, *mon chère*, need to—how do the young persons say?—hook up with someone?"

I laughed.

"You forget," Pepe continued, "what it is like to be in love."

"'Love is a bad habit—it's much safer to have the measles—they ain't near as painful.'" Archie quirked an eyebrow at me. After a few beats of silence, he supplied the quote's answer. "*Daddy-Long-Legs*. 1919."

"That movie was a little before my time," I said.

"Rub it in." He fluffed his wings.

There had to be a story behind his quote, one of love lost. Maybe one day he'd tell me. I tapped the notebook with the pencil. "How did Patrice take the breakup?"

"Devastated," Pepe said with mournful eyes.

"'Tis true," Archie added. "Her heart was broken. She believed they would be married one day."

"What about Roger Merrick? Anything about him I should know? Besides that he looks like a backwoodsman?"

Archie said, fanning his face with a wing, "If he's a backwoodsman, he can cut down my tree any day." He looked at us. "Do not stare like that. He's a very handsome man under all that hair."

My estimation of Archie just dropped several notches.

Pepe looked horrified, too. "He's a Halfcrafter, a former Geocrafter who has been married to Yvonne for over twenty-five years. He and his son work at the Museum of Science."

I took a wild guess. "A rock and minerals exhibit?"

Pepe laughed. "*Oui.* They are experts, after all."

"Have there been any rumors about something going on between Roger and Patrice?"

"No. Was there something going on?" Archie looked ready to latch on to some juicy gossip.

"I'm just speculating," I said.

"Yvonne would maim him," Pepe declared.

"Indeed," Archie agreed. "Since he is not missing any limbs, I don't believe he has ever strayed."

But, I thought, that didn't mean he didn't want to. It was something to think about. I switched tactics. "Do either of you know about the Anicula?"

Pepe nodded. "It's a legendary amulet, full of great power."

Archie added, "Full of great evil."

"Why do you say so?" I asked.

"It can turn the shy into a braggart; the humble into an egoist; a servant into a god," Archie said with emotion.

I let his words settle. "You're saying the power of the

amulet changes people in a negative way. The power goes to their head?"

"Some," Archie answered with a slow blink of his eyes. "The Anicula's past is fraught with abusers of its magic. The power is too much for most to handle."

"What about Patrice?" I asked them. "Was it too much for her?"

Pepe said softly, "I heard rumors of misuse."

"I, too," Archie added.

Elodie had mentioned the rumors, but she claimed they were false. Was she simply in denial? Or had someone purposefully started the rumors so that when Patrice went missing it would be assumed that the curse was to blame?

I wrote "rumors" in the notebook, then tapped the pencil against my lips.

"Do you really think she was cursed?" I asked them.

"She's dead, isn't she?" Archie said. "If that's not cursed, I don't know what is."

I could have argued that maybe there was a crazed murderer on the loose—and that he or she was the reason Patrice was dead. Not a curse. But I didn't want to be thinking about crazed murderers.

One more thing, however, needed to be asked. "Do either of you know what the Anicula looks like?"

They looked at each other, then shook their heads.

"Does anyone?"

"Its shape and design are kept in the highest of confidence," Pepe said, "so no one attempts to steal it."

"If it were mine, it would be locked away in the safest of places," Archie said. "Because there are many who would do anything to own that amulet."

Which left me wondering if that included killing for it.

Chapter Nine

After Pepe and Archie left to continue their rounds, I checked on Ve (who was still feverish and trying to downplay how ill she was), laced up my jogging shoes, and took Missy out for our morning run. The village green was just starting to wake up. Shop owners were cleaning windows, watering flowers, and unfurling awnings. Locals were on their morning walks or stopping in the Witch's Brew for their morning cups of coffee and warm scones.

It reminded me that Starla was meeting her date for coffee this morning. I glanced at the Roving Stones tents, at the people milling about, and wondered which vendor she had a date with. Starla deserved a little love in her life, so I really hoped it worked out. But I did question what would happen when the fair moved on to the next city. . . .

It was a beautiful morning with hardly a cloud in the sky. Birds tweeted high in the trees, and dew sparkled on the gorgeous flowers planted around the square. I headed for Mrs. P's bench under the birch tree to stretch out and wasn't the least bit surprised to find Mrs. Pennywhistle sitting there enjoying the morning sun. A rolled newspaper was tucked under her leg, and a cardboard coffee cup sat next to her. Its rim was liberally colored in deep red lipstick. Mrs. P loved her cosmetics.

"Good morning, Darcy! How's Ve this morning? Any better?"

Mrs. P and I had become fast friends after we'd been mixed up in a murder case. She was eighty if a day and was one of the most energetic people I'd ever met. Rarely did she wear anything other than a hot-pink velour tracksuit, and today was no exception. When I'd first met her, she'd reminded me of Phyllis Diller, and that impression hadn't changed. Her hair stuck out in points, starburst-style, she wore too much makeup, and her laugh was almost identical to the famous comedienne's. But one thing that was quite unique to Mrs. P was the fact that she was a Vaporcrafter—she had the ability to vaporize into thin air. It was a seriously impressive talent.

"Not better at all. I'm starting to get really worried." I put my foot on the bench and stretched my calf. Missy was on a mission to sniff every blade of grass in the vicinity.

Worry pulled at the wrinkles around Mrs. P's eyes. "Wasn't Cherise supposed to stop by yesterday?"

"She did come by, but so far nothing's changed. Aunt Ve is still feverish, she's not eating, and she keeps saying she's fine. I'm going to call Cherise later on—maybe she can explain."

"Should I bring over some soup? I make the best turkey and wild rice soup around. Ask anyone."

I smiled. "That would be wonderful. Lay on the guilt about how hard you worked to make it. Make sure she eats it."

Mrs. P laughed her outrageous cackle. A few of the Roving Stones vendors looked our way.

The talk of food reminded me that I had my first cooking lesson tonight. I also had to check in with Evan at the Gingerbread Shack to make sure Ve's wedding cake was on track and pop in at Bewitching Boutique with Harper to try on our maids of honor dresses for final fittings.

But I suddenly realized that a big chunk of my day was on hold. I was supposed to start cleaning out Patrice Keaton's house. What was going to happen there was anyone's guess at this point. I couldn't exactly call Elodie and ask. I'd have to wait for her to come to me.

"I'll do that," Mrs. P was saying. "I can work the guilt like no one's business. It's all in the voice's quiver." She demonstrated. "I'm just a poor little old lady. . . ."

"That's good," I said, awed. "Really good. I'd buy what you were selling."

She winked at me. "I'll remember that." Her voice sobered. "I heard you had quite the day yesterday, finding that mummy and everything."

I glanced around at all the shops lining the square. "Does everyone know?"

"I'd say so," she said. "I heard it from at least three people. It's a shame what happened to that woman."

"Did you know Patrice?"

"In passing," Mrs. P said. "She was one to keep to herself. Loved that girl of hers something fierce." She glanced up at me. "I've been hearing rumors that her death had something to do with the Anicula. That Patrice had misused it and had suffered the consequences."

I tipped my head. "Unless the amulet could stuff a grown woman in a suitcase, then cover her with tons of clutter, I'd say that theory is a stretch."

Mrs. P nodded absently. "Magic can be dangerous."

"Not that dangerous. Someone is behind her death. Maybe someone who wanted the Anicula."

"Is it missing?" Her eyes went wide. "If that amulet falls into the wrong hands . . ."

"Good question. Elodie says the Anicula was stolen

six months before Patrice died. No one seems to know where it is—or what it looks like. Do you?"

She shook her head.

"Someone has to know what it looks like," I said, stretching my other leg.

"Elodie, I should think."

Pretty much the only person I couldn't pester right now. I bit my lip. "Do you think the library would have any information on it?" The village library had an extensive section on witchcraft. Historians all over the world traveled here for research.

"Not likely." She tapped her chin, then snapped her fingers. "The Elder might know."

I remembered my last trip to see the Elder. The time she revoked my powers for a day because I'd broken a Wishcraft Law. Seeing her again wasn't high on my priority list. "Anyone else?" I asked weakly.

Mrs. P laughed, obviously understanding my reluctance. "There is someone else who may know."

"Who?" Anyone was better than seeing the Elder.

Mrs. P motioned to the tents. "Andreus Woodshall. The Anicula originated with his family."

"It did?"

"A few centuries ago."

"How did it end up with Patrice?"

"No idea," Mrs. P said, taking a sip of her coffee. She patted her spiky hair to ensure it was still in place (it rarely moved), and said, "But I bet there's a good story there."

Yvonne had mentioned that Mr. Macabre had dated Patrice only because he wanted the Anicula. . . . If it had rightfully belonged to his family, he was probably trying to get it back.

"Is he as creepy as people say?"

She cackled again. "Creepier."

Great. Just great. Maybe the Elder wasn't such a bad option after all.

"Are you working today?" I asked.

"Of course. Someone needs to keep an eye on Vincent Paxton. Keep your enemies close, right, Darcy?" Mrs. P winked.

True. So true. Through her late granddaughter, Mrs. P had close ties to Lotions and Potions and had given herself the part-time job of looking after Vince, the shop's new owner. Not only did she want to ensure that he blended his lotions and potions properly (which had been a problem with the prior management), but she wanted to keep an eye on what Vince was up to. As a Seeker, he was desperate to learn everything about the Craft and had made it clear that he would stop at nothing to get some answers to whether the village was truly magical.

I harbored more than a little suspicion that he might be the village's Peeper. Only because of his desperation. He had convinced himself there was witchcraft afoot in the village—and was out to prove it. It was easy to picture him breaking into village homes to look for evidence of the Craft. It would also explain why nothing had been taken during these "burglaries." They were fact-finding missions only.

But before I openly aired my suspicion (in case I was wrong), I wanted to do a little investigating of him first. "Right," I said. "And if you could, find out if Vince whittles."

"Whittles? Wood?"

I nodded.

"Why?"

"Just curious."

"What's going on in that pretty head of yours, Darcy Merriweather?"

"Too much." I laughed.

Missy tugged on her leash. She was ready to run. "We should go. I'll talk to you later, Mrs. P."

She saluted us and said, "I'll let you know how it goes with Ve."

"Don't forget the guilt," I called over my shoulder as I started jogging away.

"My specialty," she yelled back.

As Missy and I circled the village green, I could feel a pair of eyes on me, watching my every move. Yet every time I looked, I couldn't single out one person openly staring.

I ran faster and thought about the Anicula. I was going to have to meet with either Andreus Woodshall to find out more about the amulet and its powers ... or the Elder.

Neither sounded particularly inviting, but I figured Andreus was the lesser of two evils.

As I let that thought settle like a lump of cold oatmeal in my stomach, I realized I was starting to doubt the Anicula's existence.

Was it legendary, as Pepe had said?

Or mythical?

For half an hour I jogged through the village's neighborhoods, staying well clear of the Enchanted Trail's path, which branched into the woods. I had to admit that I was a little bit skeeved out by the possibility of someone watching me. And for as much as I turned it over in my head, I couldn't figure out why someone would be, either. Why me? Why now? Were the person's motives somehow tied to me finding Patrice's body? Too many questions for which I had no answers at all.

The neighborhoods were enough to take my mind off the matter. Each house had an off-the-scale quaint factor. Most homes throughout the village were historical in style—usually Victorian based. There was a whole street full of colorful gingerbread houses, another of quaint cottages. Large oak trees were in abundance, full of leafy branches this time of year. Come autumn, acorns would be gathered—not just by squirrels but by Crafters, as well, to be used in spells, fashioned into talismans, or placed in the windows of their homes to ward off evil and bring good luck.

I ran for a little longer, trying my best to focus on my pace, which after two months of running could be described only as leisurely.

Missy bounced along beside me, her tiny tongue hanging from her mouth, as I slowed to a stop in front of Harper's bookshop. The colorful pastel-striped awning overhead offered welcome relief against the bright sunshine. Ivy cascaded over the edges of a long rectangular wrought-iron window box, which also held an abundance of commonly found annuals. Pink petunias, purple salvia, and white verbena were in full bloom, along with a silvery spiky plant that offered height and texture. Harper had done well.

As I turned to go into the shop, I noticed Marcus Debrowski coming my way down the sidewalk carrying a to-go cup from the Witch's Brew.

When he spotted me, he came to an abrupt stop.

"Do I look that scary?" I asked, running a hand over my damp hair.

He took a step backward. "I'm beginning to think you're bad luck, Darcy. First Alexandra Shively a few months ago, and now this?"

"Ah. You heard the news about Patrice."

"Everyone's heard the news." He came closer. Missy wagged her tail, and he bent and patted her head. "I told you not to take that job."

His suit was impeccably pressed. His hair was combed neatly to the side and slicked back with gel. His belt matched his shoes, and I would bet my life's savings that his socks matched his shoe color as well. He probably ate a high fiber cereal for breakfast. He was just that kind of guy.

"I know," I said. "So you're really not going to like the favor I'm going to ask."

He folded his arms. "No, I'm probably not. But ask anyway."

"I kind of sort of need a private investigator's license."

His eyes grew wide. "Why?"

"I was kind of sort of hired by Elodie to find her mother's killer."

He didn't look as taken aback by the idea as I feared.

"And she doesn't think the police are capable?" he asked.

I thought of Nick. "She didn't say that. She thinks the killer was after the Anicula, and I might be able to snoop in a way the police can't."

"Among Crafters," he said, understanding.

"Mostly."

"You do know that a private investigator's license isn't easy to come by. There's all kinds of training you have to go through, including—since you have no experience— apprenticing under another PI for years."

"I know. That's the case for mortals, at least." I blinked sheepishly at him. As a Lawcrafter, he could magically get me a license, no questions asked. To a mortal, it would look like I'd done all the requirements.

My blinking seemed to have no effect whatsoever. He was shaking his head. "No."

"Please?"

"No."

A flash of movement inside the shop caught our attention. Harper moved about, dusting books and shelves.

Marcus couldn't take his eyes off her. He rubbed his chin. "Maybe we can make a deal."

"What kind of deal?" I asked reluctantly, not sure I liked where this was going.

His green eyes sparkled. "I get you the license, and you get me a date with Harper."

My jaw dropped. "That's bribery!"

"No, Darcy, that's *bargaining*. We lawyers are good at that."

I glanced at Harper.

"And," Marcus added, "you have to promise me that you'll actually study how to be a proper PI. Learn the rules, go to a shooting range. If you're going to act as a PI, you need to know how to be a PI. Take it or leave it."

"Well, since we're bargaining, if I agree to this deal, you have to make some concessions yourself."

I liked Marcus, and I thought that Harper would too if she just got to know him a little better. It was the only reason why I was even contemplating his offer.

"Like what?" he asked.

I told him.

His eyes widened. "You think it would help?"

"Definitely."

"All right, then. Shake?"

We shook hands, and he strode off, a little kick in his wingtips.

If Harper found out what I'd just done, she would kill me. I just had to make sure she never figured it out—which was easier said than done. I didn't know anyone smarter than she—or anyone who knew me better. I tapped on the window and she smiled when she saw me, making me feel a teensy bit guilty.

After unlocking the door and letting me and Missy in, she folded her arms and said, "For the love, Darcy. I'm getting really jealous."

In the small kitchenette in the back of the shop, I filled a bowl with water and set it before Missy, who lapped with enthusiasm. "Why?"

Harper held up her hands, fingers popping up one by one as she ticked off reasons. "First, two weeks after moving here, you find a dead body. Second, yesterday, you find another dead body. Third, you have some crazed woodsman in your backyard watching you. Fourth, Nick Sawyer is a serious catch. And fifth"—her thumb shot out—"give me a sec and I'll think of a fifth."

"You're demented," I said with a smile. "You know that, right? Only you would think those first three were reasons for envy." I didn't want to talk about Nick and how he was definitely a great catch. But there was a big, glaring issue with that comment. He wasn't the least bit caught—not by me at least.

Her brown eyes widened with excitement as she not-so-patiently pressed for details. "Any idea who was in the woods?"

"No."

"Is it true the person had a knife, that he was carving something?"

"Probably."

A little of the excitement left her eyes, and a thread of fear wove into them. "Carving *what*?"

"Wood."

"Oh, thank God. I was worried it was a small animal or something."

My stomach rolled at the thought. "Way to make me feel better," I said, erasing any guilt I'd been feeling.

"Sorry," she mumbled, not really sorry at all. Her face pinched. "Why wood?" Her brows were drawn in concentration as she tried to wrap her brain around the situation. She liked to have all the answers—even when there were none to be had. "And what kind of wood?"

Was she serious? "I have no idea. Brown wood."

"You need a crash course in forensics, Darcy."

I disagreed. I'd leave the forensics stuff to her.

She shook a doggy biscuit out of a box she kept under the counter and gave it to Missy. "Do you think it was a message of some sort?"

I wasn't sure what kind of message wood shavings sent. "Again, I have no idea, Harper."

"Don't get cranky with me. Someone has to figure out what's going on."

Missy crunched away. I kind of wished I had a cookie, too. A big one. "The police are looking into it."

"Be that as it may, I'm going to do a search on wood-carving serial killers. See if there's a chance of any being in the area. Wood carving. So strange."

I held in a smile at her renewed enthusiasm. "You do that."

"You're mocking, but you never know what might turn up."

"The person in the woods could have been someone who likes to randomly sit in the woods at night and whittle. For fun."

She rolled her eyes.

I didn't blame her. No one just sat in the woods and whittled in the dark. I had been only trying to make myself feel better. "Or it could have been the Peeper Creeper, who is simply creepy and not dangerous."

"True. Whittling is kind of creepy."

I laughed.

"What?"

"Whittling isn't creepy. It's an art form."

"Well, it's creepy when the whittler is watching you." She had a point.

"It would be nice if we could figure out who the Peeper was and rule him out as the person who was in your backyard," she said.

"Actually . . ."

"You have an idea? Who? Who?" She bounced up and down like a giddy schoolgirl.

"Are you up for a little investigating?" It was an unnecessary question. Harper was always up for a little investigating.

"Am I breathing? Who are we investigating?"

"Vincent Paxton."

She drew in a breath. "You think . . ."

"I *suspect*. I don't know anything for sure. That's why we need to investigate."

Nodding, she said, "I'm in."

We made plans to snoop later, and I clipped on Missy's leash and headed for the door. "Don't forget our fitting this afternoon."

"How could I?" She bent down to give Missy love and affection.

Harper wasn't exactly a fancy dress kind of a girl, and it was only her love for Ve that was getting her into one of Pepe's chiffon confections for the wedding.

As she pulled open the door to see us out, she stuck out her thumb. "Number five. You have Missy. I miss her."

It had been hard for Harper to leave Missy behind when she moved out, but we all thought it best that Missy stayed with me and Ve since we worked out of the house and had more time for her.

I tipped my head. "Are you doing okay on your own? You know, you can always move back to Ve's and lease your apartment upstairs."

Harper waved away the suggestion. "I'm fine. Just a little lonely sometimes without Missy to play with."

Missy turned in circles, yapping, her tail wagging.

Harper had said nothing about missing her big sister, but I could read between her lines quite well. I made a mental note to spend as much time with her as I could. But when? Then I had a thought. One that would help me on two fronts.

"How do you feel about cooking?" I asked.

"If you mean microwaving, I'm a pro."

That, I knew. "The Sorcerer's Stove is giving cooking classes. The first one starts tonight. I'll be there. You should sign up."

Missy barked as if in agreement.

"I don't think so," Harper said. "Kitchens and I don't get along. Remember the time I tried to make you a birthday cake and nearly burnt the house down?"

"You were six."

"My culinary skills haven't changed much."

She was so stubborn. I was going to have to play dirty. I wanted her to be there, not only to get her out of her apartment, but because Marcus would be there as well. I had a date to finagle. Getting them in the same place at the same time was half the battle.

I put on my best innocent face and set the bait. "That's a shame, especially since Jonathan Wilkens will probably be there. Maybe he'll say something about dating Patrice Keaton. Or reveal why Roger Merrick blames him for Patrice's death. I guess I'll just have to give you all the details tomorrow. If I remember them. Unless, that is, you change your mind about those classes . . ."

Harper narrowed her eyes. "You know me too well."

"So?"

She smiled. "I'm in."

Chapter Ten

On my way home, I stopped at Mrs. P's empty bench. I sat and pulled my cell phone out of the tiny pocket in my jogging shorts. I didn't usually run with my phone, but I had a call to make. One that had to be out of Ve's earshot.

Missy sat at my feet, enraptured with the Roving Stones vendors moving about their tents and setting out their wares. As I found the number I was looking for on my contact list, I glanced around, hoping to see Starla and her mysterious date. Unfortunately, they were nowhere to be seen. I couldn't wait to get the scoop from her later.

I dialed Cherise Goodwin's number, all the while hoping the Curecrafter would have an explanation as to why Aunt Ve still wasn't feeling better. I'd once been "cured" by Dennis Goodwin, Cherise's son, and I could attest firsthand to how miraculous their powers were. What was going on with Ve didn't make sense.

Cherise answered on the first ring.

Birds chirped happily overhead as I said, "Hi, Cherise. It's Darcy Merriweather."

"Darcy! I was just getting ready to call you. Is Ve any better this morning? I spoke to her last night, and she still seemed unwell."

My stomach was suddenly in knots. "Not at all. In fact, she seems to be getting worse. What's going on?"

There was a long pause before Cherise said, "I don't know."

"What do you mean you don't know?"

In the subsequent silence, I thought about what I knew of Cherise. Once upon a time, Cherise and Aunt Ve had been married to my next door neighbor Terry Goodwin (not at the same time, thank goodness). Ve first, then Cherise. Both had divorced the man, which left me wondering why. My gaze slipped to his house. I hadn't met Terry, a Numbercrafter, yet, though I had been told— many times—that he was an "interesting" man. I had no idea what that meant.

Cherise sighed. "I cast a spell, Darcy. That it didn't work is perplexing."

"Shouldn't all your spells work?"

"Of course, Curecrafters cannot cast spells that do harm, but there are other reasons why my spell might have failed."

Her voice held a note of alarm that had panic threading through me. I was almost afraid to ask, "Like what?"

Missy suddenly growled low in her throat, snapping my attention away from my growing dread. She was staring across the green at all the tents, but her focus seemed to be on one spot in particular. I, however, couldn't pinpoint what. Her ears flattened and she bared her teeth.

Suddenly, goose bumps rose along my arms. I felt eyes on me. Staring. Assessing.

I could barely focus on Cherise as she said, "Well, there could be another Crafter at work."

I scooped up Missy and set her on my lap. Whatever had caused her distress had passed. She flopped down onto my legs and set her head on her paws. Still on alert, I rubbed my hand over her head, her ears. My gaze swept the green, searching for anything out of place. I found nothing. "How so?"

"If someone didn't want Ve to get well and cast her own spell, a recantation spell."

"A recantation spell? What's that?"

"It's basically a spell that nullifies my spell."

I was shocked. "And anyone can cast it?"

"As with all spells, anyone who knows it can cast it."

"And who knows it?"

"Just about everyone. It's a common spell."

I couldn't believe my ears. "But what about 'do no harm'? How could a spell that makes Ve remain ill be cast? Doesn't that go against everything Crafters stand for?"

Missy lifted her head, yawned, and put it back down. I was still on edge. I could hear the brittleness in my own voice.

"You need to look at the shades of gray, Darcy," Cherise said. "Imagine this scenario. Someone out there, a Crafter obviously, believes Ve is better off being ill."

I couldn't hold in a disbelieving laugh. "Who on earth would want that?"

Her tone was serious as she said, "I can think of only one reason."

"Which is?" I really wanted to know, because I couldn't think of one. Ve was clearly suffering.

"If Ve remains under the weather, there will be no choice but to postpone her wedding. My guess is that someone doesn't want Ve to get married. Someone who truly believes her spell is keeping Ve from making a big mistake. In that person's eyes, there is no harm being done. And obviously, if the spell worked, then there really is no harm being done."

I let the repercussions of that statement sink in. What I deduced from what she said stunned me. "Does that mean Ve *shouldn't* be marrying Sylar? That it's a mistake?"

"That's the conclusion I came to."

"Wow."

"But . . . ," Cherise said.

I almost didn't want to know what came after that "but."

"As I explained to Ve last night when I called to check on her, there are two other reasons why the spell might not have worked."

I pulled in a deep breath. "Go on."

"One of my limitations is that I can only cure physical ailments, not mental issues."

"Are you saying that Ve might be making herself sick? That it's all in her head?" *Why* also went through my mind, but I wanted to hear Cherise's explanation. "How did Ve feel about hearing that?"

Cherise laughed. "She mentioned how many people already thought she was a bit touched in the head."

Ve's eccentricities didn't go unnoticed in this small village.

"The brain is a powerful organ. It is a theory that cannot be ruled out; however, I don't believe that's what we're dealing with."

I was beyond grateful that Curecrafters weren't bound to the Hippocratic oath—or to any HIPAA laws. "So what do you think we're dealing with?"

"Darcy, I think we need to be extra vigilant. If my instincts are correct, then there is a greater power than mine at work."

"What kind of power?"

"An evil one. Ve could be in very real danger."

With Cherise's words ringing in my head, I headed home to As You Wish.

My thoughts were spinning. Was Cherise right? Was there evil at work? Or was it only a theory?

I couldn't shake the word "evil" from my thoughts as I opened the back gate. No wonder Ve kept saying she was fine. She probably hadn't wanted to worry me.

Too late.

Archie, safely ensconced inside his outdoor cage (which he could easily escape), let out a high-pitched trill.

I jumped and winced. Sarcastically, I said, "I don't think that was loud enough."

"Smarty pants," he said. "I was just trying to get your attention. I thought you were going to stroll on by without a single glance my way, and that would not do for my ego. You look to be a woman on a mission."

I let Missy off her leash and gave Archie the quick recap of what Cherise had said. "I just want to figure out what's going on. I hate the thought that Ve might be in danger." My mama-bear instincts had kicked into high gear.

He dropped his voice. "'Finding out the truth is only half of it. It's what you do with it that matters.'"

"*The Secret Life of Bees*," I answered absently as I thought about the message behind the quote. I felt like he was telling me something I should pay attention to. I eyed him. "Do you know something you're not telling me?"

He blinked innocently, his bright black eyes shining. "Not at all."

Missy barked as if she didn't believe him. I happened to agree with her. "Spill it, Archibald."

"I'm offended," he squawked. "My integrity is of the highest caliber. I pride myself on my—"

A twig snapped behind me. I spun around in time to catch someone hopping the back fence and running toward the Enchanted Trail. Someone who'd apparently been hiding in the backyard the whole time.

Acting out of pure instinct, I yelled, "Stop!"

The person—clearly a man—didn't so much as break stride.

Before I could think twice about it, I took off after him.

Archie started mimicking a car alarm, then switched to a loud "*whoop, whoop, whoop!*"

I'd clearly lost my mind, giving chase. What was I going to do if I caught up to him? Bean him with my cell phone? I jumped the back fence and yelped at the way my ankle turned in upon my landing. My hurdling skills needed work.

For a second, I lost sight of the man as he darted into the woods. I broke out into a full-on sprint to try to catch up with him. As I ran, skipping over tree roots and dodging branches, I realized I didn't necessarily want to *catch* him. I only wanted to see who he was. I wasn't a confrontation kind of girl. But I could dial 911 like no one's business.

In hindsight, maybe that's what I should have done—before I lost my mind and gave chase. But now that I was running full tilt, I didn't want to turn back. The man would be long gone before I could even dial. I had to see who it was. . . .

From what I could tell, he was about six feet tall, dark-haired, and fair-skinned. He wore only a pair of short shorts (that looked a lot like boxers) and a T-shirt. Was he the Peeper Creeper? And if he was wearing only boxers and a T-shirt, was the Peeper Creeper not a Seeker like I'd suspected but some sort of pervert? I didn't even want to think about that option—and why he had been in our backyard—as I powered on.

I could see him up ahead, wheezing, and I realized he was an older man. As shafts of sunlight pierced the branches overhead, it made the silver in his hair sparkle. He was slowing down, and I was gaining on him.

My chest burned as I picked up the sound of nearby flapping. I looked up and saw Archie soaring overhead.

"I thought you might want some backup," he called.

It was never a bad idea to have eyes in the sky. Especially after I looked back at the trail and realized that the man was nowhere in sight. I jogged ahead to where the trail split. I didn't know which way he had gone, and the earth was too packed to see footprints.

"Do you see him?" I yelled to Archie.

"Negative! The canopy is too thick. Hold up. I'll circle around."

I bent at the waist and tried to catch my breath. I couldn't believe I'd lost him! I'd been so close. As my adrenaline wore off, I could feel the throbbing pain in my ankle. I'd twisted it good when I'd hurdled that fence.

It wasn't long before Archie was back. "He's gone. No hide nor hair."

Great. "Thanks for looking."

He bowed. "It was the least I could do."

Slowly, I limped my way back to the house. All told, I'd probably been gone only five minutes or so. As foot chases went, it was rather lame.

Archie flew back into his cage as Missy ran in circles around my feet, sniffing my legs. She was agitated, and I scooped her up to calm her down. After a minute, I felt her heartbeat go back to normal and I set her on the grass.

"Come on," I said to her. "Let's go in. I need to get cleaned up."

I also planned to give Nick a call. He needed to know what had happened. Maybe he could find some finger-prints along the back of the house or footprints in the yard.

Missy bounded inside ahead of me, and I kicked off my running shoes in the mudroom and peeled off my socks to drop in the laundry room. As soon I stepped into the kitchen, my feet started sliding out from under me. Arms flailing, I searched for something—anything—to grab on to in hopes of breaking my fall, but nothing was in reach. My left leg went one way, my right the other.

I landed with a thud and a small "*Eeee*" in the center of the floor. A floor that was slick with water.

Ve came dashing in wrapped in a fluffy bathrobe. She glistened with wetness. "Darcy! Oh, thank heavens you're here."

I glanced up at her from my splayed position on the floor and suddenly realized she wasn't alone. Nick Sawyer stood right behind her.

Wonderful.

"Are you all right, dear? What are you doing on the floor?" She kept one hand firmly on her bathrobe lapels and held out the other for me to take. As I levered myself off the floor, I noted that she looked slightly better than she had in a while. Her eyes were bright and there was natural color in her cheeks rather than a feverish blush. Damp tendrils of hair stuck to her cheeks and her neck, and a sloppy bun drooped atop her head.

"I slipped on the wet floor."

Ve looked down. "Oh my. I'm afraid that was my fault. When I heard the ruckus outside, I leapt out of my bath and came straight down. I'm afraid I must have taken most of the bath water with me."

I could tell Nick was trying not to smile—he was nibbling the corner of his lip and his cheek was twitching.

Missy was giving him lots of distance. I didn't understand what was going on with her lately. She definitely seemed upset with him.

"What're you doing here?" I was fascinated with the way his teeth clamped his lip and forced myself to look away from his mouth.

"Ve called. Thankfully, I wasn't too far away. What happened?"

He looked at Ve, who shrugged. "All I heard was Darcy yelling and Archie squawking like a siren. When I didn't see them in the backyard, I figured it had to be something bad."

I noticed the large puddles on the stairs that needed to be sopped up as soon as possible before someone took a spill and broke a neck. At the top of the steps, Tilda stared down at us with a look of dismay. Her tail swished ominously.

"Darcy?" Nick asked.

I recounted what had happened. Nick's already dark eyes turned stormy. "I'll take a look around." He carefully navigated the puddles and brushed past me, going out the back door.

Ve sneezed and suddenly she looked unwell again. "I need to get some clothes on. I'm starting to get a chill." She headed for the steps.

"Wait!" I said. "Let me dry them off first." I wasn't sure how she'd made it down without slipping. "How are you feeling? Any better?"

"I'm fine. I keep telling you that."

I grabbed a towel from the laundry room and dried each step. "I know what you're saying, but I can tell it doesn't match with how you're feeling. You're a lousy liar."

"I'll be fine, Darcy dear."

I swiped. "I talked to Cherise this morning."

"Oh?"

"Don't act so innocent," I said. "You know what she told me because she told you the same thing."

"There's nothing to be done, no matter how we look at it. What will be, will be."

I grudgingly admitted she had a point. Nothing could be done if others were involved—except perhaps if we discovered who they were and why they were after Ve. But we could be more aware. "I still don't like it."

"Neither do I, Darcy dear. Neither do I."

At the top of the landing, I dropped the towel on the floor and pushed it around with my foot, ignoring the way my whole body now ached from that fall. There was more water than I thought possible, leading all the way to Ve's private bath. Tilda did her best to trip me up as I cleaned, twining herself around my legs.

I heard voices downstairs as I finished mopping up Ve's bathroom floor. I had to smile as I glanced at her towel bars—all covered with drying nylons, colorful bras, Spanx, and one lone paisley silk handkerchief. She didn't believe in putting delicates in the washing machine.

As I came down the steps, Nick was talking to Ve in thc kitchen.

"Bad news," Ve said solemnly. All the color was gone from her cheeks.

"What?" I asked.

"Ve says this window was locked earlier." Nick pointed to the window above the kitchen sink.

I nodded. "I locked it myself last night."

As I looked at it now, though, the sash was lifted high and the screen had been pushed out. "He tried to break in?" I asked.

Nick shook his head and locked eyes with me. "No, Darcy. He didn't break in. . . . He broke *out*."

Chapter Eleven

An hour later, Nick was done processing the kitchen and yard and strongly suggested that Ve and I vacate the premises for the time being.

We were still trying to figure out how the intruder had gotten into the house in the first place. The front door was always locked, and I'd locked the back door on my way out that morning. Other than the window, there was no sign of entry in or out, but the sill had to be a good five feet off the ground. No way to climb in without help—and there was no evidence that a ladder or some other booster had been used.

It was strange. Very strange.

I was ready to pack my bags, but Ve vehemently refused. She said she had a plan, which kind of scared me more than the intruder in the house. Okay, not really. But it was close.

Nick promised to have officers increase their patrol of the area and left.

I was quite proud of myself for not begging him to stay.

Sitting at the kitchen island, I stared at the window, which was once again locked tight. The screen was still pushed outward, and Nick's supposition that the intruder had probably heard voices in the yard and was scared off—dive-bombing out the nearest window—kept playing through my head.

What if I had been a few minutes later? What if I hadn't stopped to chat with Archie? What would I have walked in to find? I shivered.

My stomach free-fell at the thought that Ve had been upstairs alone. Vulnerable. While someone was down here . . . lurking. Waiting. It made my skin crawl.

Ve was still in her bathrobe and she fluttered about the kitchen, setting various supplies on the countertop. A few candles, a sage smudge stick (sage branches wrapped in string), a handful of gemstones. She looked frazzled, pieces of hair sticking out, her bun coming undone. There was a wild look in her golden blue eyes, and I couldn't tell if it was from her fever or her feverish determination to accomplish her task.

"Can I help?" I asked.

She clasped her hands under her chin and surveyed her supplies. Finally, she said, "I could really use an agate sphere."

"Agate? The stone?"

"A banded one."

"Why?"

"For my protection spell, of course."

Oh, of course. First recantation spells, now this?

"Agate offers the most power against our enemies," she said.

Well, I was all for that. "And where does one find an agate sphere?"

She separated the stones on the counter. Small marbles of amethyst, bright yellow citrine, and jade. "The Charmory. Could you run over?"

"I'm fairly sure it's closed today, what with what happened to Patrice and all."

Ve's eyes closed. "Have mercy. With all this hoopla, I forgot all about poor Patrice. Let me think. Let me think."

Missy was napping in her dog bed, and Tilda was swatting at the sage.

Ve suddenly snapped her fingers. "I've got it. The Roving Stones. Someone at the fair is bound to have a banded agate sphere."

I raised an eyebrow. "Really?"

"Oh, Darcy dear, those Stoners have everything."

Smiling, I said, "I'll keep that in mind and see what I can find."

Ve said, "Could I ask another favor while you're out?"

"Of course."

She held up a finger and trundled off down the hall to the office. A moment later she was back, a piece of paper in hand. "Jonathan Wilkens faxed over the final wedding menu this morning. He needs our approval by noon. Could you run this over to Third Eye and get Sylar's go-ahead?"

I took the note. "I'll be back as soon as possible."

"Take your time. We can't cast the spell until midnight."

"Why?" I asked.

"It's the witching hour, Darcy."

Of course.

I gathered up my wallet and tote bag. "I'll leave Missy here with you. She'll scare off any potential intruders."

We both looked at the small dog, who sleepily raised her head and yawned. A small pink tongue stuck out. Way out.

"I'll hurry," I said.

Ve laughed. It was music to my ears. She'd been so sick lately that there hadn't been much humor.

I headed for the door. "Oh, I almost forgot. Mrs. P is stopping by later with some soup."

"Lovely," Ve said. "And, Darcy, for the agate?"

I didn't like how she wouldn't quite meet my eye. "Mmm-hmm?"

"There's one vendor in particular who's bound to have it."

"Who?" I asked, even though I knew. I just *knew*.

"Andreus Woodshall."

Of course.

Archie's cage was empty as I walked out the back gate. I glanced at Terry Goodwin's house. It was a simple two-story red-shingled gambrel with cozy window dormers. A flagstone path twined to the front door, and a picket fence lined the yard. Hedges had been neatly trimmed, perennial gardens bloomed throughout the yard, and it made me wonder who kept up with the landscaping. Because as long as I'd lived next to the man, I'd never laid eyes on him.

A sign dangled from a lamppost that read Terrence Goodwin, CPA, but I'd never seen a customer go inside. In fact, the only person I'd ever seen enter the home was Dennis Goodwin, Terry and Cherise's son.

Interesting. Several people told me Terry was an "interesting" man, but would never elaborate. As I walked past, I noticed that as always, the drapes had been pulled tight. It reminded me suddenly of Patrice Keaton's house, and I couldn't help but wonder what lurked inside Terry's home.

It might just be time I paid him a friendly visit. Say hello. Maybe bring him some brownies or something. No, not brownies. Tartlets. After all, since I was going to learn to make them tonight at the Sorcerer's Stove, I might as well put that knowledge to work.

I looked both ways before crossing the cobblestone street, headed for the green. Glinda Hansel's pink village police car cruised past. She gave me a finger wave and kept on going.

It reminded me that I wanted to find out more about her mother and what she had to do with Ve and Sylar.

Why would she have any reservations about attending the wedding? Was there a history there?

Honestly, after Sylar had been accused of murder, I'd thought I knew pretty much all there was to know about him. Widower, philanthropic optometrist, casual gambler (he liked to occasionally bet on the dogs), and generous with jewelry (but had poor discretion with inscriptions).

But obviously I was missing something. Maybe something big. Maybe not. I had to find out which, because it might be important to what was going on with Ve's health.

On the village green, I looked around. Ve had told me that Andreus Woodshall's stall was called Upala. I limped my way through the maze of tents (among those: Gemtastic! Hot Rocks, Gold Diggers, Natural Elements, Geode Dude), looking for the right one. Some vendors were already hard at work, pitching their merchandise to anyone who walked by. Others simply sat back, allowing their products to speak for themselves and customers to come to them.

I tried not to get distracted by all the shiny baubles. A few steps ahead, set slightly apart from the other tents, I finally spotted a fluttering gold banner stamped UPALA. Three of the four tent walls had been rolled up, leaving the rear wall down, and I could see the back of a man inside the booth as he chatted with a customer.

Tall, dark-haired, trim. Sounded like the description of Mr. Macabre.

So far, I hadn't gotten the willies, so I proceeded with caution.

Oh-so-slowly, I approached the stall, pretending to be fascinated with the dozens of displays. It was easy to pretend—the displays were gorgeous. There was a rainbow of color splashed in front of me. The table nearest me was full of vintage tiered stands that showed off jewelry of every kind. Antique silver boxes held loose stones and gems. On the table opposite me, I could see clusters of crystals and minerals like amethysts and citrine, among others I didn't recognize. Blues and whites and greens. They were stunning.

But the star of this booth was the front table. It was all about opals, loose ones and those that had already been fashioned into jewelry, small charms, amulets, and talismans. Common white opals were mixed with red and blue opals. There were charms, pendants, earrings, rings. The darker-hued stones, the ones streaked with vivid blues, reds, and yellows, were mesmerizing.

"See anything you like?" a deep voice asked.

Startled, I looked up and into a pair of stunning black eyes. They belonged to the man who was working the booth. A man who couldn't be Mr. Macabre, unless Andreus had learned how to turn back time—this guy appeared to be in his early twenties.

"I, uh—," I stammered.

He was gorgeous. Drop-dead. He was the kind of guy that when most women saw him they immediately started wondering if they'd shaved their legs that morning or had the foresight not to have worn granny panties.

Most women.

Not me.

I was too busy thinking that a man that pretty was too good to be true. From his jet-black hair, olive skin tone, perfect five-o'clock shadow (at ten in the morning), full lips, and strong jaw, there had to be something wrong with him.

Something. Anything.

"You like the opals?" he asked, trying to lead me along. His voice was cool, confident, charming.

I nodded and absently pointed to a blue opal set in gold and rimmed with diamonds.

"You have good taste. The black opal is the rarest of the opals, and one of this clarity . . . it is almost impossible to find."

I found my voice. "How much is it?" It would be perfect for Aunt Ve. Just her style. Maybe I could get it for her wedding and fulfill the whole "something blue" part of the day.

"Twenty-eight thousand."

Shocked, I snapped out of my stupor. "Say what?" At that price, Aunt Ve was going to have to do without.

He laughed. "It is rare, as I said."

"You have a twenty-eight-thousand-dollar gem out in the open? Aren't you afraid someone will steal it?"

His black eyes narrowed, and his whole countenance changed from one of friendliness to one of danger. Imminent danger. "No one would dare."

With a look like that, I believed it. I shifted my weight, trying to resist the urge to take a giant step away from the table.

In a blink, he was back to looking more personable. "There are more affordable options. There are plenty of reasonably priced genuine stones. And, if you must, the white opal is a nice choice, as are"—he said this with some distaste, I could tell— "synthetic opals." He shuddered.

"Why sell them if you don't like them?"

"They pay the bills. Not many have the means to purchase the black opals."

"I may be slow on the uptake, but isn't this opal blue, not black?"

"The base of the gem is black. What you're seeing is the play of color within the gemstone. Because it's a dark stone, most sunlight is absorbed, allowing the colors within to really shine. This one happens to have much blue inside. But there are others that burst with color."

He pointed to several examples that appeared, to my untrained eye, to be made of every color of the spectrum. They practically glowed with their brilliance. "They're beautiful."

"Would you like to try something on?"

I shook my head. I had a feeling that if I put one on, I wouldn't want to take it off. "No, but thank you. I actually stopped by looking for Andreus Woodshall. Is he around?"

Again, the man's eyes darkened into black beads. "He will be back any moment now."

Why that made me want to hurry right along, I had no idea. I reminded myself that he might have some answers about Patrice Keaton's death. "I guess I'll come back."

"Is there something I might help with? I am, after all, his son. Lazarus Woodshall at your service."

I *knew* he had been too good to be true. The son of Mr. Macabre. Why hadn't anyone warned me? "I, ah, need a banded agate sphere. Do you happen to have one?"

There was curiosity in his eyes as he sized me up. I supposed there weren't too many mortals who asked for banded agate spheres.

He nodded. "Certainly." As he bent and rummaged beneath the tablecloth, he said, "Have we met before?"

"No."

"Are you a local?" he asked.

"Yes." I glanced over my shoulder, suddenly feeling eyes on me again. Goose bumps popped up on my arms, and I wished he would hurry.

He peeked up at me. "New to the village?"

"Yes." My gaze swept the area. I couldn't see a single person looking my way. Rubbing my arms, I said, "Having any luck down there?"

Laughing, he stood, holding a beautiful stone orb the size of an apple, and set it on a small wooden pedestal. "Agate, a good protection stone."

"So I've heard."

"Are you in need of protection, Ms. Merriweather?"

The hair on the back of my neck rose. I was just about to ask him how he knew my name when I heard someone calling me.

"Darcy!"

I broke Lazarus's hard stare and turned to find Starla heading my way.

"Shopping?" she asked, looking bright and peppy in a pastel pink miniskirt and white blouse.

"Kind of," I said. "Are you working?" She should be, but she didn't have her camera with her.

She blushed and quietly said, "No, I'm on break."

"Oh, right! The coffee date."

She stomped on my toes, yet kept a tight smile on her face.

"Yow!" I said. First my ankle, now my toes? "Why'd you do that?"

"What?" she asked innocently. Then she turned and blinked her eyelashes at Lazarus. "Are you almost ready to go?"

My mouth fell open as I looked between them. Lazarus was Starla's date?

She kept mooning at him, yet his hard gaze never left my face.

I shivered.

I had a bad feeling about this. A very bad feeling.

Chapter Twelve

The agate orb, safely wrapped in plastic, was tucked into an Upala shopping tote as I headed for Sylar's shop to get his approval of the wedding menu.

I kept looking over my shoulder at the Upala tent, where I'd left Starla with Lazarus. Andreus still had not returned—for which I was oddly grateful.

Apparently, I needed to work on the confidence part of my sleuthing tactics. I mean, after all, how bad could the man be? Surely, everyone was exaggerating his creepiness. *Macabre. Dracula.* People like that just didn't exist.

Did they?

I was going to have to find out if I wanted to uncover what had happened to Patrice Keaton—or find out exactly what the Anicula looked like. I glanced at the Charmory. Crystals sparkled colorfully in the window, but a large CLOSED sign hung on the door.

Up ahead, I saw Mimi going into the Gingerbread Shack and decided to drop in as well. I wanted to see how Evan was faring after his knock on the head last night.

Bells tinkled as I pulled open the door. I inhaled the delicious scents inside the cozy shop. Chocolate, vanilla, cinnamon.

"Darcy Merriweather!" Evan cried. "What is this I hear about another run-in with your stalker?"

Mimi's eyes lit. "You have a stalker? Cool!"

I stepped up next to Mimi and put my arm around her as I rolled my eyes. "One, we don't know that he's *my* stalker. Two," I said, addressing Mimi, "it is not cool. You've been hanging out with Harper too much."

Thankfully, no one else was in the shop, so I quickly filled them in on what happened this morning. The bump on Evan's head had shrunk a bit, but was now colored a dark blue. "Is your head okay?"

"Just sore to touch, and I have a tiny headache. You two want the usual?"

Mimi and I nodded. Her long curly hair had been pulled back into a ponytail, and she wore a simple pair of denim shorts and a light blue V-necked tank top. She wasn't into makeup or boys quite yet, but I was sure the time would come—very soon—that boys would take notice of her. She was growing into quite the beauty.

"I have a question." Mimi's nose wrinkled and her eyebrows snapped downward. "Did your stalker—"

"Stop calling him that!" I interrupted.

She took a deep breath. "Did your *visitor* hear you talking with Archie?"

My mouth dropped open. The thought hadn't even crossed my mind. What if the intruder was a mortal? Or worse, a Seeker? "What if it was overheard?" I asked Evan. It would be hard to explain how a macaw could carry on a conversation with me. "Could I lose my powers?" It was, after all, what I'd always been told.

He set four mini devil's food cupcakes on a plate and slid it across the counter. "I don't know, Darcy."

As I paid (I always insisted), I could feel dread curling in my stomach. I was suddenly a nervous wreck about possibly losing my powers. I hoped that the intruder didn't realize who the voices belonged to—that would be the best outcome.

"If the Peeper heard something he shouldn't have, the Elder will let you know," he said. "So, for now, try not to worry. No news is good news for you."

That was easy for him to say.

Mimi and I sat at a high pub-style table. I couldn't help but notice she had her mom's diary with her again. I'd warned Mimi many times that she probably shouldn't be carrying it around the village, but she confessed that she hated letting it out of her sight. It was like having a bit of her mother with her at all times.

Which, of course, was hard to argue with.

"Maybe," I suggested to her, "we should get a book jacket for your mom's journal." I bit into the cupcake and let the chocolate melt on my tongue. Evan was a cupcake master. As a Bakecrafter, he should be. "So it doesn't look quite so important."

"Maybe," Mimi said, popping one of her cakes into her mouth whole.

I made a mental note to see if Harper had any book protectors in stock.

Mimi looked up at me, her brown eyes full of curiosity. "How did Starla's date go? Have you heard anything?"

"Starla?" Evan piped up. "She had a date? What date? When was this date? With whom?"

I didn't blame her for not telling him with whom. I kind of wondered if she would have told *me* if I hadn't seen her at the Upala booth. The son of Mr. Macabre. I shivered. "One of the Roving Stones vendors. For coffee. No big deal," I said, lying through my teeth. There was no reason to freak him out—he had an overprotective streak where his sister was concerned. It was just coffee. One date, done. Lazarus would be moving on before long.

I know I wouldn't be sad to see him go. How had he known my name? *Why* had he known my name?

"Maybe she'll fall in love with him and he'll fall in love with her, and then he'll stay in the village and they'll live happily ever after," Mimi said.

I stared at her, trying to hide my horror at the thought. "I think it's just coffee."

She pouted. "Well, they *could* fall in love."

"She is ready for a relationship," Evan said, wiping the table next to ours.

Suddenly my cupcake wasn't sitting so well.

"Do you think he brought her flowers?" Mimi asked. "Or candy?"

"I don't think so," I said.

"What's Starla's favorite flower?" she asked Evan.

He shrugged. "She likes them all."

"And candy?"

I eyed her. What was going on in her head?

"Chocolate-covered cherries," he answered.

Mimi turned to me, her brown eyes big and wide. "What're your favorites, Darcy?"

"Mine? Why?"

Evan shot me a party-pooper look.

I sighed. "Flowers? Well, I'm a simple daisy kind of girl. And candy? York Peppermint Patties."

"Cheap date," Evan murmured with a smile on his face.

"And you?" I pushed some crumbs around my plate.

"Well, since you asked. I've never had a date bring me flowers. Mine tend to bring alcohol." He pulled a wry face. "You think that says something about me?"

I laughed. "Would you prefer flowers?"

"Actually, I'm rather fond of gin. I do like my martinis. That being said, I think I'm a single red rose kind of guy."

Mimi sighed happily with a dreamy look in her eye. She was apparently a hopeless romantic.

Smiling, I grabbed my bag and stood up. "I need to go see Sylar about the wedding menu. Everything all set with Ve's cake?"

Evan made an a-okay sign with his fingers. "I'm going to start the layers this afternoon."

Ve had chosen a beautiful three-tiered chocolate fondant-covered wedding cake decorated with colorful sugar flowers. The cake was in good hands with Evan.

I said my good-byes, reminded Mimi about a cover for her mom's diary, and headed toward Sylar's shop across the green, taking the Enchanted Trail around the square since I didn't want to cut through the Roving Stones' tents.

Thankfully the path was well traveled and someone was always in sight, or I might have been worried about big bad wolves in the woods.

Though a thick tree line separated the path from the backs of village businesses, I could still see the outline of the shops that surrounded the square. I was behind the Sorcerer's Stove when I heard a loud crash and two people taking part in a restrained argument.

I couldn't make out who the voices belonged to, but it was clearly a man and a woman. Curious (okay, nosy), I hurried to an intersection in the trail. A wooden arrow with "Sorcerer's Stove" engraved on it pointed to a narrow dirt path. It would lead me to the back entrance of the restaurant. I tiptoed carefully as I tried to pick out words—or see who was doing the arguing.

As the path widened and opened to a small garden behind the restaurant, I took a good look around. Nothing seemed amiss. Butterflies flirted with flowers, birds chirped, bees buzzed. All had quieted. Then, suddenly, I jumped at another loud bang. It sounded like the lid of the Dumpster being slammed closed. I glanced toward the six-foot L-shaped fence that blocked the Dumpster from public view. The voices started up again, and I heard a man say, "The police will never find out, so please stop worrying."

I crept closer. It sounded like Jonathan, but I couldn't be sure.

"Tally ho, Darcy!" Archie swooped by.

"Shhh!" I said, Mimi's earlier concerns about being overheard fresh in my thoughts. I waved him toward the tree line and out of sight of anyone who might be watching.

Pepe clung to the macaw's back as he landed on a low-hanging branch. "*Ma chère*, what's wrong?"

I quickly filled them in. "Are you two out patrolling?"

"Indeed," Archie said.

Pepe dusted off his tiny red vest and readjusted his glasses. "The Creeper is still at large."

This sentence, said in Pepe's French accent, made me smile.

I glanced over my shoulder at the Dumpster. The voices had suddenly faded. Had the couple gone back inside? Or had they overheard Archie's approach?

"Could you do me a favor, Archie? Could you see if there's anyone over by the Dumpster?"

"I will check," Archie said. "Pepe, do you wish to come along?"

Pepe declined and hopped onto the branch. He wobbled and I scooped him up in my palms. "*Merci*." He bowed.

"You're welcome." I set him on my shoulder—one of his favorite lookouts.

Archie saluted with his wing, then flew off, a bright red dot in the blue sky.

"You think something is amiss, *ma chère*?" Pepe asked.

"I heard arguing a few minutes ago." I was going to make up some excuse about investigating Patrice's murder and how Jonathan might be involved, but ended up shrugging. "I'm being nosy."

Pepe laughed. "It is not a crime."

"Thankfully, because it's becoming a habit."

"Thankfully," he echoed, "because if not for your inquisitiveness, a murderer might still be roaming free and innocent people locked away."

He was referring to the murder that had happened a few months ago. I smiled. "Inquisitiveness. I like that word. Thanks, Pepe."

He bowed again as Archie's squawk pierced the air.

"What's he saying?" I asked, trying to make out the high-pitched words. He sounded distraught.

"I'm unsure," Pepe said.

Archie flew circles over the Dumpster, his voice repeating the same phrase. I moved closer to try and make out his words. Finally, my brain registered what he was saying.

Squawk. "Man down, man down." *Squawk.* "Man down, man down!"

Chapter Thirteen

I broke into a run. Pepe clung to my collar. The first thing I saw when I cleared the fence surrounding the Dumpster was a man crumpled facedown on the ground.

I tossed aside my purse and Upala bag and dropped to my knees to roll the body over. I gasped when I saw Jonathan's pale face. I did a quick check for blood and found none. He had no visible injuries at all.

Archie landed on the Dumpster. "Is he dead?"

"Must you be so morbid?" Pepe asked.

"It's a fairly obvious question to ask," Archie retorted.

"He's breathing," I said, relieved. His pulse was strong under my fingertips, but he didn't look well at all. Sallow skin, hollow eyes, sunken cheeks. His skin was cool and clammy. "Jonathan!" Placing my hand on his chest, I gave him a little shake.

After a long second, his eyes fluttered open and he moaned. Blinking at me as if trying to focus, he said, "Darcy?"

I had pulled out my cell phone. "I'm calling an ambulance. Don't move, okay?" I didn't know whether he had a head injury I couldn't see. I didn't want to take any chances.

Completely disobeying me, he sat up and put a hand on the phone. "No. I'm okay."

I noticed his hand shook slightly. "I'm not sure your definition of 'okay' and mine are one and the same, Jonathan."

He smiled wanly. "Be that as it may, I'm fine."

"I'm not sure your definition of 'fine' and—"

He raised his hand, cutting me off. "No ambulance."

I let out a frustrated breath. "You could have a head injury."

"My head is much too hard for that."

"In more ways than one," I mused.

Pepe said, "Perhaps a house call from Cherise Goodwin?"

Jonathan looked at the little mouse as if just noticing he was there. "A good idea, Pepe." He stood shakily, nodded to Archie as well, and said, "I will do just that."

"What happened?" I rose, too. "Did someone knock you out?"

He laughed. "What? No. What makes you think so?"

"I heard you arguing with someone," I said, bluffing. I had no idea if he'd been one of the people in the disagreement, but hoped I could flush out the truth.

His eyes narrowed, and he glanced around. "Overheard, you say?"

Suddenly, I felt as though I'd done something terribly wrong. "Not what was said, per se." Except that bit about the police never finding out. "Just voices raised in anger."

Slowly, he nodded. "I see." After a beat, he added, "It was of no concern. Zoey and I were disagreeing about a business matter with the restaurant."

Ah. Zoey.

Had she knocked him out? I gave him another once-over. Not a mark on the man, except for a few pebbles from the ground.

By the stony set of his jaw, I knew I wasn't going to get anything else out of him. I couldn't help but wonder what "business matter" the police would be interested in.

And if it had nothing to do with the restaurant at all, it meant he was lying to me.

Why would he do that?

Was he hiding something that hit a little closer to home?

Like the murder of his ex-girlfriend?

Pepe cleared his throat. "If I might inquire, why were you on the ground?"

Inquisitiveness. Apparently, it was contagious.

Swiping his forehead with a handkerchief, Jonathan said, "It must be the heat."

We all looked skyward. Sure, the sun was out, but it was a mild day. Skeptical, I looked back at him.

"Or," he said, shifting on his feet, "perhaps I've caught the same illness as your aunt. Is she feeling better?"

Even though he truly looked ill, I could tell he was lying. His darting gaze and his fidgeting gave him away. But why? "Not really."

"That's too bad. Well, it's been nice to—"

He was cut off by the shriek of a nearby siren's wail. And another. They grew louder, closer.

Had someone else seen Jonathan and called an ambulance?

But no, the sirens passed the restaurant and soon faded into a faint bleat.

I peeked down the street. "I wonder what's going on."

"Leave it to me." Archie flew off, circled above the restaurant, then came back in a hurry. "Two village police cars are racing down Incantation Circle. There looks to be something amiss at Patrice Keaton's house."

All I could imagine was that someone had uncovered another dead body in the mess at Patrice's.

I hurriedly hobbled down the trail, emerged at the corner of the square, and rushed toward Patrice's quaint blue house.

Checking with Sylar about the wedding menu was going to have to wait a little bit longer.

Ahead, in front of Patrice's, I could see a crowd gathered and two village police cars (neither were Nick's Bumblebee) with their lights flashing. Above me, I caught a flash of red as Archie and Pepe took in the scene from the sky.

As I neared, I could hear someone shouting. I skirted the edge of the crowd and stood on my tiptoes to get a glimpse of what was going on.

It was Elodie. And by the looks of the lawn and the sound of the yelling, she was in the middle of a hissy fit.

I spotted Yvonne near the front of the crowd and worked my way through to her. "What's going on?"

Yvonne had her hand over her mouth and tears in her eyes. "Grief, I think."

I remembered what Elodie had said the night before, about how she'd already grieved. This, I thought, might be a manifestation of another stage. Anger.

A pile of goods—boxes, a toaster, clothes, magazines, anything and everything—was mounded on the lawn. Elodie appeared in the doorway, shouted something about stupid, stupid records, and tossed another box out. Pristine LPs spilled out onto the grass.

"Has anyone tried to stop her?" I asked, taking in the gawking crowd.

"She won't listen. We're waiting for Connor to get here. She'll listen to him." Across the crowd, I saw a very hairy Roger Merrick talking to Glinda Hansel. She was taking notes. He was staring at me. I got the shivvies and looked away.

"Does she have any friends we can call in the meantime?" I asked.

"Not really," Yvonne said. "Elodie is a lot like her mother was. Very private. She was close to Zoey

Wilkens growing up, but Zoey has been so busy since getting married—they don't see much of each other anymore."

Plus, I imagined it was hard to be friends with someone who was married to the person who broke your mother's heart.

Elodie stepped into the doorway, cursed a blue streak about pumpernickel, and tossed a boxed Cuisinart bread maker into the pile.

"This is so sad," Yvonne said.

Elodie went back into the house. Through the open drapes I could see movement among the clutter mountains. I noticed that all the police tape had been removed from the door, the yard. Had Nick finished his investigation so soon? I would have thought that with all those boxes it would take forever to process everything.

Another box came flying out. It split, and a dozen or so plastic bins fell out. Each looked to contain gems. Or maybe they were beads. It was hard to tell from this distance until one of the plastic lids popped open and dozens of opals rolled out, glistening in the sunshine. There had to be thousands of dollars' worth of opals lying in the grass.

I recalled what Elodie had said about her mother's clutter. How there were treasures mixed in with the trash. She hadn't been kidding.

Suddenly the hair rose at the back of my neck again, and I could feel someone watching me. I glanced at Roger, but he had his back to me as he continued his conversation with Glinda.

On tiptoes, I looked around as goose bumps rose on my arms. My gaze skipped from face to face. Some I recognized; some I didn't. My eyes widened as I saw Vincent Paxton. He cautiously waved.

I wasn't sure what to make of him. Why was he being overtly friendly these days? There seemed to be no maliciousness in his eyes, and I felt no agitation when I looked at him. No one else seemed to be the least bit interested in me. Until . . . there. A man in the back of the crowd. I could see only part of his face—the rest was hidden by a woman in front of him. A tall man. With dark silver-streaked hair. As soon as I spotted him, he ducked away. But my goose bumps remained.

I started to go after him, but Yvonne had latched on to my arm. "Here comes Connor," she said, her voice tremulous.

True enough, Connor sprinted down the street. He ignored the crowd, the police, his father. His sights were set on one person only. Elodie, who had emerged from the house with an armful of, of all things, wooden hangers.

She was about to toss them when Connor shouted, "Elodie."

Frozen in place, she stared at her fiancé as he approached. He was breathing hard by the time he reached the bottom of the front steps.

Elodie stood on the landing, staring down at him.

"Elodie, baby," he said softly. He held out his arms.

Her bottom lip trembled and her eyes filled with tears.

"Come on," Connor coaxed.

She dropped the hangers, rushed down the steps and into his arms. Where she burst into tears.

"It's okay," he said, rubbing her back. He carefully led her back up the steps and into the house. Away from prying eyes.

I had a lump in my throat the size of an orange. At least it felt that way. I was suddenly seven years old again, school clothes shopping with my less-than-enthused father and a newborn Harper. He was frazzled, and I knew he'd rather be anywhere else. I'd thrown a temper tantrum over not wanting his choice of a red plaid skirt. I'd cried, kicked, screamed.

He let me. Then he gathered me in his arms and my anger dissolved into anguished sobs.

Because he'd known it hadn't been about the skirt at all.

It had been about my mother not being there.

I still had that skirt somewhere, packed away in a box in Ve's garage. It had been one of the few times I'd felt my father and I were on the same wavelength. That he understood my grief. That I understood his.

The air stirred around me, snapping me out of my memories. I turned and found Nick standing next to me, quietly watching.

He reached out and gently touched my arm. "Are you okay?" he asked softly.

I realized there were tears in my eyes. I quickly swiped them away. "Yeah."

He nodded. After a few seconds, he said, "Everything okay here now?"

Yvonne said, "I hope so."

I thought she would have rushed right inside the house. I was impressed by her restraint, but noticed how she was fidgeting. It was killing her to stay out here.

"I think everything will be fine now that Connor's here," I said.

"Are there any leads on the case, Nick?" Yvonne asked pointedly. "I think it would help Elodie to know her mother's killer is behind bars."

Nick's dark eyes gave nothing away as he looked at her. "We're working on it."

"Any clues in the house?" Yvonne asked. She was practically rubbing her hands together, looking for a juicy tidbit.

"I can't comment on an ongoing case, Mrs. Merrick." She pouted.

I was pouting inwardly, too. I wanted to know what Nick had learned.

The crowd slowly dispersed, and as it did so, I noticed that Jonathan and Zoey stood across the street, holding hands, taking everything in.

What had they been fighting about? What would the police never find out? What was wrong with Jonathan?

I rubbed my temples. I was getting a headache.

Suddenly, a man boomed, "Come to revisit the scene of your crime, Wilkens?"

Next to me, Yvonne murmured, "Oh no."

Roger Merrick advanced on Jonathan, who didn't budge an inch.

I was impressed, because if I'd seen Roger coming at me like that, I'd be sprinting down the street.

Yvonne grabbed Nick's arm and thrust him forward. "Stop him before he does something stupid."

Nick darted off.

I rubbed my arms, still feeling like someone was watching me with malicious intent. I glanced around again. There weren't many people left. The police officers, Yvonne, Roger, Jonathan, Zoey, and Connor and Elodie in the house. I scanned the woods, but didn't see anyone.

A flash of orange caught my eye, and I saw the tabby cat peeking out from under a front bush. It blinked at me lazily, and I wondered if it lived nearby. I wondered, too, if it was a familiar—but there was no way of knowing on sight. The animal would have to speak for me to be sure.

"Have you come to confess?" Roger shouted.

Nick jumped in front of him just before he reached Jonathan, sandwiching himself in between the two men.

Jonathan tucked Zoey behind him. Her eyes were wide and frightened.

Yvonne and I inched closer as Glinda ran over, her hand on her gun, and motioned for Zoey to come to her. She went to Glinda's side, and they looked almost identical from behind except for the clothing. Same height, same hair color. I'd take them for sisters, except from the front they looked absolutely nothing alike. Glinda was angelically pretty, while Zoey was what some would call a plain Jane. With her unusual looks, if she was about a foot taller, she would be on runways in Paris where couture models weren't necessarily the prettiest but rather striking and memorable. But here in the Enchanted Village, she blended in. Especially next to the striking Glinda.

"You're demented," Jonathan said. He hadn't shouted it, which seemed to make Roger more angry.

Roger strained against Nick's outstretched arms. "You deny your role in her death?"

"Her death," Jonathan said calmly, "was not at my hands."

"That's not what I said," Roger growled.

Nick seemed inclined to let them keep talking—as long as it didn't become physical.

"Perhaps, Roger, you doth protest too much." Jonathan took a step closer to the furry beast. He no longer seemed like an ill man, but one who had the strength of ten men. "A reflection of your own guilt in this situation?"

Yvonne's hand flew to her mouth to cover her gasp. I was trying my best to keep up with everything going on.

Roger roared, his eyes wide and wild. He drew in a deep breath as he prepared for his attack. Nick threw a look at Glinda.

She calmly stepped over and Tased Roger.

He immediately fell to the ground with a whine.

My jaw dropped.

Nick let out a breath and shook out his arms. To Zoey, he said, "Take Jonathan home."

She nodded and pulled on his arm. He didn't budge. His gaze was fixed on the doorway of Patrice's house.

I followed it, and found Elodie staring at Jonathan, her gaze just as strained as his.

"Jonathan," Zoey said softly, tugging. "Let's go."

"Oh my God!" Yvonne cried, rushing to Roger's side. "What just happened?"

I heard Glinda say, "He'll be fine. It was a very low voltage."

Finally, Jonathan turned away.

And when I looked back at the doorway, I saw that Elodie was gone, too.

Chapter Fourteen

An hour had passed.

Roger had recovered and lumbered like a giant grizzly, walking in circles around the yard with Yvonne by his side.

Glinda remained, kind of floating around. Her blond hair had been tied back in a stylish ponytail, and her light blue eyes looked saintly in the late-morning light.

I'd busied myself by organizing the mess on the lawn.

Nick had just finished interviewing everyone and had come over to me. He had barely been by my side for a few seconds when Glinda approached.

"Chief?" she said. "We all done here?"

Nodding, he said, "You can head on out."

"What?" Roger said, having overheard. "You're not charging her with anything?"

I wasn't sure if he was referring to Glinda, for Tasing him, or Elodie, for causing the ruckus in the first place. "The girl's gone crazy."

Ah, had to be Elodie, since Glinda had only been doing her job.

Technically, I supposed Nick could have charged Elodie with disturbing the peace, and I was thankful he hadn't. She had enough to deal with.

Roger shook his head. "Girl's gone plum crazy."

Yvonne elbowed him in his gut. "Stop that. She's grieving, is all."

He didn't look convinced. A bristly eyebrow rose, and he scratched his beard. He didn't look any worse for wear after being zapped. Being big was obviously a perk in that situation. "I say it's a good thing Connor hasn't married the girl yet. He needs to get out while he can."

Yvonne glared at him, *tsk*ed disgustedly, and stomped into Patrice's house.

I wanted to follow her. Roger gave me the heebies. Instead, I took a step closer to Nick, who didn't seem to mind in the least. I saw his lip twitch as he suppressed a smile, and I would have sworn that he moved closer to me as well. Our elbows bumped, then settled against each other.

I resisted the urge to snuggle right up next to him. It was harder than it seemed.

"What did I say?" Roger asked, perplexed, as he watched his wife go.

Nick ignored the question and asked one of his own. "Has Elodie acted out before?"

Roger folded his arms across his massive chest and shrugged.

Interesting. Roger had apparently adored Patrice — but not her daughter?

Nick jotted in his notebook. "Did she ever show aggression toward her mother?"

"She'd get mad about the clutter, sure."

What normal person wouldn't? I wondered.

"Did they fight?" Nick asked.

Roger grumbled. "Once they had a big fight. Didn't talk for months."

"What did they fight about?" Nick asked.

"I don't know. I should go check on Yvonne," he said and lumbered off.

Nick glanced around. "Hansel? You still here? I thought you left."

Glinda hurried over. "I was waiting for you?"

I couldn't help but notice the way she looked at him. I had a feeling it mirrored the way *I* looked at him.

She liked him.

I glanced his way. He didn't seem to notice.

"Why?" he asked.

"I—" She blinked long lashes. "I thought we were done?"

He gave an abrupt nod. "We are. I'll meet you at the station."

She still stood there.

"You can go now," he said softly.

"Oh. Okay." She turned and hurriedly walked away.

I waited for him to say something about her obvious adoration, but he didn't.

And if he wasn't going to mention it, neither was I.

Looking for something to talk about other than my growing jealousy, I said, "Do you already know what Elodie and her mom had a fight about?"

Nick smiled. "I can't discuss the case with you, either, Darcy."

There was one case he could talk about with me—since I was somewhat involved. "Any leads with the Peeper Creeper?"

"Not yet."

Lots of good news today, I thought sarcastically.

The screen door slammed, and Connor came down the steps toward us.

"How's Elodie?" I asked.

"Embarrassed," he said. "I'm going to take her home so she can lie down. She spent the morning working on funeral arrangements, and I think it all got to her."

Understandable.

He said, "Darcy, is there any way you can stay and bring this stuff back into the house?"

"I have a couple of quick errands to run. I can do it after that. Give me fifteen minutes?"

"Take your time," he said, throwing a look at the pile on the lawn. "I don't think this stuff is going anywhere."

As I headed off to Sylar's office, I couldn't help but think about those opals glistening in the sun. And I couldn't help but wonder what else might be hiding in all that clutter. Were there more treasures? Secrets? Or perhaps the answer to who had killed Patrice.

Chapter Fifteen

Much to my dismay, Third Eye Optometry had a CLOSED sign on the door. I shaded my eyes and peeked in, but everything inside was dark and closed up tight.

Weird. I checked my watch. It was close to eleven thirty. I had only a half hour to track down Sylar and get his approval on the wedding menu.

Sitting on a bench in front of his shop, I pulled out my cell phone and dialed Ve. She answered on the third ring, her voice sounding tired.

I got right to the point. "Sylar's not at work."

"Don't be silly," Ve said. "Of course he is."

I glanced over my shoulder at the shop. Still dark. "Nope. He's not."

"Oh dear," Ve murmured. "Give me a minute. I'm going to call his cell and then give you a call back."

I hung up and glanced at the village green. The Roving Stones had a good crowd browsing the booths. I stared at the Upala tent and watched as customers stopped, chatted, and bought. I couldn't tell from here if it was Lazarus or his father doing the selling, however. And I didn't particularly want to find out.

Chicken of me, I knew. Especially since Mr. Macabre was probably the only one, other than Elodie, who knew what the Anicula looked like. If the amulet was mixed in with Patrice's treasures, it would be nice to know what I was looking for.

My cell phone rang. Ve. "Did you find him?" I asked.

"He's not answering any of his phones. I'm worried, Darcy. What if he caught what I have and has fallen ill? What if he's collapsed somewhere, waiting for someone to find him?"

Sylar was too stubborn to get sick. "I'm sure that's not what happened."

"But we must be certain."

I had a sinking feeling about where this conversation was headed. "How?"

"Can you look for him?"

I drew in a deep breath. "Where?"

"First check the store, then his house. After that, I guess we'll have to get Nick involved."

I hated the worry in her voice. "Do you have keys to his office? And his house?"

"I do, but he has spares hidden. It will save time if you just use those. Are you at the shop still?"

"Sitting out front."

"Go around to the back entrance. There's a security light next to the door. It has a faux panel. Simply push downward on the top of the lamp and you'll hear a click. A little compartment will pop out that has a key in it. It will unlock the back door. Give me a call if you have any trouble or to let me know what you find."

Seemed vaguely like a wild-goose chase to me, but I couldn't say no to Ve, especially when she was so worried. But I was also feeling torn. By now I should have been back at Patrice's house, helping to clean up Elodie's mess.

So I did my best at being in two places at once. I called for backup.

My first call was to Mrs. Pennywhistle and I had to

laugh when I found out she was with Ve, dropping off soup. Sometimes the village felt like a small, small world.

Mrs. P was more than happy to head over to Elodie's, and since Elodie trusted Mrs. P, I knew she wouldn't mind me asking her for help. I also called Starla to see if she could lend a hand, but she didn't answer her phone. As I left a quick message, I couldn't help but wonder if her coffee date had turned into a lunch date.

I really hoped not.

After I hung up, I walked around the side of the building, following a stony path to the back of Sylar's shop, a stand-alone business not too far from the Sorcerer's Stove. The store was a cute little cottage with a faux thatched roof. At the rear of the building were a couple of trash cans tucked behind a picket fence, a narrow driveway, and another wooded dirt path leading to the Enchanted Trail.

After I set my bags down by the picket fence, I started looking for the spare. I felt a little strange inspecting Sylar's back door and security light, like I was some sort of criminal. That feeling was made even worse when I realized I wasn't tall enough to reach the top of the light. I glanced furtively around for something to stand on, but didn't see a thing. Not so much as a wooden crate or cardboard box in sight.

I was debating whether to run home for a step stool when my gaze fell upon the trash cans. They were the metal kind, which would be strong enough to hold my weight yet small enough for me to drag over to the door.

One of them would have to do.

Looking left, then right, then left again, I moseyed over to the cans like I had every right to be removing them from their picket pen.

One of them was heavier than it looked, so I left it in place and grabbed the other one. It banged against my shins as I carried it over to the back door. As I set it down, the lid popped and clanged like a cymbal. Guiltily, I checked to make sure no one had spotted me and was calling the police. All clear.

Climbing atop the can took some doing. I had to balance one foot on the ground, hold on to the doorknob for leverage, then haul myself up. As I pulled, the doorknob turned. The door swung open, and I screamed as it pulled me off-balance. I fluttered and flailed and jumped before I toppled over. I landed with a wince as pain once again shot through my ankle. The trash can teetered, and I reached for it just a second too late. It fell with a crash.

For the love, as Harper would say.

I glanced at the now-open door. The door that had been unlocked. *Huh*. I probably should have checked that before the whole trash can thing. Live and learn.

I took a quick peek around the building to make sure no one had heard the cacophony. Apparently, as the police were not descending, no one had. I quickly went about setting things back to rights in case anyone happened along.

Trash had spilled out of the can. Mostly shredded paper products, thank goodness. As I went about scooping everything back into the containers, a flash of bright purple on the ground caught my eye. I picked up the sliver of paper and realized I recognized it.

It was part of Ve's wedding invitation—the RSVP card. Crouching, I found many more purple strips. Not just from the RSVP cards but parts of the entire invitation. Sitting back, I wondered why on earth Sylar had shredded wedding invitations in his trash. Were these extra invitations? Or was this the reason why Ve hadn't heard back from so many of the people she invited?

It was puzzling, but I didn't have the time at the moment to stress over it. I finished cleaning up the mess and dragged the can back to its pen. I'd just wrestled it in when I heard voices. People were coming down the dirt path from the Enchanted Trail.

I dropped to the ground and duck-walked behind the trash can corral, out of sight. My gaze shot to the back door of Sylar's shop. It was still open. Not terribly wide but certainly noticeable.

I gulped and wished with all my might the door would swing closed.

Nothing, nada, zilch.

Where was that Anicula when I needed it?

A couple emerged from the tree cover, their arms linked.

I frowned, feeling the skin on my forehead dip into an angry vee.

I didn't recognize the woman, a short sexy-secretary type with plump cheeks and a sharp chin. Her white-blond hair was swept into a claw clip, and she wore hardly any makeup at all—and didn't need any with her fair, flawless skin. Her wrap dress accented a curvaceous figure. She was Betty Boop cute.

What wasn't so cute was the way she gripped the man's arm so possessively.

Sylar's arm.

And to think Ve had been worried about him.

This was when I realized the importance of the Craft's "do no harm" motto. Because if I'd known a spell for putting a pox on a man, I'd have cast it. The swine.

Sylar patted her hand and removed it (somewhat forcibly) from his arm. "Dorothy, I'm glad we had this chat, but we should be getting back to work."

Aha, so this was Dorothy. I should have known—I could see Glinda looking just like her in thirty years.

"Sy, you don't understand," she said.

Sy? I wanted to gag at her cotton-candy tone.

Sylar looked truly perplexed. His bushy white eyebrows dipped. "Understand what?"

She heaved a sigh, then stood on her tiptoes and kissed him. At first it was just a peck, but Sylar seemed to melt into her and it became a steamy embrace.

My jaw dropped.

Sylar, thank goodness, finally came to his senses and extricated himself. He took a step back, looking slightly stunned. He was shaking his head.

Dorothy-the-hussy said, "If you go through with marrying Velma, Sylar, I'll be forced to quit." She dragged a hand down his chest, taking hold of his tie. "You don't want that, do you?" She cuddled up closer to him.

Yes. Yes, he did. I was getting a clearer picture now. This woman was after Ve's man. And by the looks of it, he was weak. As Dorothy leaned in for another smooch, he didn't back away.

Something had to be done. Fast. I felt around for a rock and found a small stone. I tossed it at the door.

Sylar's head snapped up—the trance he was under finally broken.

Dorothy pouted.

Sylar, his tie askew, marched toward the back door. "Call the police, Dorothy. It looks like we've had a break-in."

As they cautiously entered the shop, I snuck away, wondering just how I was going to break this development to Ve.

Chapter Sixteen

I was halfway to Patrice Keaton's house when I remembered the menu.

Sighing, I spun around and headed back to Sylar's shop. I heard the sirens just as I approached the front door.

Trying to look innocent, I turned and found the Bumblebee pulling up to the curb.

Nick got out and gave me a searching look. "Why am I not surprised?"

"I don't know what you mean."

He smiled a smile that melted me from the inside out.

Sylar came hurrying out the front door and stopped short when he spotted me. "Darcy! What are you doing here?"

I fussed around in my tote bag and came up with the wedding menu. "Ve sent me over for your approval of the wedding menu." I glanced at Nick. "Is there something wrong?"

"Someone broke into the store." Sylar was short of breath, his cheeks pink, his tie still askew from when Dorothy had tugged on it.

My jaw locked, then loosened, and I tried for my best bashful voice. "The back door?"

Sylar blinked. "Why, yes. How'd you—"

Looking between the two men, I said, "I think I'm at fault."

"Maybe you should explain, Darcy." Nick's lip was twitching with amusement again. I tried not to stare at it. Or wish that it was touching mine.

"Well, Ve sent me over with the wedding menu"—I flashed it for them to prove I was legit—"and when the store was closed, Ve was worried because Sylar was supposed to be working. She became very concerned for his well-being." I gave him the hairy eyeball for worrying Ve while he was out traipsing around with that baby-booming bimbo, Dorothy. "She asked me to go inside and make sure Sylar hadn't passed out or anything."

"So you broke in?" Nick asked, eyes wide.

"Nooo," I explained patiently. "I used the key that's hidden in the security light by the back door." Okay, so I fudged the truth a wee bit. What they don't know about me falling off a trash can wouldn't hurt them. "Ve told me where it was. I must not have closed the door tightly on my way out. Sorry," I said to Sylar.

He coughed and tugged at his collar. "Quite all right. It was nice of you to check on my welfare."

I rocked on my heels. "If you don't mind me asking, where were you? Ve was beside herself trying to get in touch."

His already-pink cheeks flamed crimson. "I, ah—a doctor's appointment. Yes, the doctor. To make sure I'm fit as a fiddle for the upcoming wedding!"

"And all is well, I take it?" I asked, twisting the knife.

"Fine. Dandy! Fit as a—"

"Fiddle. Right, got that. And no one was covering the shop? Don't you have an assistant or something?"

"Dorothy," Nick supplied, nodding.

Sylar fidgeted with his pocket watch. "I"—he coughed—"gave her the day off."

Over Sylar's shoulder, Dorothy and her white-blond hair could be seen peering out at us. I lifted my eyebrows.

Sylar followed my gaze. "The *morning* off. Morning! My apologies. The break-in has me rattled."

I was about to protest the words "break-in" when Nick touched my elbow. "So we're all good here?"

Sylar clapped him on the shoulder. "Seems so. Nothing is missing from the shop, and I'll go call Ve right this moment. Thanks for coming so quickly, Nick. It's nice to have someone competent on the job." He turned to go.

"Wait!" I cried.

He turned around, a bit of panic in his eyes. "Yes, Darcy?"

"The menu." I passed it to him.

He lowered his glasses to the end of his nose and peered at the paper. "Good. Very good. I approve."

I bet he did. There could have been mud cakes on that menu and he would have said it was fine. He just wanted to be away from us as soon as humanly possible.

He thrust the menu back at me and retreated into the shop, leaving the CLOSED sign still hanging on the door as it slammed closed.

Nick smiled his half smile. "Any reason you gave him the grand inquisition?"

"Promise not to tell?" I said.

This time he fully smiled. "Cross my heart."

"Sylar neglected to mention that he was playing tonsil hockey with Dorothy behind the shop." I shuddered at the memory. Some things a girl just didn't need to see. "He hadn't been to the doctor at all—he'd been on a walk with her."

Nick's eyes widened. "You're kidding."

"Nope. And that's not all. There are shredded wedding invitations in the trash. And I don't know if they're extras or if the invitations were never mailed in the first place."

Nick held up a hand. "Do I want to know why you were snooping in his trash?"

"It wasn't snooping. It . . . it's a long story. And doesn't really matter."

He ran a hand through his hair. "So Sylar is cheating on Ve?"

"I don't know if I'd say that. It looks like Dorothy has her sights set on him, though, and he . . . he's just weak. Men. Sheesh."

He elbowed me. "Hey. Not *all* men."

Suddenly, I felt bashful myself. "You'll have to convince me of that."

He held my gaze. "Maybe I will."

My heart was pounding. In a good way.

"Do you," he began, but was cut off by his radio. He gave a little shake of his head. "It's been one of those days."

Didn't I know it.

"Sawyer here," he said into his walkie-talkie thingy.

A voice crackled. "Chief, they need you back at the Keaton house."

Nick winced as he asked, "Why?"

"Report of a robbery."

"Be right there," he answered. To me, he said, "I've got to go."

"I heard. I'm on my way back there, too."

He stepped off the curb. "Guess I'll see you there."

"Guess so." I rocked on my heels.

He opened his car door, then looked up at me with that half smile. "Do you want a ride?"

I smiled. "I thought you'd never ask."

On the two-minute drive to Patrice's house, I called Ve to let her know that Sylar was in fact safe and sound.

For how long he remained that way was to be determined.

When Ve found out about what had happened with Dorothy, there was going to be hell to pay.

I was beginning to think that I shouldn't tell her . . . just so there wouldn't be another murder in the village anytime soon.

On the phone, Ve sounded relieved to hear the news but somewhat distant. Distracted.

"What are you doing?" I asked.

"Watching reality TV," she said. "It's really quite compelling."

I smiled at the thought of her watching some of the more outrageous programs. "I'll be at the Keaton house for a while. There was a bit of an incident there this morning."

Nick cast me a sideways smirk.

Okay, "a bit" might have been an understatement.

"I heard." She *tsk*ed. "That poor girl."

That's right—Mrs. P had been with her when I called for help. I told Ve I'd check on her in a while and hung up as Nick parked near Patrice's house.

Mrs. P was marching around in her bright pink tracksuit, her hands in the air as if calling for help from the heavens. Elodie and Yvonne sat on the front steps, in almost identical positions. Elodie had her elbows propped on her knees and her head in her hand as she stared forlornly at the lawn. Yvonne had only one elbow on her knee, her hand cupping her chin.

Mrs. P came to an abrupt stop. "One minute they're here, the next they're gone. Couldn't have been more than thirty seconds that I was in the house."

Nick said, "Slow down. What's gone?"

"The opals!" Mrs. P said as if we should have known.

"This is all my fault," Elodie murmured.

"Now, now." Yvonne patted Elodie's knee. "It's no one's fault but the thief's."

Elodie's hair was mussed, sticking out in lumps and bumps. "We all know who the thief is."

"You do?" I asked.

Nick stepped forward. "Who?"

"Andreus Woodshall, of course," Elodie said. "Who else?"

Mrs. P shivered.

So did I. The man's name was popping up with alarming frequency.

"We don't know that for certain," Yvonne said, stretching out her legs.

Elodie threw her a "be serious" look. "Who else would it be?"

Yvonne pondered for a moment. "Perhaps you're right. It was Andreus."

Nick looked like he needed a stiff drink. Or a nap. Or both. "Did any of you see him take the opals?"

All three women shook their heads.

"Then how can you be sure?" Nick asked.

Completely serious, Elodie asked, "Who else would it be?"

I felt like we were talking in circles. I was starting to get dizzy.

"Maybe you should talk me through what happened," Nick said.

Mrs. P said, "I was out here, separating piles. Trash from treasure. Elodie and Yvonne were in the house." Her voice rose. "I heard a crash from the backyard."

"We heard it, too," Yvonne piped in.

"So I went a'running. Well" — Mrs. P grinned — "a'fast-walkin.'"

Which, despite her age, was pretty fast.

"A flowerpot had been knocked over on the back deck. By the time we got that sorted out and I came back out front, the box of opals was gone."

"Just the opals?" Nick asked.

Mrs. P nodded firmly. "Just."

"Which proves that it was Andreus," Elodie said. She glanced at Yvonne. "He's not usually so careless. He should have taken some of the other gems, too, just to throw off some suspicion."

My head was starting to spin. I sat on the grass.

Yvonne nodded in agreement. "Sloppy. But desperate times—"

Nick coughed. "Ladies."

They all looked at him.

"Perhaps a little more clarification?" He had a pencil poised on a notepad. "What's this about desperate times?"

"And what do you mean by usually?" I asked. "He's broken in before?"

Yvonne said, "Andreus is desperate to get his hands on the Anicula."

"And since we've had several break-ins over the past eighteen months—whenever the Roving Stones are in town—we assume it's Andreus. He doesn't usually take anything, though. He's just looking for the Anicula."

I looked at Yvonne. "So yesterday when we found the front door broken . . ."

She shrugged. "I assumed it was Andreus again."

That would have been nice to know yesterday. But then again, there hadn't really been any time to discuss the break-in after Patrice's body had been found.

"The Anic what?" Nick asked.

"The Anicula," I said. "It's a magical amulet that grants wishes to its owner." My mind kept replaying Elodie's statement—the one where she said he breaks in but doesn't take anything. Could *he* be the Peeper Creeper?

Nick went a little pale and looked like he wanted to sit down, too, but resisted. "Amulet?"

"Actually," Elodie said, correcting me, "it doesn't have to be its owner. It will grant wishes to whoever is within its immediate proximity. About six inches."

"I didn't know that," Yvonne said.

Elodie glanced at her. "Not many people do. And technically . . ."

"What?" Nick asked as if he didn't really want to know.

"It's not an amulet."

"It's not?" Yvonne and I asked at the same time.

Elodie shook her head. "At one time it was, but then it became too recognizable and was dismantled. Now it's just a solitary shaped gemstone awaiting a new setting."

"Who dismantled it?" Yvonne asked.

She seemed a little overeager to know, if you asked me.

"My father," Elodie said. "A long, long time ago."

Nick rubbed the spot between his eyebrows and cut her off. "What does this have to do with the robbery today?" His eyes widened. "Let me guess. The stone is an opal."

I drew in a breath. "A black opal?"

"How'd you know?" Elodie asked.

"I was at Upala this morning and there were a lot of black opals."

"Andreus collects them," Elodie said, "in hopes that one might just be the magical Anicula."

But that made no sense. "Why so many when he knows what he's looking for?"

Elodie stretched her legs. "But he doesn't. He doesn't know what the Anicula looks like."

Well, there blew my plans to ask him about its appearance.

"How is that possible?" I asked. "Didn't his family create it?"

"Long before he was born. Generations," Elodie said. "He knows the Anicula is a black opal. He knew my mother owned it. When he learned it was stolen, he slowly began acquiring as many black opals as he could, hoping that eventually he'd stumble across the right one."

"Then why break in here?" Mrs. P asked. "Why take the opals that were on the grass?"

Elodie sighed. "Because a part of him doesn't believe it was stolen. He thinks my mother has it hidden inside the house."

Nick said, "The Anicula was stolen? When?"

"Six months before my mother died," Elodie said.

"So," he said, "as of right now, no one knows where the Anicula is?"

We all nodded.

He shook his head in disbelief. "But it is an opal?"

"It is," Elodie affirmed. "Did you know that Upala means opal in"—she glanced at Yvonne—"Greek?"

"Latin," she said.

"What *does* the Anicula opal look like?" Yvonne asked. "Is it big? Little?"

I eyed her. She was definitely fishing for information. Was she after the Anicula for herself?

Elodie's eyes took on a distant look, as if she were remembering something specific from her past. "The last time I saw it, I was little, maybe four or five. But I'll never forget that day, holding that stone in my hand." Her voice grew strong. "Feeling the power, even though the opal wasn't very big." Her tone shifted, and now it was filled with sorrow. "The Anicula is shaped like a small teardrop. Because, my father said, it brought so much pain to those who abused it."

She hadn't seen the Anicula in twenty years? That didn't make sense. "I thought your mom wore the Anicula every day," I said.

"She did," Elodie answered. "Tucked inside a velvet pouch."

Ah, that made more sense.

I bit my lip. Most people would think that endless wishes would be a good thing, a great thing. But with that power came responsibility. And that responsibility could turn into something depressive—or egomaniacal.

I, for one, was very glad my powers were limited.

"Is it possible the Anicula stone was in with the opals that were stolen?" I asked.

Mrs. P said, "There weren't any tear-shaped stones that I saw—most of them were round—so I think it's safe to say it wasn't there."

Thank goodness.

"You'll go talk to Andreus?" Yvonne asked Nick.

"Yes, I'll question him. But without an eyewitness or his confession, it doesn't look good for getting those stones back."

Elodie said, "I don't care about the stones. Or the Anicula. I hate that stone. If he finds it, he can keep it. I never want to see it again."

Chapter Seventeen

The mess Elodie had made outside was nothing in comparison to what I discovered inside the house. I hadn't thought it could be much worse than it had been the day before, but Nick and his team had gone through every box—and left the contents to fall where they may.

Nick's team had confiscated the suitcase that Patrice had been found in, but given the time that had elapsed between Patrice disappearing and finding her body—there was little hope that any evidence remained.

Mrs. P said, "Ve seemed to be feeling a bit better by the time I left her earlier. Could be my presence cheered her right up."

"Or you scared the virus right out of her," Evan joked.

He had come over to help clean. Unlike Harper and Starla, he had employees to cover the shop when he wasn't there.

Mrs. P cackled and gave him a hearty shove. "Oh, you. It was probably the soup. It has healing powers."

"Really?" I hoped I didn't sound naive. It was hard to know what was magical in this village and what wasn't.

She winked. "Or it could be the bottle of vodka I brought along."

I pushed a box aside to make room for another. Shocked, I said, "You got Ve drunk?"

"Just a little tipsy." She sorted through a pile of clothes. "Just enough for her to forget how sick she was feeling."

"Until tomorrow when the hangover hits." Evan would be mortified to know he had a fine sheen of dust covering his reddish blond 'do.

I was going to have to ply Ve with as much ibuprofen as she could take.

"Until then," Mrs. P said, "there's today. By the time I left, Ve was looking like her old self."

"Fit as a fiddle?" I asked, thinking of Sylar and Dorothy in their steamy embrace.

Mrs. P snapped her fingers. "Exactly."

Ve and Sylar's wedding was Sunday afternoon. The ceremony was to take place on the village green (the Roving Stones would be gone by then), in front of all Ve and Sylar's friends and family.

My stomach hurt thinking about it. Was Ve saying "I do" a big mistake?

True enough, I wasn't that fond of Sylar. He was a nice man, but I wasn't sure he was right for Ve. From what I'd seen over the last couple of months, she put more into the relationship than he did. Lots of take and no give on his part.

I'd been in a similar relationship and it hadn't turned out well.

But I had to keep my feelings to myself. Ve was happy and that was all that mattered.

She was happy, wasn't she?

As I made another trip outside to gather an armload of clutter, I thought about what Cherise had said yesterday. Was Ve's illness a psychological manifestation of her misgivings about marrying Sylar? If vodka could cure her ailments, even temporarily, it would seem likely.

At this point, I wanted to believe it.

The other choices weren't so great.

Either another Crafter's recantation spell was counteracting Cherise's curing spell, or something evil was at work.

Mental problems had never looked so good.

No matter what, I was glad Ve was feeling a little better. She was going to need her strength when she found out about Dorothy.

And I had to tell her. Didn't I?

I was debating that when I caught a flash of orange in the bushes. Bending down, I made kissy noises to the tabby and duck-walked closer. The cat's golden eyes watched me warily. It wore no collar and gave me a hard stare. Suddenly, it bolted and disappeared around the back of the house. If it was a stray, it obviously lived around here somewhere. And if it was a familiar, it wanted to be left alone.

As I carried another box inside, I was still thinking about Ve and decided to get a little advice from my friends. "Hypothetically, if you two knew a secret that might hurt someone but felt that person should know what's going on around her, would you tell?"

"Yes," Evan said.

"No." Mrs. P's crazy hair didn't budge as she shook her head.

I looked between them.

"What kind of secret?" Evan asked, his eyebrows waggling. "What do you know about whom? Share!"

"Hypothetically," I said.

"Yeah, right." He tossed a bunch of old newspaper into a black trash bag.

"I say stay out of it," Mrs. P said. "The odds of you being caught in the crossfire are too great. Let the people involved work it out themselves."

I bit my lip. "What if I said I saw a certain optician's assistant kiss a certain optician behind his shop just days before he was due to be married?"

"Oh my goodness," Mrs. P cried. "You have to tell Ve!"

"Wait, wait." Evan held up his hands. "Are we still being hypothetical?"

I threw him a withering glance.

He grinned, delighted with this bit of gossip. "Are you saying Dorothy Hansel planted a big one on Sylar?"

I nodded, wishing I could banish the image from my mind.

"Did Sylar initiate it?" Evan asked.

"Not really. But he didn't exactly push her away."

Mrs. P cackled. She had a spot of bright red lipstick on her tooth. "Oh, honey, he's a man, after all."

Evan frowned. "I don't think you should tell Ve, then. Not yet, at least. Sounds to me like Dorothy is just stirring up trouble. She's had a thing for Sylar for years. She's probably desperate to stop the wedding."

"Do you think Sylar has a thing for her?" I asked, picking a dust bunny off Evan's shoulder.

Both shook their heads.

"If he did," Mrs. P said, "he's had plenty of time to act on it before now. I believe he thinks of her as just a good friend."

"So don't tell Ve?" I asked.

"Wait a day or two," Mrs. P advised. "You might be surprised that the situation works itself out. Ve and Sylar will be married on Sunday, as planned."

Evan squinted at me. "You don't look happy about that."

"It's just—" I hefted the box to place it atop a growing pile. My cell phone rang, cutting me off. It was Ve, speak of the devil.

"Darling girl," she said. "Sylar just called. He found a bag with an agate ball behind his shop and thinks it might belong to you. I think he might be right."

I winced. I must have accidentally left my Upala bag

behind the trash cans. Had Sylar figured out I'd been spying? "I hadn't even realized I left it behind. I'm almost done here at Patrice's for today. I'll pack up and head over to pick it up and will be home soon."

"I'll be here," Ve said loftily as if she hadn't a care in the world. How much vodka had she drunk?

I hung up and said, "I think we should wrap up for the day." The mess on the lawn had been cleared, transferred now inside the house, where it blended in with the rest of the clutter. Elodie had given me free rein to come and go as I pleased. Even after all that had happened, she still wanted the house cleared out as soon as possible. I shoved some boxes aside. "I have to go pick up my agate sphere I accidentally left behind Sylar's shop. Apparently, he found it."

"You're going back there?" Evan asked.

"I have to. I need the sphere for Ve's protection spell."

"From the Peeper Creeper?" Mrs. P asked.

I had told them what happened this morning.

"Well," Evan said with a smile. "You might want to let Dorothy borrow that agate."

"Why?" I asked.

"Because," he said, raising an amused eyebrow, "when Ve finds out what Dorothy has done, she's going to need all the protection she can get."

Chapter Eighteen

I wasn't looking forward to seeing Sylar.

Especially if he suspected that I'd seen what had happened between him and Dorothy behind his shop earlier.

As I hurried along the Enchanted Trail toward the Third Eye Optometry Office, I tried to process all I'd learned in the last two days, starting with finding Patrice's body and ending with Roger attacking Jonathan Wilkens.

Really, what it all boiled down to was that I was no closer to figuring out who had killed Patrice. Or why.

As I turned onto the wooded path leading to the back door of Third Eye, I thought I heard footsteps behind me. I turned to look back at the trail, but I couldn't see anyone coming in either direction.

Paranoid.

Intuition?

I glanced back again, but there was still no sign of anyone.

Strange.

At least the footsteps hadn't come with that heebie-jeebie feeling I'd been experiencing lately.

I circled around to the front of Sylar's shop and was surprised when I saw the CLOSED sign on the front door.

I shaded my eyes against the glass, but even though there was a faint light coming from the rear of the store, I didn't see anyone inside. I rapped on the glass and waited, but no one answered.

I backtracked to the rear door, in case Sylar was in the back storeroom and couldn't hear my knocking out front. As I neared the door, I heard a scurrying behind me and whipped around. "Who's there?"

No one answered.

Of course not. That would be too easy. "Vince?" I called out. For some reason, I had the feeling he was following me around. I just didn't know why.

There was no reply. No Vince. No bogeymen. No big bad wolves.

I was really beginning to question my sanity as I knocked on Sylar's back door.

A second later, the door swung open and Dorothy peered out. "Who're you?" she asked with a tone of voice that clearly conveyed a high level of crankiness.

I wasn't exactly comfortable talking to her. "I'm Darcy Merriweather. I think Sylar is expecting me? I left—"

"Oh. *You're* Darcy."

I didn't care for the dulcet tone of her voice. It was way too sweet to be sincere.

She leaned against the doorframe, a hip cocked, her arms folded across her ample chest. "You're a pretty thing, aren't you?"

"Um, thank you. Is Sylar here?"

"No."

Uncomfortable, I shifted. I wished I'd thought to ask Mrs. P to tag along.

Pointedly, she asked, "Is it true you're dating Nick Sawyer?"

Again, I heard a rustle behind me. I tossed a look over my shoulder. Not only to see if anyone was there (there wasn't), but to see if I could spot any hidden cameras. Surely, someone was playing a joke on me. Dorothy wasn't really quizzing me on my love life, was she?

"I left a bag here earlier . . . ," I said, trying to distract her from whatever mission she was on.

"He's a handsome man, that Nick." She examined one of her long, painted nails. "Marriage material."

"It's a brown bag." I held my hands apart a foot. "About this big?"

One of her eyebrows rose as she studied me closely. Then she abruptly turned around and picked up the Upala bag. She dangled it in front of me. "This bag?"

Relief flowed. "Yes." I reached for it and she yanked it back.

I'd never been in a catfight in my whole life, but I was seriously considering it at this point. I was pretty sure I could take her. After all, I was a good twenty years younger, but she had a meanness in her eyes that I couldn't discount. She would fight dirty—I was sure of it.

"I really should be going. Very busy," I said, trying to hold my temper in check.

"So I've heard. Busy, busy, busy," she sang.

She actually had a nice voice. I kind of hated that about her, since I couldn't sing my way out of a paper bag. Speaking of which, she had stepped closer to me, invading my personal space. Which I tolerated only because now she was near enough for me to snatch the Upala bag. I grabbed it out of her hands and clutched it to my chest.

She smiled. Apparently, I was amusing.

I, however, found no humor in this situation whatsoever.

"You're just a busy little bee. Busy with the wedding coming up. Busy helping Elodie Keaton. Busy"—she shimmied her hips—"getting busy with the chief of police?"

What was it with her fascination with Nick?

Her eyebrows snapped together. "And busy spying on me and Sylar?"

I felt a guilty flush sweep over my neck.

With a determined look in her eye, she took another step closer, tottering on impossibly high heels. When she reached out to jab me, she suddenly let out a cry and pulled her hand back. She cradled her hand.

I wasn't sure what had just happened, but was more than a little relieved that I wasn't going to have to break out the self-defense skills Nick had taught me. Though, I had to admit, I kind of wanted to rip the hair right off her head and wondered, absently, if that made me a bad person.

She hissed like a wounded feral cat as she eyed the bag. "You may be protected right now, Darcy Merriweather, but let me tell you this: If you don't keep that pert little nose of yours out of my business, then there's not enough protection in the world that will keep you safe. Stay out of my way, little girl. Keep your mouth shut about Sylar; quit the job at the Keaton house so the police can do their jobs; and back off of Nick Sawyer. Do you understand me?"

Had the agate protected me by somehow zapping Dorothy? If so, there was no way I was going to let her borrow the agate as Evan had suggested. I kind of wanted Ve to wallop this trollop.

When I didn't answer, Dorothy jabbed a finger in my direction. "You've been warned." She stomped away in her high heels and slammed the back door behind her.

Behind me, I again heard the rustling. I'd had enough. "Really, Vince, if that's you, just come out already."

I spun around to find a tall man standing at the trailhead. Slashes of sunlight spilled across his handsome features.

He wasn't Vince.

This man was older, mid-to-late forties, I guessed,

with black eyes, olive skin tone, the barest hint of silver in his black hair. He had an aristocratic nose, high cheek bones, and a friendly smile. He wore a dark suit with a white shirt and black tie—and he wore it well.

"Who—who are you?" I asked.

He bowed. "Andreus Woodshall, and you are quite welcome."

My first thought was that he didn't look like Dracula at all. Well, maybe a handsome Dracula, but certainly not a creepy one.

I tipped my head. "Welcome for what?"

He nodded to the bag.

I held it up. "The agate ball?"

"More specifically, the protection spell I placed upon it when I realized that the woman was going to accost you. The ball itself doesn't have that level of power without the help of other elements."

"Like magic?" I asked. I'd forgotten he was a Charm-crafter, and I hadn't realized that Dorothy was a Crafter—she had to be if she knew she'd been blocked by a protection spell.

He nodded in acquiescence.

"Well, then yes, thank you. I really didn't want to kick her ass."

His eyes flared; then his head tipped back and he laughed.

I blushed. "Sorry. I'm out of sorts right now."

"Quite all right, considering what just happened."

"You saw it all?"

He nodded.

"Have you been following me?"

He tipped his head. "No. Why would you think so?"

I didn't have even the slightest bit of apprehension around him. No goose bumps. No hair rising on the back of my neck. Nothing. "No reason."

As he studied me, it felt like his gaze was going right through me, burning with its intensity. It was as if he was trying to see what was at the very core of my being, what kind of person I was, with one look. Yet I still felt no malice. It was a strange sensation. One I wasn't entirely comfortable with.

Again, I shifted. "How did your son know my name earlier?"

Smiling wanly, he said, "You were hired to work at the Keatons' house. I'm very interested with anything—with *anyone*," he stressed, "going in and out of that home. And therefore, so is Lazarus."

"Walk with me?" I asked. I wanted to get away from Third Eye.

His arm swept out with a flourish. "After you."

Limping only slightly, I headed up the small path leading to the trail. "Why are you so interested in the Keaton house?"

His voice rumbled behind me. "The Anicula, of course."

I was surprised he confessed so freely. Glancing back at him, I let out a small cry. Here, in the shade, his features had changed. Long gone was handsome, replaced with sinister. Beady eyes, hollow cheeks, sharp little piranha teeth.

A chill swept down my spine, and I picked up my pace. "Darcy?"

We emerged from the path into the sunshine. I spared a glance. He was handsome again. I shuddered, not sure what had just happened. "I'm okay. Uh, stubbed my toe."

He walked stiffly beside me, like a ramrod undertaker, and I wondered how far he'd take his honesty. "Did you steal those opals this morning from Patrice Keaton's lawn?"

"Would I do such a thing?" he asked, nodding his head in the affirmative. "I felt as though there was no other option. I couldn't believe my luck when I saw the opals on the ground. For years, I've tried to get into that house to look for the Anicula, and to have the stones laid out as such . . . It was too good to be true. I acted quickly, but alas, none were what I was seeking. I will return the merchandise to Elodie at once."

I latched on to something he said. He'd *tried* to get into the house. "You've never been in the Keatons' house?"

"Not once."

"You haven't been breaking in every time the Roving Stones are in town?"

His eyes widened. "No."

I stared at him.

Holding his hands up in surrender, he said, "Do not be misled. I would have broken in—if I could. I cannot."

"Why?" *Someone* had been breaking in.

"There is a spell cast upon the house that prohibits my entrance."

I stumbled a bit and he grabbed on to my elbow to steady me. "A spell cast by whom?"

"Geer Keaton." There was venom in his voice.

"I don't understand," I said. There was a lot of that going on today. I wasn't liking it one bit.

"The Anicula belongs to my family," Andreus said.

We were walking under a shady stretch of the path, so I made sure to keep my gaze averted. However, a jogger happening by must have taken a look at him because she let out a yip when he bade her a "good afternoon" and she sprinted at an Olympic pace past us.

I knew just how she felt.

Andreus seemed to take no notice.

"The Anicula's enchantment was a wedding gift from my great-great-great-grandfather to his bride," he said. "It has been in my family for generations. That is, until Geer Keaton, the grave robber, stole it."

"Really?" It seemed too outrageous to be true. We had stepped into the sun again, so I felt safe looking at him.

"Really. I have been trying to recover it since."

"Geer dug up a grave? Literally?"

Humoring me, he smiled. "Literally. We were friends you see. Best friends. Years and years ago. A lifetime, it seems. In high school, right here in the village."

Geer, Patrice, Yvonne, and Roger . . . and now Andreus. All had gone to school together. Were all bound by the Anicula in some way?

"Our families were close. Geocrafters and Charmcrafters practically go hand in hand. Geer had heard the legend of the Anicula. He knew it had been buried with my grandmother. When her mausoleum was broken into, it didn't take much deduction to figure out that it had been Geer behind the crime."

A squirrel darted across the path. Two more joggers went by and a young woman with a baby carriage. It was just another day in the village to most. To me, I couldn't help feeling that my life was about to take a turn. Whether for good or bad remained to be seen.

"Especially," he added, "when Patrice suddenly broke up with Roger and started dating Geer. Patrice and Roger had been due to get married after graduation. They were madly in love. Soul mates."

I stopped walking and looked at him full-on (thank goodness we were in a sunny spot). "You're saying that Geer used the Anicula to steal Patrice from Roger? That he *wished* it?"

"Yes."

"Wow."

He started walking again, and I followed.

This explanation revealed to me Roger's infatuation with Patrice and also Yvonne's dislike of her.

"Immediately after the theft, Geer had a spell commissioned that kept me from entering his home. He made sure to never bring the Anicula out of the house. I have a feeling it's still inside."

"You don't think it was stolen, as Patrice claimed?"

He shook his head. "I doubt it."

"But you don't know for certain?"

"No, I don't know, but I will do just about anything to return the Anicula to where it belongs."

"With your grandmother?" I asked. "Or with your family, in general?"

I really wanted to know. Because I could feel myself falling for his woe-is-me story of injustice. If it was true, it was horrible what Geer had done. But if Andreus wanted the Anicula back so he could use its power . . .

"With my grandmother. She wanted the power to be buried with her, never to harm anyone else. She was a wise woman."

I wanted to believe him, I really did. But I didn't quite.

"Why are you telling me all this?" I asked, though I had a feeling I already knew the answer.

"I would like your help in convincing Elodie to return the Anicula to my family if she has it."

I didn't think that would be a problem after her proclamation earlier. We'd reached the turnoff path to As You Wish. "There's one problem with that."

"Which is?"

"Elodie doesn't know where the Anicula is, either. She says she hasn't seen it since she was a little girl, maybe four or five, and she believes it was stolen, as her mother claimed."

"Four or five?" His lips pressed into a thin line. "Is that so?"

"It's what she said. Why? You don't think so?"

"What I think, Darcy, is that she is lying to you."

Chapter Nineteen

Godfrey Baleaux, Cloakcrafter extraordinaire and owner of the Bewitching Boutique, was in the process of pinning my maid of honor dress and had already poked me three times. "Ow!" Make that four.

It was only four o'clock and I felt as though this day was never going to end. I'd already dropped off the agate ball with Ve, who looked slightly better, asked Archie to keep an eye on her, and then hightailed it to Bewitching Boutique.

"Sorry, sorry," he said, his white hair tickling the back of my neck as he worked on my sleeve. "My nerves. They're shot. So tell me again. Andreus didn't elaborate as to *why* he thought Elodie was lying?"

We'd been through this three times already. Coincidentally, each time was accompanied by a pinprick. I checked for blood on my shoulder near the sleeve he was working on and said, "He told me to ask Elodie."

Only a tiny pinprick of blood, thank goodness. Anything more and I was sure to faint dead away. He handed me a handkerchief and I pressed it to the spot.

Harper caught my reflection in the dressing room mirror and said, "If Elodie already told you she hadn't seen the Anicula in years, I doubt she's going to fess up to making any recent wishes."

Pepe, working on Harper's hem, made a *tsk*ing sound. His whiskers twitched. "Quite true."

"I've been trying to think of why she would lie." Our dresses were really quite lovely. Amethyst in color, cocktail length, and fitted (or would be soon) in all the right places. Mine had cap sleeves while Harper's was strapless.

"I can think of a reason," Harper said.

We all looked at her expectantly.

Smiling, she tapped her chin, pretending to be in deep thought. She was enjoying the attention—a rarity for her. Usually she shied away from anyone paying her any kind of interest. Of course, talking about a murder case was also a rarity—one Harper, a forensic nut, reveled in. Not the murder—but the solving of the crime.

"She absolutely does not want anyone to know what she wished for. And admitting to seeing the Anicula might precipitate a conversation about her *using* the Anicula."

I didn't want to ruin her moment, so I kept it to myself that I'd already figured out that, if Andreus was right, Elodie probably made a wish she didn't want anyone knowing about. It was *what* she wished for that I wanted to know. "What kind of wish wouldn't you want people to know about?"

Godfrey guffawed. His jowls jiggled. "Many, many things."

"Like?" I pressed.

"Weight loss, for one," he said. "I would want people to believe I did it on my own."

Pepe eyed Godfrey's belly. "Obviously not a wish you've made recently."

"You're a fine familiar to talk," Godfrey countered with a touch of humor in his voice. The two were always bickering, but most of the time it was a friendly give-and-take. Most.

Rubbing a paw over his chubby belly, Pepe said, "Touché."

"Has Elodie lost a lot of weight recently?" I asked.

Both shook their heads. I was back to square one.

"Money," Harper said. "I wouldn't want people to know I wished for money."

"Well, Elodie doesn't have any. At least not until she sells her mother's house and its contents." I turned slightly so the light would catch the shimmer in the dress. It was stunning.

Pepe had finished with Harper's dress, and she slipped behind a curtain to change into her street clothes. "Well, there goes that theory."

Godfrey groaned as he knelt to pin my hem. "My word," he gasped. "What happened to your knees, Miss Darcy? Oh! And your ankle?"

I peeked down. "The ankle I twisted when I ran after the Peeper Creeper trying to break into—or as it turns out, break out of—the house this morning, and I skinned my knees when I fell off a trash can this afternoon behind Third Eye."

The curtain slid open from the dressing area, and Harper came out with a look of astonishment on her face. "And what were you doing behind Sylar's shop?"

Pepe waved his paw. "*Non, non.* The more important query is why were you atop a garbage can?"

"Or, perhaps," Godfrey said with a chuckle, "we do not want to know."

"I want to know," Harper said, sitting in a deep leather chair. "Spill it."

"Which part?" I said, teasing them. "The part where Ve thought Sylar might be dead inside the shop and told me to break in? Or the part where I found shredded wedding invitations in the trash? Or"—I drew out the word—"the part where I saw Dorothy proposition Sylar with a steamy kiss?"

"Ew," Harper said.

"Ew," Godfrey echoed, shuddering.

Pepe whistled. "Perhaps you should explain all three."

I did. And asked them, too, if I should tell Ve what I had seen.

"Definitely," Harper said. "Since you've been blabbing about it all around town, it's bound to get back to her."

I opened my mouth to debate the word "blabbing" when I realized she was right. I had been. I sat on the ottoman. "I've turned into the town gossip."

"No, *ma chère*; that is Archie's title. You're seeking counsel. There is a difference."

Harper snorted. "A subtle one."

I frowned. I was going to have to tell Ve. I put my head in my hand and looked at them. "I should probably also tell you about the threats."

"What threats?" Harper balled her fists like she was getting ready to throw a punch on my behalf.

"From Dorothy." I recounted what had happened behind the shop.

"I never liked that woman," Godfrey said.

Pepe laughed. "Only enough to ask her to marry you."

My eyes widened. "What?"

"Temporary insanity," Godfrey said, tucking away his pins. "I had sense enough to call it off."

"When was this?" Harper sat on the edge of her seat.

Godfrey stroked his snow-white beard. "Between her second and third husbands, about ten years ago."

"Why did you call it off?" I asked, ducking into the changing room. I carefully took off my dress, trying to avoid the pins.

"Oh, the usual reasons," Godfrey said. "It was clear she was in love with Sylar, even back then. She was always stealing my supplies for her hobbies, of which she had many. And she tried to burn down my house."

I poked my head over the curtain. "Seriously?"

"A wee little fire." Godfrey didn't sound too traumatized by the event.

"My tail was singed while putting out the flames," Pepe said with dismay. "I loathe that woman."

"Was she arrested?" Harper asked.

"No. No." Godfrey took the dress I handed out. "I didn't press charges."

"Why not?" Harper demanded.

"Simple," Godfrey said. "She said if I did, she would return with a gallon of gasoline."

I came out of the dressing room. "And you believed her?"

"Wouldn't you?" he asked.

I recalled the look in her eye when she warned me and suddenly felt queasy. "She really is crazy, then."

"Oh, *oui*," Pepe said. "It's best you heed her warning and keep your distance."

Unfortunately, that was going to be impossible. "Is she a Crafter?"

Godfrey said, "A Broomcrafter."

Harper and I stared at him. I'd never heard the term.

He waved his hands. "You know, she makes witches' brooms. So we can fly?"

Harper lit up. "We can really fly on brooms?"

Oh, dear Lord. She was going to be doing loopde-loops in the night sky before I knew it. Another thing to worry about.

"Alas, only on certain dates," he said.

I was grateful he didn't elaborate and hoped beyond hope that Harper would let the matter drop. My mind was whirling with all this information about Dorothy, doing its own loopdeloops. "Is it possible she can cast a recantation spell?"

"Certainly," Pepe said. "Any Crafter can if she knows the proper spell."

"What are you thinking?" Harper asked, eyeing me warily.

I tied my sneaker. "I'm just wondering if Dorothy is the reason why Ve isn't getting better."

We all sat in silence for a moment, weighing the gravity of my statement.

"It wouldn't surprise me," Godfrey finally said. "It wouldn't surprise me at all."

Chapter Twenty

Later that night, the Sorcerer's Stove was quiet as Harper and I entered.

She said, "By the way, I couldn't find any reports online about any woodcarving serial killers."

"Good to know."

"But that doesn't mean you should let your guard down."

"Okay."

"Wood shavings," she muttered. "It's just plain strange."

Several tourists and a couple of locals sat eating dinner. The bartender was cleaning glasses and looked at us hopefully as we approached.

"Sorry," I said. "We're here for the cooking class."

Harper said, "Speak for yourself. I need a drink." She climbed onto a stool.

I pulled her off. "After the class. Your knife skills are dangerous enough without involving alcohol."

The bartender, a young woman named Ula, said, "I'll be here. And there will probably be plenty of seats."

"Why's it so quiet?" Harper asked as we headed toward the kitchen.

Jonathan stood near the demonstration kitchen, talking to an official-looking man with a clipboard.

I didn't want to mention the food poisoning issue to Harper if she hadn't yet heard about it. I was afraid she might turn around and walk out the door. "Probably just a slow night."

The cooking class was from seven to eight. After that, we had plans to stake out Vincent Paxton's house to see if he might be the Peeper Creeper.

Jonathan greeted us with a smile, looking none the worse for wear after his episode behind the restaurant this afternoon. Which was to say, he didn't look *worse*. He still looked terribly unwell.

Jonathan didn't make introductions to his clipboarded friend, but as we passed, I saw a badge clipped to his shirt that read HEALTH INSPECTOR.

Uh-oh.

The demonstration kitchen was small, but big enough for eight cooking students. Three long and wide peninsulas designed in a U shape filled the room. Two of them, the legs of the U, had four stations apiece, and the bottom of the U was where Zoey Wilkens stood in a spotless white chef's jacket and toque, prepping ingredients. She barely looked up as we came in, and I noticed stress lines creasing her forehead, drawing down on the corners of her mouth.

No wonder. The health inspector had the power to close down the restaurant. I thought back to Jonathan's explanation of his and Zoey's argument. That it had been a business dispute.

Had he been telling the truth? Was there something going on with the restaurant that would involve the police *and* the health inspector?

Zoey looked up and managed a smile. "Come in. Come in."

Marcus nodded to me from his spot at one of the tables, and I held in a smile as I went and sat next to him. He'd taken almost all my advice from this morning.

Gone were his tightly pressed suit and tie, his shiny loafers. He was wearing dark jeans, blue suede sneakers, and an argyle sweater vest. His hair was gently tousled, sticking up in little tufts. The only thing he hadn't done was remove his contacts in favor of glasses.

"Good job," I whispered. He was utterly adorable. "But where are your glasses?"

He leaned in and whispered, "They need adjustment and Third Eye was closed. Hi, Harper," he said as she sidled up next to me.

She did a double-take, and I really had to bite my lip to keep in my smile as her eyes filled with sudden interest in the lawyer.

I knew my sister well.

As she did me. Her gaze shifted to me. Her eyes had filled with suspicion as she said, "Marcus, I barely recognized you."

"Really?" he said, playing dumb.

"The clothes . . ." Her cheeks were turning a soft pink.

Being bribed had never felt so good. The only thing left was for my sister to say yes to a date with Marcus and my PI license would be on its way.

"This is the casual me," he said. "Did you think I wore suits all the time?"

She coughed. "No, no. Of course not."

I was silently gloating when the next student walked into the room. I hoped my gasp of surprise wasn't too loud.

Vincent Paxton gave a friendly wave and took a spot on the other side of us, next to Harmony Atchinson, the owner of the Pixie Cottage, and two villagers, Angela and Colleen Curtis—a mother and daughter I'd seen around but had never met. We all said friendly helloes as we investigated our ingredients.

A few minutes before seven, Starla rushed in, completely out of breath, as if she'd run the whole way.

"I'm here!" she cried, quite unnecessarily, and took the only empty spot left — next to Harper. Starla leaned forward. "Marcus! Hubba-hubba."

"Indeedy-Pete," Harmony echoed. "If I wasn't taken . . ."

"I'm sitting here," Angela said to her, good-naturedly.

Harmony put her arm around her. "I said *if*."

I smiled at the pair, who I'd had no idea were a couple.

Colleen, who looked to be nineteen or twenty, rolled her eyes.

Marcus smiled, laughed, and blushed. "Thanks."

Harper snapped her head to look at Starla, as if weighing whether she was competition.

Starla was oblivious to the scrutiny. "Vince! You like to cook?"

I wondered how her date had gone with Lazarus Woodshall. I hadn't had a chance to talk to her since this morning — which felt like an eternity ago.

"I have no idea," Vince admitted. He had big puppy-dog eyes, tousled hair, and a nerdy air about him. Harper had once had a crush on him, but it hadn't lasted long. "But I know I can't afford to keep eating out. That's why I'm here. I need all the help I can get. I can burn water."

"Been there, done that," Starla said. "The pan never recovered. Thankfully, Evan does most of the cooking."

Both siblings were Cross-Crafters (part Bakecrafter, part Wishcrafter), but Evan had inherited the bulk of baking abilities and Starla the ability to grant wishes. Her baking skills were terrible, and Evan's wish-granting was extremely limited.

Not that she'd say anything about that aloud. We were in mixed company. Vince was a Seeker, and though I was pretty sure Harmony was a Crafter, I didn't know about the Curtises.

I glanced at Zoey. I wasn't sure about her, either.

Jonathan was a Foodcrafter. Was she? Her skills certainly rivaled his in the kitchen.

"Darcy," Harmony said, "is it true that Evan ran into the Peeper Creeper in the woods behind your house?"

"What?" Starla said. "Why haven't I heard about this?"

"Probably the same reason he hadn't heard about your date." They were keeping secrets from each other. There seemed to be a lot of that going on in the village lately.

It was Starla's turn to flush.

"Date?" Angela asked, latching on to this latest development. "With whom?"

Starla waved her hand in dismissal. "Doesn't matter." She glanced around nervously. "Isn't it time to start?"

I glanced across the U to find Vince frowning at his bowls of fruit, but I wasn't sure what had caused his change of demeanor.

"Almost," Zoey said. "We're just waiting on Jonathan." She looked toward the door and bit her lip. "You'll see you have several options for the tartlet. Pears, apples, or apricots. Or you can go wild and mix and match. The choice is yours."

She drummed her fingers on the countertop and looked at the clock again.

Harmony said, "Darcy, what's it really like inside Patrice's house? Is it as messy as everyone's saying?"

I wasn't really comfortable talking about business. "Let's just say she liked to collect things."

Colleen leaned forward. "I heard she has all kinds of jewelry in there. Gems and stuff."

"Some," I said.

"What was the call today about some opals being stolen?" Angela asked. When I looked at her with a question in my eyes, she said, "I have a police scanner."

"Opals were stolen from Patrice's today?" Marcus asked.

I said, "They've been recovered and are back where they belong."

"Who took them?" Colleen asked.

Harper said loudly, "Zoey, why is the health department here?"

Sometimes I loved my sister more than I could express.

"The health department is here?" Angela asked, glancing around. "You don't have rats again, do you?"

"Rats?" I gasped, resisting the urge to hop atop my station. Ve had mentioned a rodent problem, but I'd been picturing a mouse or two—and they'd looked a lot like Pepe.

Zoey broke out in a sweat. She wiped her forehead with the back of her sleeve, disturbing the little blond hairs that poked out from beneath her hat. Her blue eyes had grown wide. "No, we don't have rats."

"But you *had* rats?" Harper asked.

"I'll be right back," Zoey said, wiping her hands on a towel. She rushed out of the room.

Harper looked from face to face. "They had rats?"

"Hundreds," Harmony said, shuddering. "I had to put my permanent article relocation on hold for a long time after that."

What Harmony called "permanent article relocation" others called "Dumpster diving." Her hobby had come in handy a few months ago when she overheard something that helped solve a murder investigation.

Angela nodded. "It was an epidemic. The restaurant was forced to close, kids couldn't walk to school, and all the businesses in the village suffered when the tourists got word."

"Evan was on twenty-four-hour alert," Starla said, "trying to keep them out of the bakery. It was horrible."

"I remember that," Vince said. "It was what, two years ago? Three?"

"Two and a half," Colleen said. "I was a senior, and I was so glad I could drive to school instead of having to take a shuttle bus like the younger kids. Homecoming was canceled, though, because of all the rats under the bleachers." She pouted. "I was up for homecoming queen."

Angela patted her arm in sympathy.

I had been thinking that the term "epidemic" was a bit of an exaggeration, but now I wondered if it wasn't extremely accurate.

"What happened to them all? The rats?" Harper, I noticed, had her gaze glued to the floor as though a rodent might run by at any moment. She had a history with rats—having freed dozens of them from a science lab in college. Not that there had been enough evidence to charge her with anything.

"They just disappeared one day," Colleen said, shrugging.

"All of them?" I asked.

"Every last one." Angela was once again looking down at the floor.

Intuition had me glancing at Marcus, and I found that he wouldn't look my way. I wasn't surprised. Since when did rats suddenly disappear overnight?

When magic was involved, that's when.

Had it anything to do with Patrice? I had to ask—in a roundabout way. "Was that around the time when Jonathan was dating Patrice Keaton?"

Marcus shot me a look of dismay—probably because I'd said her name aloud.

Harmony nodded. "They'd been dating for a while at that point." She looked toward the door before adding, "Cute couple, those two."

"Do you think the rats are back?" Harper asked. "It might explain why business is so slow."

"I haven't seen any or heard anything about a return," Angela said. "This place seems so spotless."

Colleen rolled a pear between her hands. "The health department is probably here because of the food poisonings."

"The food poisonings?" Vince echoed.

"I've heard about three cases just this week," Colleen said. "All of the people affected had eaten here last Friday night. I work at the library shelving books," she said to me and Harper in an aside. "I hear a lot of gossip."

"Did you hear what caused the problem?" Marcus asked, eyeing his pears suspiciously.

Colleen shook her head.

Vince, looking a little green, said, "I ate here last Friday night. . . ."

I was about to reassure him that he'd probably already feel the effects when Zoey rushed into the room at a fast clip, her color high.

"It looks like Jonathan isn't going to make it to this class, after all. We should go ahead and get started on our tartlets."

"Is everything okay with Jonathan?" I asked. "Is he feeling all right?" I couldn't quite shake that image of him by the Dumpster.

"Fine, fine. Just held up with the some paperwork. Now, we'll start with our crust. Have any of you made your own crust before?"

We all shook our heads.

"I see," she said, looking at the clock. I had a feeling she was counting the minutes until class was done.

Twenty minutes later, we had all managed to avoid any mention of rats or food poisoning—no easy feat. As I pulled my bowl of pears toward me, I couldn't help but notice how beautiful the bowl was. Burled walnut, hand-carved. The cutting board, too, was beautifully crafted. Even the mixing spoons. They were all stunning and I said so.

Zoey said, "Thank you."

I blinked. "You made them?"

She nodded shyly. "My mother taught me how when I was little. It's kind of a family hobby."

Harmony nodded appreciatively, yet had a bit of snark in her voice as she said, "You certainly learned from one of the best."

Zoey picked up a knife and jabbed it into a pear. She savagely dragged the knife down the pear. "Very true."

Okay, then. Apparently she and her mom didn't have a good relationship.

Ula came running into the room. "Zoey, come quick."

She dropped her knife. "What's wrong?"

"It's Jonathan. He collapsed."

Chapter Twenty-one

An hour later, Harper and I started our stakeout of Vince. After class ended, we decided it was the perfect time to follow him, to see where he went next and to determine if he was up to no good.

Which turned out to be a lot harder than we thought because he didn't seem to want to leave the restaurant. He'd spent the ten minutes since class ended standing around staring at passersby, the sky, his shoelaces.

I couldn't help but think about Jonathan. By the time we'd all rushed out of the classroom to tend to him, Jonathan had recovered and insisted that he'd merely stumbled and fallen—not collapsed.

Zoey insisted he go home and rest, and she had gone with him, abandoning our little cooking class to a sous chef who looked like he'd rather be eating glass than teaching us how to make a tartlet.

Despite all that had happened, I was quite pleased with how my tartlets had come out and was happy to have some leftovers to take to Terry Goodwin, my *interesting* neighbor and Archie's caretaker. I was determined to meet the man before the week's end.

Harper had burned her tartlets to a crisp, giving Marcus the perfect excuse to share his bàtch with her. She held her takeout box carefully, like a prized box of chocolates.

I was getting restless, waiting for Vince to budge from his spot by the Stove's front door. He looked at his watch, then checked his cell phone. At this rate, we were going to be standing here all night.

"What's he waiting for?" Harper asked.

"Us to leave, I think." I explained how I suspected he'd been following me lately.

"Why would he do that?"

"My best guess? He suspects I'm a Crafter."

"If that's true, why follow just you?" she asked with a pout in her voice. "And not me?"

Only Harper would get miffed at not having a stalker of her very own. "Probably because you never go anywhere."

She looked about to argue, then changed her mind and smiled. "I think we should test the theory. Have a little fun with him."

I was all for that. It would be nice to know for certain if he'd been the one following me around lately.

We started walking, taking the long way around the village green. "I saw you talking with Marcus after the class. Anything new?" I asked, testing the waters.

I had been talking to Starla at the time and unable to eavesdrop. She was being coy about her date with Lazarus, and I was really worried she liked him. A lot.

"Nope." Harper kicked a pebble.

"Nothing at all?" I pressed.

"Not a thing. Why are you acting so strange about it?"

I forced a laugh. "Just curious."

"Right," she said.

Had he chickened out and not asked her on a date? Or was she toying with me because she suspected she'd been set up?

With Harper, I couldn't know for sure. We neared the

Third Eye, which was closed for the night. Harper stopped for a moment, lingering in front of the shop. She said, "Is it wrong that I don't care for Sylar all that much? At first I thought he was this cuddly grandpa kind of guy, but the more I get to know him . . ." She made a sour face.

"Is it wrong that I don't care for him, either?"

She stopped short. "Really?"

"I just don't think he's right for Ve. Be that as it may, he's her choice. We have to respect that."

"Are you going to tell her about Dorothy?"

"I think I have to, despite Dorothy's warning."

If you don't keep that pert little nose of yours out of my business, then there's not enough protection in the world that will keep you safe. Stay out of my way, little girl. Keep your mouth shut about Sylar; quit the job at the Keaton house so the police can do their jobs; and back off of Nick Sawyer. Do you understand me?

Harper continued to kick at the pebble. "I can't believe she threatened you. Who does she think she is, anyway? I think we should investigate her past." Coyly, she added, "Marcus mentioned something about you getting a PI license."

I swallowed hard. "He told you about that?"

She gave me a sly look. "Was it a secret?"

"Not at all," I fibbed.

"I think it's the perfect side job for us," she said.

I was going to kill Marcus.

Trying to change the subject, I said, "Is Vince behind us?"

She tossed a surreptitious look over her shoulder. "About fifty yards. If he's the Peeper and somehow learns that you're a Crafter, what then?" she whispered.

I wasn't sure. If he had overheard my conversation with Archie this morning, then he had to know something truly magical was going on in the village. Grudgingly, I said, "I'm going to have to talk to the Elder and find out."

"The sooner the better," Harper said.

"Well, certainly not tonight."

"Why?"

"The woods are creepy in the dark." Plus, there might be a knife-wielding maniac on the loose. But I didn't want to remind her of that. "Tomorrow will be soon enough."

I heard a loud *woof* and looked up.

"Well, look who had another break-out," Harper teased.

Headed our way, Nick had his Saint Bernard's leash in one hand, and in the crook of his other arm . . . a wriggling Missy.

She had escaped once again.

Higgins strained and pulled in an effort to reach me and Harper. Nick's demands of "heel!" went completely unheeded.

I braced myself for impact as Higgins threw his paws on my shoulders and licked my face. Suddenly, his attention shifted to my take-out box, and before I knew it, he'd knocked it out of my hands and was eating every last pear tartlet.

Harper was laughing herself silly.

Nick apologized profusely, then cursed as Higgins started eating the Styrofoam. Nick shoved Missy at me and wrestled the box away from Higgins. The enormous dog then lunged for Harper's box.

Harper jabbed a finger at Higgins. *"Pzzt!"*

Higgins stopped dead in his tracks.

"How'd you do that?" Nick asked, amazed. "A spell?"

"A little Dog Whisperer magic," she said. "You need to show Higgins who's pack leader. He's totally taking advantage of you."

I tipped my head and smiled. "Totally."

Nick's dark gaze met mine, and a little zap of heat shot through my body. I liked it. Maybe a little too much. Again, Dorothy's warning went through my head. Would she try to burn my house down if I didn't stay away from Nick? Away from Patrice's house?

Was I going to let her affect the way I lived?

"And someone needs to figure out how you're escaping," Harper was saying to Missy as she rubbed her head.

"Thanks for bringing her back, Nick. Again." I looked into Missy's innocent eyes. "I didn't even know she had escaped."

"I came home to check on Mimi and found them together." Nick's gaze fixed on something over my shoulder. "Is there any reason why Vincent Paxton just did a complete one-eighty when he saw me?"

"Probably because he's stalking Darcy," Harper said.

Nick's gaze zipped to mine. "He's what?"

I patted Missy's head. "We don't know that for sure."

"We think he's the Peeper Creeper," Harper added.

I rolled my eyes. "We don't know that, either."

Harper glared at me. "You're going to be a lousy PI."

"Do I need to sit down?" Nick asked. "What's this about a PI? And why do you think Vince is the Peeper?"

"We don't need to get into all that right now," I said.

"That's right. We've got to follow Vince. Looks like he's headed back to his store." Harper strode off.

"Darcy?" Nick said, holding Higgins tightly.

"Yeah?"

"Do I want to know?"

"No."

"Should I know?"

I tipped my head, weighing options. "Not yet." We started walking, following Harper, who was zigzagging through the Roving Stones tents. "Anything new on the Peeper case?"

"Nothing good," he said, sounding weary.

"What's that mean?"

"You know the bag of shavings Officer Hansel collected?"

I nodded.

"It's missing."

I stopped short. "What do you mean missing?"

It was a stupid question. I knew what missing meant. I just didn't understand how something like that could happen.

"It disappeared from her vehicle before she could log it into evidence."

My mind spun. "Someone stole it out of her car? When? How?"

"This morning. I'm looking into it."

If anyone could find out what happened, it was Nick. Still, I was uneasy. I was about to tell him of Dorothy's threats when he said, "I have a big favor to ask."

"Ask away."

"I have to work all night, and ordinarily I wouldn't mind Mimi staying home alone, especially with the alarm system and Higgins, but . . ."

He didn't even have to finish his sentence. "She can stay with me. Higgins, too. Where is Mimi now?" I shifted a fidgeting Missy to my other arm.

We'd emerged from the tents and were walking toward Harper, who sat on a bench across the street from Lotions and Potions. Subtlety wasn't her strong point.

"At Lotions and Potions, visiting with Mrs. P." He touched my arm. "Are you sure? About tonight?"

"Absolutely. It's been a long time since I've had a sleepover. It'll be fun."

Softly, he said, "No sleepovers, huh? Me either."

My insides went gooey at the look in his eyes. Slowly, his hand slid down my arm and settled in my palm. He left it there, and I suddenly felt lighter than air.

Smiling, we walked hand in hand to where Harper sat.

She looked up, zeroed in on our hands, and broke into a goofy grin.

Thankfully, she didn't say anything other than, "He just went inside."

We looked through the plate-glass windows. Mrs. P was sampling one of Vince's tartlets. Mimi was sitting on a stool at the workstation where Mrs. P concocted a lot of Vince's stock.

I set Missy down and she commenced in sniffing Higgins, who didn't seem to mind the intrusion.

"Humor me. Why would you suspect Vince as the Peeper?" Nick asked.

"What if the Peeper was a Seeker looking for evidence of the Craft?" I asked.

"You can't just think of mortal motivations in this village," Harper added.

Inside the shop, Mrs. P had slipped on a sweater and was headed out the door with Mimi.

Nick was quiet for a minute, then said, "But nothing was taken."

"Probably because most Crafters don't have much evidence of their Craft. There's nothing to find. Except . . ."

My gaze shot to Mimi's hand. Her empty hand. Abruptly, she stopped short, spun around, and sprinted back into the shop.

Not soon enough. As I looked through the window, my heart sank. Vince was sitting on the stool Mimi had just vacated.

He was flipping through Melina's journal.

Chapter Twenty-two

"Am I in trouble?" Mimi asked as Higgins dragged me across the village green. We had gone back to her house to pack an overnight bag and were now on our way to As You Wish. "Are you mad at me?"

The Roving Stones tents looked ominous in the twilight as I dragged Higgins to a stop and searched her face. "Why would I be mad at you?"

She lifted one of her shoulders in a delicate shrug. "You warned me about the journal."

I had, but now wasn't the right time to say "I told you so." Sometimes the hardest lessons were the ones you had to learn yourself. We started walking again. "No, I'm not mad." *Concerned* was more like it. "I don't think he saw much, if anything at all."

He couldn't have in the few seconds he'd flipped through the diary. But still. If he had seen *any* information about the Craft, it was too much. Mimi didn't need to hear that right now, though.

Missy trotted along between us. It had turned dark, but the night was clear and the stars were sparkling. Harper and Mrs. P had taken on the challenge of watching Vince. Mrs. P had been more than enthusiastic about the stakeout, even going to the extreme of running (well, speed-walking) to the Pixie Cottage, where she lived, to change from her pink tracksuit to a black one.

She and Harper were two peas in a pod.

"But now," I warned Mimi, "more than ever, you need to keep special track of that diary. Find somewhere to hide it."

"But what if the Peeper breaks in and finds it?"

She had me with that one. If Vince was the Creeper and he'd just peeped at that diary, he wasn't going to back down until he got his hands on it again. "We need to make sure we find a very good hiding place."

"But where?" she asked.

I pushed open the back gate and saw that Archie wasn't in his cage. I glanced at Terry's house and noticed a curtain shifting. Someone—Terry?—was watching. "Let's sleep on it tonight, and make a decision tomorrow."

"Okay."

Missy and Higgins bounded into the house, and I heard a squawk from the family room. "Oh, the indignity! Get him off me. Get. Him. Off. Me!"

Mimi's curls bounced as she chased after Higgins. I rushed into the fray. In the family room, I found *Survivor* on the TV, Tilda atop a bookshelf, Ve giggling, Mimi tugging Higgins's collar, Missy doing circles, and red feathers sticking out from beneath Higgins's fur.

"Tell me that's not drool!" Archie squawked in a high-pitched voice from beneath the dog.

I yanked Higgins backward, gave him a stern look and a "*pzzt!*" He abandoned his new feathered squeak toy and went over to Ve. He climbed up on the couch next to her and plopped his head in her lap.

Maybe Harper was onto something with the *pzzt*-ing stuff.

Ve was simultaneously wiping her eyes and blowing her nose.

"This is not amusing, Velma," Archie chastised.

"From my vantage point it is," she countered, sounding completely congested. Her nose, the area around her eyes, and her cheeks were various shades of red. All of which contrasted badly with her coppery hair.

Despite her obvious good humor, she looked, as Harper would say, "unfortunate." Not at all her normal pulled-together self. I wished I could make her better—I hated seeing her suffer like this.

If only I could grant my own wishes. Or if only I'd found that Anicula . . .

Archie looked up at me dolefully as he lay on his back, his wings spread out, his little feet up in the air. "Tell me," he said dramatically.

"It's drool," I said, watching it ooze off his feathers and onto the floor.

He whimpered. "Put me out of my misery."

"Mimi," I said, "grab me some paper towels from the kitchen, please."

"Just let me die," Archie said. "I feel so violated."

Mimi was back in a flash. I used the paper towels to wipe down Archie's feathers.

He chuckled. "Not there; it tickles."

I rolled my eyes. "All done."

Very ungracefully, he picked himself off the floor and surveyed the damage to his plumage. "I must bathe. Immediately. I am going home." He stooped into a bow. "Farewell, ladies." He flew to the mudroom, perched on a coat hook, and waited for me to catch up.

I made sure to keep the back door closed so that if anyone was lurking outside they couldn't see us talking. "Thanks for keeping an eye on Ve."

"I should get hazard pay," he declared. "Drool. I'll never recover."

I leaned against the wall and said, "Name your price." His currency was usually easily affordable.

"There is no price to cover the cost of my wounded pride."

"A James Bond marathon?" I tempted.

He twitched. "How cheap do you think I am?"

"Plus Broadway show tune karaoke. That's my final offer."

He contemplated for a moment, then said, "It's a deal. Just so you know, I would have settled for the James Bond marathon. That Sean Connery shivers me timbers." He fluffed his wings.

I opened the back door. "You're a strange bird."

"Darcy darling, you have no idea. Velma, tell me if that hoodlum finds the immunity idol!" he called out.

"I will," she shouted back, sounding raspy.

"Have the two of you been watching *Survivor* all day?"

"No," he said. "For a while we watched a *Real Housewives of New York City* marathon. Those women are a hoot. Oh!"

"Yeah?"

"Ve had a visitor."

"She did? Who?"

"Sylar came by." Archie leaned forward and dropped his voice. "Between us, she didn't look too happy about what he was telling her."

"Did you hear what they were talking about?"

"Are you accusing me of eavesdropping? I'm offended!"

"Archie."

"Something about Dorothy Hansel." He blinked. "Now, there's a piece of work."

Tell me about it.

"I didn't hear the whole of the conversation, however, as I was hiding under the sofa."

It would have been hard for Ve to explain to Sylar, a

mortal, why her neighbor's macaw was watching a *Survivor* marathon with her. "Understandable."

"You may want to ask her about it." He bowed again and said, "Call me if you need anything."

With that, he flew out the door. I closed and locked it behind him.

When I went back into the family room, the TV was muted and Mimi was in full explanation about what had happened with the diary.

I sat on the love seat and yawned. It had been a long day. One that wasn't over yet—we still had to cast the protection spell at midnight. The agate sphere sat on the coffee table, and seeing it reminded me of Andreus Woodshall and what he'd said about Elodie.

I didn't know who to trust.

For some reason, my instincts told me to believe what he said. But if I did, that meant Elodie was lying to me. And if she was lying to me, did that mean she knew more about her mother's murder than she let on? I didn't like thinking about that, but couldn't help my thoughts from wandering to the falling out she'd had with her mother not long before she died.

But . . . but if Elodie had something to do with Patrice's murder, why would she hire me to look into what happened to her mother?

That part made no sense unless she was innocent.

Or was using me.

I didn't like thinking about that, either.

Ve was saying, "It sounds as though a trip to see the Elder is in order. She will know how to deal with the likes of Vincent Paxton."

Tilda hopped down from the corner bookshelf and onto the back of the couch. She eyed Higgins as if contemplating how to displace him from her usual spot next to Ve.

Good luck to her. Higgins was snoring.

Mimi sat clutching her mother's diary. "What's the Elder like?"

"She's very nice," Ve said at the same time I said, "She's scary."

Mimi's dark eyes widened, and Ve gave me a withering look.

"What?" I said. "She is. In a benevolent way, of course. She's kind and wise and ... scares the bejeebers out of me."

"What does she look like?" Mimi yawned so widely her small hand couldn't cover it. I wondered when her normal bedtime was. It was only nine o'clock now.

"Actually, I've never *seen* her. I've only *heard* her. She hides in a tree." I explained my trips to see the Elder. "Have you seen her?" I asked Ve.

"Of course." She yawned and petted Higgins's head.

Mimi and I stared at her, silently begging for more information.

Ve smiled. "She's beautiful."

This told me nothing. Ve thought every woman was beautiful.

"You're not going to tell us anything about her, are you?" I asked.

"Not a thing. It's not for me to tell. You both will learn when the time is right."

"Aw," Mimi whined.

"Aw," I echoed.

Ve tugged her shawl tighter around her shoulders.

Tilda walked along the edge of the couch, her ears back as she stared at the mammoth dog on *her* couch. I had a feeling her claws were soon to make an appearance.

When Mimi yawned again, I said, "We should get you settled in upstairs."

After that, I would ask Ve about Sylar's visit—and what he had said about Dorothy.

When I stood, I picked up a strange scent. Sniffing, I said, "Do you smell that?"

Ve smiled weakly. "I can't smell anything."

Missy had stirred from her spot on the love seat. Her fur rose and she growled low in her throat.

"What is it?" Mimi asked, sniffing the air like a bloodhound.

I rushed into the kitchen. The scent was stronger in here — and much more identifiable.

Smoke.

I went to the kitchen sink, raised the window shade, and peeked out. "Fire!" I yelled, panic rising.

I couldn't see the flames — only their orange glow. It flickered around the house's foundation. I ran back into the living room to find that Ve was up and holding an unusually calm Tilda. Mimi had Higgins and Missy leashed.

"Go out the front door and call 911," I said. "I'm going to grab the extinguisher and see if I can stop the fire from spreading."

Neither argued with me. As they hurried past, I spotted Melina Sawyer's diary sitting on the coffee table. Shaking my head, I quickly picked it up and tucked it into my waistband. There was no way I was leaving it unattended.

In the kitchen pantry, I grabbed the fire extinguisher we kept in case of emergency and rushed out the back door.

The air was acrid and smoky, and I coughed as I rounded the corner, ready to do battle with the flames — and bumped into someone who was already extinguishing the fire.

Sirens began to wail in the distance as the tall man turned and waved a hand in front of his face to clear the air.

I blinked in surprise, sure I was seeing things.

When I rubbed my eyes, the apparition didn't disappear.

"It's nice to finally meet you, Darcy," he said in an accent I couldn't quite place. "Though"—he smiled—"the circumstances could have been better. I rushed over as soon as I saw the flames."

Maybe I'd inhaled too much smoke. I stepped backward, took a deep breath, and rubbed my eyes again.

The image didn't change.

Elvis was in my backyard, wearing a fancy dinner jacket complete with a pocket square, tight satin pants, and slippers, and he was holding a fire extinguisher.

Chapter Twenty-three

In light of the fire, we packed up all necessary items (Ve's lipstick, the dog and cat food, my stash of peppermint patties) and moved out.

I would have told Harper we were coming, but she wasn't answering her cell phone. She was probably still on her Vince stakeout, which must have taken her out of the village, because between the police force and the fire department arriving on our doorstep, there was no missing that Something Big had happened at As You Wish. It seemed like every villager had taken up residence on the sidewalk in front of the house.

Now, an hour after the fire was out, everyone had dispersed except for Nick and the fire chief. Ve, Mimi, Higgins, Missy, and Tilda and I were trekking across the village green toward Spellbound Books with two rolling suitcases dragging behind our sorry group.

Nick, poor Nick, had said he'd stop by when he was done with his preliminary investigation but agreed that it was best we didn't sleep at home tonight.

"You could have warned me," I said to Ve.

"How exactly?" She dabbed her nose with a white handkerchief. "It's not exactly something that can be forewarned. You must experience it firsthand."

"A simple, 'Terry Goodwin is the spitting image of Elvis' would have sufficed."

And damn if he wasn't. Okay, yes, a gracefully aged Elvis (not the chubby seventies version), but Elvis nonetheless, right down to the lip curl.

Now I understood why he was such a recluse. Looking like he did, he'd be mobbed with curiosity-seekers wherever he went.

Mimi said, "Who's Elvis?"

We both stopped and stared at her. "You're not serious," I said.

Her eyes were wide and blank.

"Oh, dear Lord," Ve said. "I feel old. Ancient. Is there moss growing on me?"

The Roving Stones tent flaps were making strange noises again. It gave me the heebie-jeebies. "No, and keep those old bones moving." The sooner we were settled in Harper's apartment above the bookshop, the better I would feel. As soon as we started our little caravan moving again, I said, "We're going to have to indoctrinate Mimi into the Elvis fan club, that's all." Never heard of Elvis . . . It was un-American, even for a twelve-year-old. "Should we start with the movies or the music?"

Ve smiled and said, "I could go for a little *Blue Hawaii* right now."

It was the perfect distraction from the fact that someone tried to burn our house down.

With us inside it.

No, not someone.

Dorothy.

It had to have been her. After all, she had a history of being a firebug. Godfrey could attest to that. Plus, she was seriously ticked off at me. This little fire was probably another warning to me, especially since the fire chief said it had been started in such a way as to remain in the garden and not spread to the house.

Inwardly, I seethed. The chief's news didn't make me feel any better. Mimi had been inside the house. If the wind had shifted or a spark jumped . . . Anything could have happened.

The mama bear in me wanted to shake Dorothy until her teeth popped out.

My jaw ached from clenching, and I forced myself to release it as we crossed the street and trekked down the alley behind the shops.

My mind raced, plotted. This act of Dorothy's would not go unpunished.

Her fiery warning had backfired on her. It hadn't scared me away. It had ticked me off.

We rattled up to Harper's back door. Thankfully, I had a spare key to her place. As I slipped the key into the lock, I was surprised to hear voices at the top of the steps.

"Slow, slow! Gentle," Harper was saying loudly enough to be heard over the music (the Beatles) playing.

I swung open the door and Higgins charged in ahead of me, galloping up the steps, his tail wagging at full force. My heart suddenly broke for him as I remembered that this used to be his home. He and his former owner used to reside in this apartment before a murder case had shattered both their worlds. Nick and Mimi had adopted Higgins and given him a new place to live, but it was obvious he still remembered his old house.

"What the h—," a man started to shout. Then there was a loud crash and a scream from Harper.

I rushed up the narrow stairs to find Marcus flat on his back underneath a bookcase.

"Pzzt! Pzzt!" Harper shouted at Higgins, who was tearing around the apartment. His tail knocked over a lamp and the wine bottle on the table. Harper let out a small cry as red seeped into the carpet.

Missy bounded into the room and started yapping. Mimi appeared next to me, carrying a hissing Tilda inside a cat carrier. Ve came in behind her, wheezing.

"Honey," I said. "We're home!"

Harper curled her tiny fists. "What is going on?" she yelled. She stomped over to her iPod dock and turned off the music.

Suddenly, except for Ve's and Higgins's panting and Tilda's hissing, it was deathly quiet.

I bent next to Marcus. "Are you okay?"

"Do you think you could get this bookcase off me?" he asked, looking pale.

Mimi helped as I levered the heavy oak case off him. The bookshelf looked none the worse for wear, but I couldn't say the same for Marcus.

"That's going to leave a mark," Mimi said sagely.

He sat up and surveyed the damage. Bruises were already beginning to form on his jaw and cheek. "I'm okay."

Harper dropped beside him and took his face in her hands, closely giving him a once-over.

He didn't seem to mind one bit.

In fact, when she bounced up to get him an ice pack, he waggled his eyebrows at me. "Good timing," he whispered.

Yep. He was fine.

Harper came back with some ice cubes wrapped in a washcloth. Gently, she held the compress to his cheek. "Look what you all have done. Why are you here? Haven't you heard of calling?"

I opened Tilda's cage door to free her and she refused to come out. "I called. You didn't answer."

Harper frowned and glanced at her cell phone on the coffee table. Next to two wineglasses.

I lifted an eyebrow and gave her a smirk.

She gave me the evil eye. "Marcus very nicely offered come over and do some heavy lifting."

"I see that," I said.

Ve laughed as she rolled her suitcase into the apartment and plopped onto the couch. Missy hopped up next to her, and Mimi sat on her other side.

Marcus eyed the suitcases. "Are you staying?"

His tone made it clear that we'd interrupted his plans for the night.

"We're moving in," Mimi said.

"You're *what*?" Harper cried.

Ve said, "Just temporarily, until we can cast that protection spell."

"And the arson investigator finishes his report," I added. I headed to the kitchen to look for something that would get the red wine stains out of the carpet.

"Arson?" Harper said, her voice high.

"Someone tried to burn down As You Wish," Mimi said nonchalantly as she checked her cell phone for text messages. "You didn't hear the sirens?"

Harper lost all color and looked on the verge of a nervous breakdown, so I took pity on her and explained everything. I finished with, "By the time I made it outside, Terry Goodwin had already put out the flames."

"You finally met Terry? What's he like?" Harper asked.

"Very 'Jailhouse Rock'-ish."

Marcus laughed, then abruptly stopped and pressed the ice closer to his cheek.

"What's that mean?" Harper asked.

"You have to see for yourself," I said.

"Ha!" Ve exclaimed. "I told you so."

I dabbed at the carpet with a damp cloth and laughed. She had been right.

Harper shook her head. "I'm so confused."

The stain wasn't budging. "Never mind that. I thought you were supposed to be following Vince?"

"Vince?" Marcus asked. "Why?"

"Long story," I said. I was saved from telling it by a firm knock on the door downstairs.

Higgins and Missy started barking and nearly fell over themselves to get down the steps. Tilda went back to hissing, and Harper threw her hands in the air. "Who now?"

Ve rubbed her temples and said loud enough to be heard over the barking, "Do you have any more wine?"

The knocker had been Nick. And he'd been very agreeable to talking outside of the chaos in Harper's apartment.

We were currently walking around the green, the dogs leading the way. It was late—almost midnight—and the green had cleared of all gawkers and emergency personnel.

Nick's polo shirt was half untucked, his pants wrinkled, the bags under his eyes starting to look like the suitcase I'd hauled to Harper's.

"You look tired," I said, stating the obvious.

He dragged a hand down his face. "It's been a hell of a night. Four break-ins so far, then the call about the fire. The one night I let Mimi out of my sight . . ."

I was suddenly feeling guilty. It was my fault Mimi was in danger at all. Well, kind of. Mostly it was psycho Dorothy's fault. I had told him all about the threats, including the one about him, and he'd promised to look into them. "You know I'd do anything to protect her, right?"

As he glanced at me, the moonlight bounced off his dark eyes. "I know." He paused a beat, two. "What did Harper mean earlier when she said you'd make a lousy PI?"

I didn't like keeping secrets from him, but he really didn't need the whole truth. "Elodie hired me to look into her mother's death."

He swore under his breath. "You said no, right?"

I bit my lip.

"Right?" He slowed to a stop. "Darcy."

I blinked innocently. "Nick."

He wasn't buying it. "You need a license, training. . . ."

"I'm working on it."

"I'm not going to talk you out of this, am I?"

"I don't think so. No."

We continued walking. Missy and Higgins were sniff-ing happily.

Finally, he said, "Have you learned anything?"

I bumped his shoulder with mine. "I'll tell you mine if you tell me yours."

His eyes flashed in the darkness. "Isn't that saying, 'I'll *show* you mine. . . .'"

Oh. Well. There was that, too. My mouth went dry. "Work with me here."

He bumped me back. "How about you share yours, and I'll share what I can."

I was grateful he trusted me enough to share what he could. "Deal."

"So?"

"I haven't really learned anything yet."

He laughed, and it echoed across the green.

Smiling, I said, "Just little bits and pieces here and there. Most of which you probably already know. But I had a chat with Andreus Woodshall this afternoon that shed some more light on the Anicula." I gave him a brief run-down of what Mr. Macabre had said, from the theft of the Anicula years ago to his statement that Elodie had lied to me.

We walked slowly. Despite a gentle breeze rustling leaves and stars twinkling, the tent flaps still clanked against their poles, sounding a little like prisoners drag-ging tin cups along their bars. It was unsettling.

"I don't like how much I've been hearing about this

Anicula," he said. "It's turning up everywhere from the Peeper case to Patrice's murder."

"Do you think the two cases are connected?"

"Maybe."

I angled toward him to look into his face. "Remember the whole sharing thing?"

"I've been doing a little digging," he said (rather reluctantly, I thought). "All the houses broken into?"

Trying to encourage him, I nodded.

"All have been Charmory customers. I contacted Elodie this afternoon, and she e-mailed me her customer list and credit card purchases for the last two years. It's extensive, but a quick search revealed that every person who had a house broken into had used a credit card at the Charmory within the last eighteen months. I suspect there have been many more break-ins that we don't know about."

"That means our Peeper somehow got hold of that list."

"Yes. Probably broke in and copied it from her computer."

"Eighteen months, you say?"

"Yes."

"When Patrice disappeared."

He didn't say anything. He didn't have to.

My pulse had kicked up a notch. The Peeper wasn't looking for items related to the Craft. The Peeper was looking for something that belonged to Patrice. "Our Peeper is looking for the Anicula."

He glanced at me. "I believe so."

I supposed that ruled out Vince Paxton as the Creeper. I silently sent him an apology.

"Why, all of a sudden, is the Peeper getting sloppy?" I asked. "Leaving behind evidence of break-ins, and like tonight—why so many break-ins in one night?"

"I can think of one reason only, Darcy."

"What's that?"

"Someone is getting desperate."

Why that person was so desperate was left unasked. There was absolutely no way to know.

"What would you wish for?" I asked him. "If you could wish for absolutely anything?"

"It seems surreal to even think such a thing is possible, doesn't it?"

"Surreal and a little scary."

I recalled what Archie had said about how the Anicula changed people.

It can turn the shy into a braggart; the humble into an egoist; a servant into a god.

"I'd probably wish that Mimi has a long, happy and healthy life. You?"

I wasn't the least bit surprised that his wish was for someone else.

"It's strange being a Wishcrafter. There are so many times I say to myself that I wish I could grant my own wishes, most recently because I wished I could make Ve feel better. But to actually have that power? I don't know if I'd want it. It's one thing to grant other people's wishes without them knowing it—it's a bit like being a fairy godmother—but at least those powers are limited. With the Anicula, you can change the course of someone's life. Interfere with matters of love, life, death. I don't think I'd want that power or that responsibility."

Crickets chirped a symphony as we circled back to the bookshop. "But someone obviously does," he said.

"We just have to figure out who wants it the most, and we'll find our Peeper."

"And possibly a murderer as well."

He was probably right. Every negative aspect in Patrice's life had revolved around that Anicula. I had to find out whether she'd abused its power. Elodie denied the rumors, but I didn't know if she was simply covering for her mother.

I could think of only one other person who might know the truth: Yvonne. I had to get her to open up to me somehow.

"In the interest of sharing," Nick said, "I'll also tell you that Patrice's autopsy report came in."

"And?"

"Inconclusive," he said. "The medical examiner thinks it was probably asphyxiation."

"She was alive when someone put her in that suit-case?"

Headlights swept over us as a car drove past. "It looks that way. She was probably knocked out or drugged beforehand. I'm not sure we'll ever know."

An ache deep in my chest squeezed my lungs, making it hard to breathe. Poor Patrice. Poor Elodie. "That's horrible."

"Yes," he said softly. We walked in silence the rest of the way.

As we neared the alleyway leading to Harper's door, I said, "Well, all in all, it's been nice *working* with you."

With a hint of mischievousness in his voice, he said, "You know what they say about all work and no play."

In the shadows of the building, we slowed to a stop again, and the two dogs glanced back at us, clearly annoyed. Nick and I looked at each other, and I was enjoying the feelings racing through me—maybe a little too much. "Play?" I asked lamely.

His hand came up and cupped my cheek. He slowly leaned in, and my heart was doing a happy jig, kicking around in my chest like a drunken leprechaun. He was going to kiss me! And right then, there was nothing more I wanted in the whole world.

I resisted the urge to throw myself into his arms and allowed myself to enjoy the tingles on my skin, the touch of his rough palm on my cheek, the scent of him, of the night air. The anticipation.

But as I slowly leaned in to meet his lips, he suddenly drew back, his gaze hard on a car coming down the street.

I stiffened. It was a pink village police cruiser, its strobe light flashing.

Glinda.

I cursed her timing as the car slowed to a stop and the window powered down.

Nick said, "Anything wrong, Officer Hansel?"

"Another report of a break-in, Chief. I'm on my way there now."

Under the streetlamp, I could clearly see the calculating way she was looking at us. A chill went down my back.

"You should get going, then," he said in a firm voice.

She nodded and said, "Yes, sir. But the homeowners insisted on speaking to you."

"Who?" he asked.

"The Merricks. Roger and Yvonne."

I drew in a breath. The Peeper had broken into their home?

Nick said, "I'll be there in five minutes."

"Yes, sir." She glared at me as the car rolled away.

I stared after it and said, "Can I come with you?"

"Why?"

At least he hadn't said no right off. "I want to talk to Yvonne, and this might be the perfect time. If she's rattled, she might open up to me."

He shook his head. "I can't. Protocol."

I bit my lip. "Is there anything stopping me from dropping the dogs off and then checking on Patrice's house? After all, it's across the street and might have been hit as well. If I happen to bump into Yvonne in the process . . ."

"Hit?" he said with a smirk.

"Hey, if I'm going to be a PI, I have to learn the lingo, right?"

He rolled his eyes. "You being a PI is not a good idea."

I lifted an eyebrow and narrowed my eyes, ready to fight it out.

Quickly, he raised a hand in surrender. "I should be going. I'll see you there?"

Nodding, I just hoped I wouldn't run into the Peeper on my way.

Chapter Twenty-four

When I ran upstairs and dropped off the dogs, I was surprised to find Ve missing.

Mimi was sleeping on Harper's bed, and my sister was sorting books on the shelf that had fallen on Marcus. He was working on trying to get Tilda out of her cage.

If that didn't make him a keeper in Harper's eyes, I didn't know what would. She was a pet lover at heart.

I couldn't hear any hissing, but that didn't mean Marcus could let his guard down and I told him so.

"Don't worry," he said. "I'm kind of a Cat Whisperer."

We both stared at him.

"It's true," he said. "Watch."

He lay down on his belly and put his head dangerously (in my opinion) close to the opening of the cage. "Come on out, sweetheart," he cooed. "I've got a nice can of tuna for you. The good stuff."

I stole a look at Harper. She had an oooey-gooey look in her eye.

Not wanting to openly gloat, I hid my smile of triumph. Unless Marcus did something to screw this up, his chances with Harper had just skyrocketed. Especially after Tilda pranced out of the cage as if she had been planning on it all along. Marcus scooped her up, and damn if I couldn't hear her purrs across the room.

Cat Whisperer, indeed.

I explained where I was off to and asked, "Where's Ve?"

Harper set a book on the shelf. "She went back to As You Wish to cast the protection spell."

Glancing at my watch, I saw it was just past twelve thirty. "Alone?"

"She called Terry. He's meeting her there." Her eyes twinkled. "It didn't sound like he minded at all when she called to ask."

I would think not. According to Ve, Terry Goodwin had been trying to win her back for years. "Really? Terry?"

Tilda had settled herself nicely in Marcus's arms. He said, "She might have been encouraged by your sister."

"Harper!" I gasped.

"What?" she asked innocently.

"Ve's getting married on Sunday."

She shrugged. "She's not married yet. I think she should explore all her options before settling down."

Ve had been married four times already. Her options had been vastly explored. But I didn't have time to argue with my sister.

I checked on Mimi, who was sleeping with her arms thrown over her head. Missy had curled up next to her and looked as happy as could be. Higgins had claimed the couch—the entire couch, and I knew I didn't want to be the one to evict him from his spot. Which left me wondering where the rest of us were going to sleep.

It was a problem to worry about later. Right now, I wanted to get over to see Yvonne. I vaguely explained to Harper what I was doing, glossing over the break-in as no big deal, and headed out.

Five minutes later, I stood in front of Patrice's house. There were already two police cars in front of the Merricks' house, but neither one was Nick's, and I didn't see any sign of him.

In the interest of keeping up false pretenses, I planned a quick walk around Patrice's house before I tried to find Yvonne. As I approached the back deck, which thankfully was lit from a globe light near the door, I stopped short.

There was broken glass on the decking. I zeroed in on the back door. The glass in the upper part of the door had been smashed and a hand-sized hole was clear. Just big enough for someone to put their arm through and unlock the door from the inside.

Carefully, I stepped over the broken shards and pushed the back door open. From a quick glance, nothing appeared amiss. But that seemed to be the Peeper's MO.

"Not here, too," a raspy voice said from directly behind me.

Letting out a squeal, I grabbed my heart, turned, and found Yvonne.

She held out a hand and steadied me. "I'm sorry. I thought you heard me coming. Did you find something?"

Adrenaline rushed, pricking my skin, making my heart throb. "The house has been broken into again."

"Seems that there's a spree going on. Nick Sawyer just left on another call."

Ah, that's why Nick hadn't been across the street. *Desperate.* The word echoed in my head. "Was anything taken at your house?"

"No, I don't think so. I woke up and found the intruder pawing through my jewelry."

I felt my eyes widen. "You saw the Peeper?"

"I couldn't believe what I was seeing," she said, rambling on. "At first I thought I was dreaming."

"Understandable."

"I wondered if I was seeing things," Yvonne said, shaking her head. Her blond hair had been pulled back in a headband, and the chain that normally held her reading glasses was absent from her neck.

My curiosity was killing me. "Did you recognize the Peeper?"

"Oh no. It was much too dark, and the Peeper was dressed all in black, hooded head to toe."

I deflated.

"The Peeper stood there, picked up a piece of jewelry one at a time, mumbled something, then went on to the next piece. It was very strange. When the Peeper turned and found me staring, the Peeper jumped a little bit. Kind of like you did a minute ago. That's when I realized it was very real and started screaming."

"You saw the Peeper's face?"

"No, thanks to a ski mask."

Damn. "What did Roger do?"

"He slept through the whole thing," she said, outraged. "He can barely keep his eyes open even now."

"He slept through the whole thing? Really?"

"Not even a snore, which is very unusual for him — trust me." She yawned. "I think he may be coming down with something — he wasn't feeling well at dinner. Maybe that's the explanation."

I had a sinking feeling. "Did you go out to eat?"

Looking left and right, as if afraid to be overheard, she said, "Between us, Darcy, I brought in takeout. But Roger thinks I made it."

Let me guess. "From the Stove?"

"If Roger finds out, I'll never hear the end of it. You know how he feels about Jonathan." She made a face. "Usually the food there is above reproach, but I couldn't eat much of mine — something was off with it. But Roger cleaned his plate, as usual."

I didn't mention the food poisoning going around and hoped Roger had an iron stomach.

She gave a little cough. "My throat is still sore from all that screaming." She smiled. "But you've never seen a person run so fast."

"The Peeper didn't take anything?"

"Not a thing. Strange, isn't it?"

"Not if the person was looking for the Anicula and didn't find it."

Her face paled in the moonlight. "You think?"

I nodded and looked at the broken back door. "I think the Peeper was here, too."

I thought about what this meant. The Peeper was on a crime spree.

"We should let the police know about this," Yvonne said, motioning to the back door.

I wasn't sure if I'd get another opportunity tonight, so I said, "Before we do that, I wanted to ask you something."

Puzzled, she lifted her eyebrows. "Me?"

Crickets chirped in the dark woods around the house. Mosquitoes buzzed annoyingly. "I spoke with Andreus Woodshall this afternoon. He told me quite a story about the Anicula."

Frown lines deepened around her mouth. "I bet he did."

"Is it true?"

She let out a deep breath and seemed to shrink inside herself. "That Geer and Roger dug up that stupid amulet? Yes, it's true. Fools."

Shocked, I said, "*Roger* helped Geer?"

Leaning against the deck rail, she stared into the sky. "Did Mr. Macabre neglect to mention that?"

He hadn't mentioned it. And I wondered why. Also, why had Roger willingly helped Geer steal the amulet with what Geer had in mind? I could only surmise that Roger had had no idea Geer planned to wish that Patrice fall in love with him—and leave Roger brokenhearted in the process.

Yvonne swatted away a bug. "Then I suppose he didn't mention my role in it, either?"

She'd stunned me. *"What?"*

How had she even known about the amulet? She'd been a mortal at the time.... Then I remembered that magical charms weren't solely limited to Crafters. Because she had known about the Anicula at the time didn't necessarily mean she had known about the Craft. That knowledge had obviously come later—when she married Roger.

Taking a deep breath, she said, "I knew what Geer had planned. I could have stopped him. And I didn't. Andreus has never forgiven me."

"You and Andreus were friends?"

She nodded. "Best friends. I betrayed that."

I put the pieces together. "Because you wanted Roger for yourself?"

Slowly, she nodded. "Geer knew how I felt about Roger, and I knew how he felt about Patrice. He told me all about his plan to steal the Anicula and wish that Patrice would fall in love with him. I didn't tell a soul. I wanted Roger and Patrice to break up because I knew Roger would come to me for comfort. However, I drew the line at actually helping Geer get the amulet." She shuddered.

"Grave robbing, you mean?"

A moth buzzed her head as she winced. "Yes." Her eyes fluttered closed. "It's so shameful. But because I refused to help and Geer couldn't do it alone, he tricked Roger into helping him. Roger never saw what was coming."

But Yvonne had known. And she'd been waiting. I didn't know how to ask what I was thinking, so I blurted it out. "You didn't mind being Roger's second choice?"

Looking into the distance, she shook her head. "No. And I still don't. I love the big ape. I just wish he loved me."

One of the Wishcraft Laws was that I couldn't interfere with love, so I felt safe in not granting that wish. "He doesn't?"

Her jaw quivered, but her voice was firm. "He never stopped loving Patrice. When Geer made the wish that he and Patrice fall madly in love, he neglected to wish for Roger's happiness. It's why Roger doesn't like Elodie." She gave me a sad smile. "Every time he looks at her, he sees Geer and is reminded all over again what he lost."

My mind spun. "Did Patrice know about Geer's wish?"

"Not for years. He finally confessed what he'd done in a letter to be read after he died."

I imagined that had come as quite a shock. "But she'd been happy with him, right?"

"A picture-perfect life."

But had it been? Really? Could the Anicula really hold so much power that it could snap Patrice out of love with Roger and in love with Geer in a flash?

It gave me the heebie-jeebies just thinking about it, about how Patrice had had no say in the matter.

I pushed my luck with Yvonne. "Why did you and Patrice have a falling out?"

"I wanted a wish, and she refused to grant it. Patrice rarely granted wishes. Not her own, or anyone's. She feared the power in that stone. She would wear it in a little pouch around her neck, day and night, taking it off only to shower. She was afraid to let it out of her sight. Rightfully so, I guess, if it really was stolen, as she said."

It had been stolen six months before she went missing.

Around the same time she and Jonathan had broken up.

The same time she and Elodie had had some sort of fight and stopped talking to each other.

"Do you know why Patrice and Elodie had a fight around that time?" I asked.

She shook her head. "I've asked Connor, but he won't say. And Elodie won't talk about it, either."

"But Patrice and Elodie reconciled before Patrice went missing, right?" It was what Starla had told me.

"Oh yes. About three months before. Elodie's and Connor's wedding drew them back together. All had been forgiven, whatever it was."

They had gone months without talking to each other.... It made me wonder if things might have been forgiven but not forgotten.

I still wanted more information from Yvonne. "What wish did you want from Patrice?"

"It wasn't for me. It was for Connor and Elodie. They were having a rough patch, and I wanted to wish them happiness together, a life full of love, laughter, babies. Patrice refused. I couldn't believe she wouldn't do it. Not only because a wish like that would guarantee her child's happiness, but because she'd denied me the only favor I ever asked of her. It ruined our friendship."

I could see why Yvonne, of all people, would be upset. She was a control freak. If she had an opportunity to guarantee Connor's happiness, she was going to take it.

But I was slightly amazed that Yvonne seemed to glaze right over the fact that she had helped sabotage Patrice's relationship with Roger to have him for herself.

If I were Patrice, I might hold a grudge about that.

But why hadn't Patrice granted the wish? Didn't every parent want happiness for their child, even if the person asking for the wish wasn't someone she cared for? "Why did she refuse?"

"She said that if the two were meant to be, they were meant to be. That she wouldn't interfere with Elodie's life like her life had been interfered with. She wanted to make sure that if the two were going to be together, it was because they wanted to be together. Not because she wished it so."

"You said Patrice hardly ever granted wishes. Do you know of any she did grant?"

"Only one, while she was dating Jonathan Wilkens." Closing her eyes, she sighed. "What a tangled web we weave."

"When we practice to deceive? Who was being deceptive?" Or rather, who wasn't being deceptive around here?

"Roger may be a blowhard about a lot of things, but one thing he's right about is how Jonathan ruined Patrice's life."

"How so?"

"After Geer died, Patrice had very little interest in dating. A couple of years passed and she started to get a little crush on Jonathan." She smiled. "Maybe not so little. Big. A big crush. He knew it, but didn't really act upon it. Not until he needed something from her."

Something rustled in the grass near the deck. I looked down and saw bright eyes looking up at me. The tabby.

"*Meow*," it said.

Yvonne looked over the railing and said, "That cat's been hanging around here for weeks now."

"Do you know whose it is?"

"A stray, I think. I've tried to lure it into the house, but it won't come near me."

As if to demonstrate the truth of Yvonne's words, the cat darted under the deck.

I could probably get a trap for it. Or call Marcus, the Cat Whisperer. For now, I wanted to hear what Yvonne had to say about Jonathan. "What did Jonathan need?"

"He had a little rodent problem."

"The rats?"

"He'd spent thousands trying to get rid of them. The village turned against him. It was ugly. Patrice agreed to grant his wish. They started dating after that, and she fell head over heels for him."

"But?"

"He was a womanizer. Cheated with every pretty

thing that walked by until he met Zoey. She changed his life. But in the process . . ."

"He broke Patrice's heart," I supplied.

"She never really recovered. She started dating Andreus. At first to make Jonathan jealous, then because she knew the power she had over Andreus. As long as she had the Anicula, he wouldn't leave her."

"Do you think he knew she was using him?"

"I believe so. He allowed it because he was using her, too. He wanted that amulet back. It is rightfully his, after all."

I took a deep breath and asked, "Do you think he would kill to get it?"

She was quiet for a moment. "I don't think so. Under all that creepiness, I think he's a nice guy."

"Let me ask you this, then. If he got the Anicula back, what do you think he'd do with it? Do you think he'd return it to its proper burial place? Or do you think he'd hold on to its power?"

She swatted at a gnat. "The power to grant wishes is incredibly heady, and I can't see him letting that go."

It was the way I was leaning, too.

I studied her. "Well, I'm glad things worked out for Elodie and Connor. They're still together and seem very much in love."

Looking like a proud mama, she nodded. "They're very happy together."

Biting my lip, I suddenly wondered if they were that way because of destiny . . . or because Yvonne had killed Patrice, stolen the Anicula, and finally granted her wish.

Chapter Twenty-five

"Tragedy!" Pepe declared the next morning, fully distraught, as he hopped off Archie's feathered back and onto the kitchen island. Pepe paced, his tail slashing out, his little mouse whiskers twitching in agitation.

Even his dramatics couldn't suppress my yawn as I set another pot of coffee to brew. It had been a long night. Most of it sleepless, as I'd tossed and turned on Harper's apartment floor, nose to nose with Tilda, who hadn't been pleased to be displaced from her usual bed.

I'd woken up early, packed everything up, brought Mimi to Nick's place, and was now back home with a still-ailing Ve at As You Wish. With my grumpy mood, I *dared* anyone to break in.

It was close to noon, and Pepe and Archie had just arrived. Starla was already sitting at the island, nibbling on scones I'd bought at the Witch's Brew.

"*Quell horror!*" Pepe cried, throwing tiny fists into the air and shaking them.

I decided he'd been hanging out with Archie too much.

Starla said, "What happened, Pepe?"

As I set out the biggest mug I could find, I gave him a closer inspection. He wasn't simply being dramatic—he was beside himself, trembling with outrage.

Archie *tsk*ed. "'Tis not good."

"I don't know how to tell her." Pepe paced.

"Tell me what?" I asked.

"Not you," Archie clarified.

"Me?" Starla asked, hand to chest.

"No." Pepe shook his head so hard his ears quivered. "Velma."

"Ve?" She was no better this morning, and the virus was taking its toll. She'd barely had enough energy to walk home from Harper's this morning. Casting that protection spell last night had taken a couple of hours and zapped what was left of her energy. She hadn't arrived back at Harper's until after three a.m.—long after I'd returned from Patrice's. I'd stayed awake, listening for her to come back like she was a teenager out past curfew.

Now I looked around the kitchen for evidence of the spell but saw nothing out of the ordinary except for the agate ball and leftover sage in a basket on the kitchen counter as if they were commonplace objects found in a kitchen, like a basket of fruit. A strong hint of sage lingered in the air, and it filled me with confidence that we were safe within these walls.

Pepe said, "It's missing."

"What's missing?" I asked. The coffeepot hissed and spat. I was on my second pot and hadn't felt the least bit of a boost from the caffeine.

Pepe took a deep breath. "Her dress."

Lifting the carafe, I poured coffee into my mug—as close to the rim as I could get without spilling. "What dress?"

When he said nothing, Starla and I looked at him. Then at Archie, who wouldn't meet my eye, then at Pepe again. I carefully set my mug on the counter.

"Her *wedding* dress?" Starla gasped.

"*Oui*," Pepe said in a tiny voice. "When I went to

sleep, it hung in the workroom. When I woke up, it was gone. Vanished."

Archie used the tip of his wing to pat the mouse's back. "It will be found; do not worry."

"I am magical, yes," Pepe said with a nod, "but even I cannot make the dress reappear. Or make a new one in three days' time. Her beading—it is exceptionally intricate."

My heart pounded. "Someone stole Ve's dress?"

"I assume," Pepe said. "But there is no sign of a break-in. It's as if the gown simply disappeared."

Gowns didn't just disappear unless magic was involved. Which most likely meant a Crafter was involved. And I could think of only one Crafter who didn't want Ve to get married on Sunday.

Dorothy.

I lifted my mug. *Scratch that thought.* I could think of several Crafters who didn't want Ve to get married on Sunday. Like me, Harper, and Godfrey. But none of us would go to the lengths of stealing Ve's dress to keep it from happening.

Dorothy, however, had a mean streak, and I could see her sneaking off with Ve's dress, no problem.

"Maybe it was the Peeper," Starla said. "The rash of break-ins last night was all the talk in the village this morning."

"Why would the Peeper want Ve's dress?" I asked. The Peeper, clearly, was after the Anicula.

"The *Peeper*," Archie said, making a noise of disgust. "I am sick of him."

I was growing weary of him as well.

"If only we could catch him." Pepe balled his fist and made a punching motion.

Smiling behind my mug, I said, "It might be easier to catch him if we had any idea at all who it is." All I knew was that it wasn't Vince Paxton. I'd forgotten to tell

Mrs. P that I'd ruled him out, and she'd continued staking him out last night, using her Vaporcrafting skills to keep an eye on him at his place. He'd gone to bed a little after eleven and stayed there until early this morning.

I silently sent him another apology. And Mrs. P, too, for wasting her time, though she hadn't seemed to mind the stake-out at all.

"What about Andreus Woodshall?" Archie asked. "Does he have an alibi for last night?"

"I don't know." I picked a blueberry off a scone and ate it. "He's an obvious suspect, but I don't think it was him. He told me that a spell had been placed on the Keatons' house that kept him out of it. The Peeper went inside last night."

Pepe said, "He has a son, does he not?"

My gaze slid to Starla. Her cheeks colored. "I, ah, can vouch for his whereabouts," she said.

Archie cooed, "Ooh la la."

"Don't make me pluck you," she warned.

His beak snapped closed.

We were back to having no idea who the Peeper was.

Pepe wrung his hands. He glanced at the stairs. "I may as well get this over with. I must tell Ve about her dress before my whiskers fall out from the stress."

"Actually, now's not a good time. She's upstairs with Cherise Goodwin." Thankfully, Cherise had agreed to an emergency house call. "Hopefully, another spell is the key to a full recovery in time for the wedding."

Pepe moaned. "Do not remind me about the wedding. How am I going to tell Ve about her dress?"

Coffee scorched the back of my throat. "You aren't." All three stared at me. "You won't need to. We're going to find that dress."

"How?" Archie asked.

Pepe's eyes widened as if seeing me for the first time in a new light. "I can *wish* for it. Brilliant idea!"

I laughed. "I'd been thinking more along the lines of practicing some private investigation skills." Which would mostly consist of me snooping around Dorothy's house to see if there was a wayward wedding dress lying around.

"Wishing would be faster, *non*?" Pepe's eyes were wide, pleading.

"Definitely," Starla said.

"But remember," I cautioned, "all wishes by Crafters must now be approved first by the Elder." She apparently had some sort of magical inbox and knew when wishes were being made. "If the wish isn't granted immediately, you must go to the Elder and explain the wish you made. She will then decide to grant or deny it."

Pepe nodded solemnly, then said, "I wish to . . ."

My nerves tingled. The word "wish" always did that to me. Starla, too, if her fidgeting was any indication. "You take this one," she said to me. She hopped off her stool and grabbed her camera, which hung in the mudroom. She came back, grabbed a scone from the plate, and said, "I've got to get back to work." Sending air kisses, she waved and ducked out the back door.

Pepe still hadn't finished his wish.

"What's wrong?" I asked.

"I am not certain what to wish. To find the dress or to have it back."

"A bird in hand, my little friend," Archie said wisely.

Pepe nodded. "I wish to have Ve's dress returned to the boutique immediately."

I said, "Wish I might, wish I may, grant this wish without delay." After a second, I said, "Shall I call Godfrey and see if it's there?"

Pepe nodded.

I picked up the phone and dialed. Godfrey answered on the second ring.

"I about had myself a heart attack," he said. "I was sitting here putting the final touches on your dress, and suddenly a wedding gown appears next to me. A little warning next time, Darcy."

I smiled and gave Pepe the thumbs-up. "Absolutely."

I hung up with Godfrey and said, "He might need a cardiac checkup, but he says the dress is back in the shop."

Pepe wiped his paw across his brow. "*Merci*, Darcy. *Merci*."

I kissed the top of his head. "You're very welcome."

Archie cleared his throat. "Speaking of the Elder ..."

I didn't like his tone. It was the one he used when acting as the Elder's majordomo. "Go on."

"She requests your presence today at one p.m."

I swallowed hard. "I haven't done anything wrong, have I?" I couldn't think of anything.

"I am just the messenger," he said. "Pepe, we should be off. It's almost time for our patrol." Archie sighed. "The Elder is quite displeased that none of the patrols spotted the Peeper sneaking through the village last night on a crime spree. It is quite the embarrassment."

I saw the two of them off, then grabbed my coffee and sat on the sofa with my notebook. Staring at the page I'd started yesterday, I frowned. I certainly had more information, but I was really no closer to knowing who would kill her.

I reexamined what I'd written.

Who was Patrice?
Why would someone want to kill her?

- *The Anicula's powers (Mr. Macabre)*
- *Greed*
- *Love (Jonathan??? Mr. Macabre?)*
- *Jealousy (Roger, Yvonne)*

Certain things I could answer. Patrice was a loving mother. I suspected her hoarding stemmed from when she "suddenly" fell in love with Geer, leaving Roger. Not of her own free will. Maybe the magic hadn't been strong enough to keep her from realizing she had lost something, even if she couldn't quite remember what. Maybe she held on to things, objects, to try to fill that void.

It was really quite sad to think about.

I jotted a quick note to myself: F*ind out why Patrice and Elodie have stopped talking.*

As to why someone would want to kill Patrice, I still didn't know. I'd narrowed it down to jealousy or the Anicula.

On a crisp new page in the notebook, I wrote: *Jealousy: Roger, Yvonne.*

Roger was jealous of Andreus and Jonathan. Roger hated that Jonathan had used Patrice and that he'd left her brokenhearted. He hated, simply, that Patrice had loved Jonathan at all—and not him. Could he have killed Patrice because he hated seeing her with other men?

Yvonne was jealous of Patrice—that Roger still loved her. She was jealous that Patrice could grant any wish at any time . . . and angry because Patrice refused to grant her wish. Could her emotions have pushed her over the edge?

Next, I thought about the Anicula and who was desperate for its powers. I wrote: *The Anicula—Andreus, Lazarus, Yvonne, Roger, Elodie, Jonathan?*

Andreus and Lazarus had family ties to the Anicula. Yvonne was controlling, and would probably want nothing more than to have the power to control Connor's future—and to guarantee her own.

I crossed Roger off my Anicula list. After all, if he still loved Patrice, he wouldn't kill her for the Anicula—he might use it to wish that she loved him again, but he wouldn't harm her.

Elodie had to be considered as well. If Andreus was to be believed (and why would he fib about it?), she had lied to me about the Anicula. I had to find out why—and if the reason behind it had anything to do with her mother's death.

I'd thrown Jonathan on the list, too, for one reason only. He'd used Patrice for a wish before—what if he asked for another after they broke up and she refused? Would he kill her to get the Anicula for himself? I bet he wished he had it right now, what with the food poisonings tied to his restaurant.

I sat up so fast I almost spilled my coffee as I thought of something. Could Jonathan be behind the recent break-ins? Was he looking for the Anicula to stop the outbreak of food poisonings?

I thought about that for a second. The recent Peeper break-ins *had* started around the same time as the food poisonings. Plus, he had silver in his hair—just like the man I'd chased into the woods yesterday morning. The man who'd been in the house.

I doodled on my notebook and wondered why he'd break into As You Wish. Then I realized he knew I was working for Elodie—he'd seen me there yesterday. Maybe he thought I'd found the Anicula?

The hair stood up on my arms, and I knew I was onto something. If Jonathan was the Peeper, it would also explain the argument he'd had with Zoey, about the police finding out about *something*.

As I let my thoughts tumble around, I recalled a bit of what Yvonne had said last night, about how the Peeper had been picking up pieces of her jewelry and mumbling something. The truth of *why* hit me so hard I sucked in a breath.

The Peeper didn't know what the Anicula looked like.

It explained why nothing was ever taken during the break-ins. The Peeper would pick up the jewels, make a wish, and wait to see if it was granted. If it wasn't, the Peeper moved on to the next item, to the next house.

But if Patrice had granted Jonathan a wish before—

the one to get rid of the rats—wouldn't he know what the Anicula looked like? Or had she granted the wish without him seeing the Anicula?

I was trying to figure out how I could find out when there was a sharp rap on the back door before it swung open. Mimi rushed in, slamming the door behind her, her cheeks red. "Darcy!"

Missy started barking and circling around Mimi's feet, looking for attention. Alarmed, I jumped to my feet. "Mimi, what's wrong?"

"Archie just came by." She huffed and puffed, as if she'd run the whole way from her house to mine.

"Did something happen to your dad?" I racked my brain, trying to think of what would cause her so much panic. "Is he hurt?"

She shook her head, sending her dark ponytail flying. "No! Archie wanted to see *me*."

A feeling of dread started in my stomach when I spotted the dark cape in one hand, her mom's diary in the other. "Why?"

She gulped. "I've been summoned by the Elder."

Chapter Twenty-six

I tried to keep calm. One of us had to. "What did Archie say, specifically?"

"Just that the Elder wanted to see me at one o'clock, and he told me to bring my mom's diary with me."

The same time I'd been summoned. I told her so.

"Are we in trouble?" she asked.

"I don't think so. When I was in trouble with the Elder before, Archie announced which Wishcraft law I'd broken when he summoned me."

"Do you think the Elder knows that Vince saw my mom's diary?"

There was no way to sugarcoat my answer. "Yes."

"How?"

"I haven't quite figured out how the Elder knows anything."

"Is she all-knowing? Like the Wizard of Oz?"

I smiled. I'd also thought of the Wizard when it came to the Elder. "I think so."

"Then if she knows everything, does she know who the Peeper Creeper is? Or who killed Mrs. Keaton?"

It was a good question. "If she knew who the Peeper was, I don't think she'd be sending out patrols." Helplessly, I shrugged. "I don't know how her powers work, so it's hard to say what she knows and what she doesn't."

"Maybe we can ask her," Mimi said.

"I'm not sure that's a good idea."

Tilda strutted into the room, her tail high in the air. She pranced by Missy and hissed for good measure. She hopped onto the coffee table and sniffed my coffee, then leapt onto the back of the couch, where she watched us with veiled interest.

"Why not?"

"Maybe we should just hear her out for now and save our questions for another time."

Mimi blanched. "Do you think there will be other times?"

I was saved from answering by footsteps on the stairs. Ve was saying, "I already feel much, much better."

Cherise Goodwin said, "Be that as it may, I still want you to rest. You've been through a lot this past week. Emotionally, you have a long road ahead of you, and I cannot help you with that. You need your rest."

Ve twirled. "But I feel good as new."

Cherise smiled conspiratorially. "That may be because of your new rela—"

Ve caught sight of me and Mimi and cut Cherise off with a squeeze to her arm. "Look who's here!"

I wasn't buying the bright smile. "What's this about an emotional long road?"

Waving a dismissive hand, Ve said, "Nothing to worry about."

"I should go," Cherise said. She kissed both Ve's cheeks.

She waved good-bye to me and Mimi, and I very clearly heard her whisper "Good luck with everything" to Ve when she left.

Huh. What was that all about?

Mimi said, "So you're all better now, Aunt Ve?"

"It sure feels that way," Ve said. She clapped her hands. "There's so much to get done."

Mimi said, "For the wedding?"

Something dark flashed in Ve's expression before she brightened again. "Among other things. First things first—a big lunch! I think I'll go out. Maybe to the Stove. Do you two care to join me?"

"We can't," I said, still studying her. Something was off. Way off. I just didn't know what. "We've been summoned to see the Elder."

Ve's face fell. "Oh? Why?"

"I think it's because Vince saw my mom's diary," Mimi said, holding up the leather-bound book.

"That would make sense, I suppose," Ve said. "When are you due?"

I glanced at the clock. "In a few minutes. I should get my cape." I stole a look at Mimi, who was flipping through the diary. "I'll be right back, Mimi. Ve, can I talk to you for a second?"

"Certainly!"

She followed me to the front closet, where I pulled my brand-new cape from within. "Is everything okay with Cherise?"

"Perfect," Ve said. "I've never felt better."

"Why do I feel like there's something you're not telling me?"

"I have no idea." She smiled wide and shrugged

Oh, she was definitely hiding something.

I let it go for now—only because I had to go see the Elder.

"Where do we stand with the wedding, Darcy dear?" Ve asked as we walked back into the kitchen.

Mimi snapped the diary closed and looked up at us. Was that a guilty flush to her cheeks?

What was going on around here?

"Darcy?" Ve repeated. "The wedding preparations? I'm still worried about the lack of RSVPs."

I winced. I'd completely forgotten to ask her about

the invitations in the trash behind Sylar's optometry office, Third Eye. "I think I might know why," I said and explained.

Ve's eyes widened. "Oooh," she fumed. "I bet Sylar gave the invitations to Dorothy to mail and she trashed most of them."

Mimi said, "But I got my invitation."

Ve curved an arm around Mimi's shoulders. "Lesson number one in being devious, Mimi dear: Don't be obvious. Dorothy probably mailed only a few invites, to the people closest to us. That way we wouldn't know anything was amiss."

"Why would she do that, though?" Mimi asked.

I winced again. "There's probably something else I should tell you," I said to Ve.

"Have mercy, child. What now?"

My heart beat wildly, and I wasn't sure I was doing the right thing. "There was kind of an incident behind Third Eye yesterday. Between Sylar and Dorothy." I cringed.

"The kiss?" Ve asked.

Shocked, I could only nod.

She patted my cheek. "Don't worry. Sylar already told me all about it yesterday. He didn't tell me, however, that you had seen it."

That's right—Archie had said Sylar stopped by. At least he was being up-front with Ve. It made me like him a little more.

"He kind of didn't know I was there," I said.

Ve smiled. "I see."

"You don't mind that Sylar was kissing someone else?" Mimi asked, slightly outraged, if her tone was any indication.

"It's complicated." Ve's eyes flashed. "I think it's time I paid Dorothy a visit. Today. Right now, in fact."

"Why don't you wait?" I said, not wanting her to go alone. "I'll go with you."

Ve laughed. "You don't have to worry, Darcy. I can handle this myself."

Missy ran to the back door and whined. I looked at the clock again—I couldn't risk her escaping when I didn't have time to look for her. "Mimi, can you take Missy out before we leave?"

She nodded, and as I watched them go, I couldn't help but think about the fire last night. "About Dorothy . . ."

"Spill it, Darcy Ann." Ve stared long and hard. "What else are you keeping from me?"

If she was going to see Dorothy—and I knew that once Ve had something in her mind there was no changing it—she had to be warned. I told her about Dorothy's threat.

"The fire last night!" she exclaimed. "I should have known after what she did to Godfrey. I had been assuming it was this Peeper person. You should have told me about her threat."

"I didn't want to worry you," I said. "Especially with you being ill."

"Well, I am better now and will take care of this matter at once."

Her tone had me worried. "There's no concrete proof Dorothy set the fire. . . ."

"Of course not," Ve said. "She's too smart for that. We shall see what she has to say for herself."

"Please be careful," I pleaded.

Ve narrowed her eyes. "Honestly, Darcy dear, I'm more worried about you."

"Me?"

"Dorothy rarely bluffs. She can be dangerous." Ve picked up the agate sphere out of the basket on the countertop and handed it to me. "Until I get this all straightened out, I want you to carry this everywhere you go." She folded my fingers over the stone. "And be careful. Very careful."

*   *   *

Mimi clutched my hand as we walked through the woods. "Why do we have to wear the capes?"

"I don't know," I said. Now I was wondering why, too. It was August. If anyone saw us, we might look a tad bit suspicious.

"Are you sure you know the way?"

"Unfortunately, yes."

Even though the day was sunny, the woods were dark. Every once in a while a sunbeam would slip through the canopy to highlight a spot on the trail or a tree root. In broad daylight, there was nothing ominous about this trip. Thank goodness. I didn't think Mimi could handle a trek through these woods at night.

"What's that ahead?" she asked.

I smiled. "That's the Elder's meadow." The woods may have been in shadow, but the Elder's meadow was bright and cheery and full of colorful wildflowers. I felt Mimi's hand relax.

"It's beautiful."

I agreed.

In the middle of the meadow was a solitary tree. Short and squat, it looked like an overgrown mushroom with willowy weeping leaves. It was the Elder's tree.

We stood side by side, taking it all in.

"What happens now?" Mimi asked.

"We wait," I whispered.

"I don't like waiting," she declared.

"Demetria," the Elder's voice boomed. "The sooner you learn patience, the better."

The voice came from inside the tree. It wasn't a young voice, and it wasn't old either. Somewhere in between. It was also distorted, to a certain degree. A disguise, I realized. Which meant the Elder was probably someone we knew. Ve once told me the Elder's identity would be revealed to me in due time.

I had no idea when that would be, but like Mimi, I was growing impatient.

"You cannot always control what is going on around you," the Elder said. "Nor should you, even if you believe you're doing the right thing. Do I make myself clear?"

Mimi sidestepped behind me and said, "I'm not controlling."

I gave her hand a squeeze to warn her to be quiet.

"I'm not," she whispered to me.

"My child, do not argue. I know everything. I see everything."

Mimi gulped.

"Sit down, the two of you," the Elder said.

Two tree stumps magically appeared behind us. Mimi's eyes grew to the size of saucers as we sat down.

"Darcy," the Elder said, "do you know why I called you both here?"

"It's either because of the diary," I guessed, "or because the Peeper Creeper overheard my conversation with Archie yesterday."

"You are right on both fronts. Let us begin with the diary." I could have sworn I heard her sigh. "Demetria, you willfully disregarded Darcy's sound advice to keep the diary hidden. It almost fell into mortal hands, which could have been devastating to the Craft."

"I'm sorry," Mimi said in a quiet voice.

I glanced at her. She had tears in her brown eyes, and they nearly broke my heart.

"I wasn't trying to put the Craft in jeopardy," she added.

"Your actions were reckless, child. Please give the diary to Darcy."

"But," Mimi began.

The Elder's voice was firm. "Right now."

"My mother . . . ," Mimi said weakly, clutching the diary to her chest.

There was a beat of silence, during which not even a bird chirped or a leaf rustled. I swore I could hear my own heart fluttering.

"I am aware of your mother," the Elder said. "She committed a grievous error in penning that diary. It should not be in existence."

"You're not going to get rid of it, are you?" Mimi cried.

"No. However, Darcy will be its caretaker until I deem you responsible enough to hold such a wealth of knowledge."

"I'm—"

I kicked Mimi to get her to be quiet. She glanced at me, and I shook my head, warning her. She clamped her lips closed and handed me the diary.

"Good," the Elder said. "You are fortunate that Vincent Paxton did not know the treasure he held. For now, the Craft's secrets are safe. They must stay that way."

Mimi's bottom lip trembled.

"Darcy, you are here forth entrusted with the safekeeping of that journal. Do not let it fall into the wrong hands."

My nerves jumped. I cleared my throat. "How am I supposed to ensure that?" There was, after all, a Peeper on the loose. Sure, it might be Jonathan—or someone—looking for the Anicula. But it might not.

"You know the answer," the Elder said.

"I do?"

I thought I heard another sigh. "Search within yourself."

"Elder?" Mimi asked.

"Yes, child."

"Why do we have to wear the capes when we come to see you?"

I rolled my eyes. What was with Mimi and the questions today?

"When you have been summoned to see me, the capes make you invisible to mortals."

"They do?" I'd had no idea.

"Yes," the Elder said with more patience than I thought we deserved. "But only when you are summoned to see me. Any other time, you are perfectly visible. It is one small way to ensure the safety of my meadow and of our meetings. Now, let us discuss the incident at As You Wish."

I winced. "Was my conversation with Archie overheard by the Peeper Creeper?"

There was another beat of silence. It was starting to unnerve me.

"The intruder did, indeed, overhear your conversation." My heart beat wildly. "You were not intentionally reckless, but you must be more careful. Be aware of your surroundings. Know that a mortal can happen by at any moment."

"Was the intruder a mortal?" I asked.

"No."

"Do you know who the intruder was?" I pressed.

"Yes."

"Who?" I asked.

"It is not for me to say."

"How can you be so passive? The Peeper Creeper broke into our home! He could be dangerous."

Mimi gave me a quick kick in the leg. I glanced at her and she shook her head, warning me. I snapped my lips closed.

"If you were at risk from that particular intruder, I would let you know," the Elder said. "However, the person who overheard your conversation was not at all dangerous."

I blinked, trying to take in what she was saying. "What

do you mean?" There was more silence. "Let me guess," I groused. "It's not for you to say."

"Correct."

I sighed. "Okay, let me ask you this. What would have happened if the person who overheard the conversation was a mortal? What then? Would I have lost my powers?"

Mimi sat quietly, enrapt with the conversation.

"It depends. There are two options for two separate scenarios. The first scenario is if a Crafter willingly tells a mortal of a Craft secret or power. The other, as in the case with your conversation with Archie, is if a mortal accidentally overhears or stumbles upon a Craft secret or power."

"What are the options?" I asked.

"With the second scenario, when the knowledge is not purposefully revealed, a spell is cast upon the mortal and her memories of the incident are cleansed."

"You can cast a spell for amnesia?" Mimi gasped.

"Yes."

"Whoa," Mimi mumbled.

"What is the other option?" I asked.

"In the case of a Crafter being willfully negligent, the punishment is severe. The Crafter would lose her powers, and the mortal would still have her memory cleansed."

"Why would a Crafter deliberately tell a mortal about the Craft?" I asked.

"The usual reasons. Drunk. Egotistical. Trying to impress. Not wanting to keep a secret from someone you're falling in love with. Losing powers is the punishment for being so reckless with the legacy. It is extreme, yes, but it is necessary."

I needed some clarification on something she'd said. "I've always been told that I could lose my powers if a mortal accidentally heard me discussing the Craft.... Are you saying that's not true at all?"

The Elder said, "The warning is in place to make Crafters more aware of their surroundings."

"So basically it's a scare tactic to keep us in line?"

"Yes."

"Sneaky," I said.

"Do you know everything that happens in the village?" Mimi asked.

The Elder had a tinge of humor in her voice when she said, "Not everything."

"Do you know who the Peeper Creeper is?" Mimi asked, and for once I was glad for her nosiness.

"My governing," the Elder said, "is limited to Crafters, Halfcrafters, and Cross-Crafters who use, misuse, or abuse their power."

"So," I tried to understand, "either the Peeper is mortal, or it's a Crafter who is not abusing her powers to commit the crime."

"Yes."

"And, as another example," I said, "if Dorothy Hansel tried to burn down As You Wish but didn't use her Broomcrafting power to do it, you have no jurisdiction in punishing her?"

"Unfortunately, yes."

"That's disappointing," Mimi said, slumping.

"Yes," the Elder said. "That is when I must trust the local authorities to do their job."

Mimi brightened. "My dad is police chief."

"I know, my child."

"You can trust him," Mimi said.

There was a beat of silence again. "I hope so, Mimi. Now, it is time for the two of you to go."

"One more question?" I asked. Something the Elder had said had been bothering me.

"One," she said.

"A few minutes ago, when we were talking about the Peeper overhearing my conversation with Archie . . . you

said the *intruder* overheard." I tipped my head. "Are the
Peeper and the person who broke into my house yesterday two separate people?"

There was definitely humor in her voice when she
said, "It is not for me to say, Darcy."

I wished I knew what she found so amusing. "Just how
many people have been sneaking around As You Wish?"

The Elder said firmly, "It is not for me to say. You two
are dismissed."

The tree went dark, and as we stood up, the tree stumps
beneath us burst into colorful particles that rained onto
the ground. Wildflowers immediately bloomed.

"Wow," Mimi said, bending to sniff a blossom.

As we walked away, Mimi took my hand again. "She
wasn't as scary as I thought she'd be. I kind of liked her,
except for the part about the diary."

I held up the diary and it slipped from my fingers and
fell onto the path. Mimi gasped. "It's okay," I said,
crouching down to pick it up.

The book lay face-up and had opened to a page that
apparently had been well read. There was even a book-
mark holding its place.

Mimi grabbed for it before I could reach it and said,
"I've got it. Here." She handed it back to me.

But not before I'd seen the heading on the page.

Spells.

I glanced at Mimi, and again she wore a guilty flush as
she suddenly felt the need to study a leaf.

But what, exactly, was she guilty of?

Chapter Twenty-seven

After I made sure Mimi made it home safely, I headed back to As You Wish. Missy and Tilda were both sitting on the back step, on opposite sides like gargoyles protecting a castle.

But who were they protecting it from?

Was there more than one Peeper?

The Elder's elusive answer told me yes, but it left me with more questions: *Who? Why?*

Missy raced down the steps to greet me, while Tilda turned and went back into the house via the dog door. "She has a bad attitude," I said to Missy.

Missy yapped.

I petted her head and went through the mudroom door. "Ve?"

No answer. I checked the whole house, but it was empty. It had been over an hour since Mimi and I had left to see the Elder.

My stomach twisted into a big knot, and I tried to tell myself not to worry. Ve had assured me she could handle her visit to Dorothy alone. An hour passed. Two. Ve wasn't answering her cell phone, either; I'd left over a dozen messages.

Taking a deep breath, I knew what I had to do.

I had to go see Dorothy.

I made sure Missy was settled and headed out the back door. On the other side of the fence, Archie was inside his cage in Terry Goodwin's yard, and I went over to him. "I can't find Ve. She went out a couple of hours ago to see Dorothy, and I'm afraid something might have happened to her."

He fluffed his feathers and glanced around nervously. "Perhaps give Ve a few more minutes? I'm sure she'll turn up."

Resolutely, I shook my head. "I've got to go look. I'm afraid that crazy Dorothy did something to her."

"I'm sure she didn't," he said. "She is not so stupid."

"Archie, she tried to burn down the house."

"You do not know that for certain."

I glared at him.

He gave in. "I will help you search for Ve. We will find her in no time. I am sure of it."

Archie unlatched his cage door with his wing and took to the skies while I checked to make sure the agate ball was in my tote bag before I set off. I also carried Melina Sawyer's diary—I didn't know what to do with it, despite the Elder telling me to "search within." I'd searched. I still didn't have a clue.

Tourists milled about the Roving Stones tents, and I spotted Starla snapping pictures. She saw me and waved. I waved back and pressed onward to Third Eye.

Suddenly, I felt that eerie sensation of being watched by something—or someone—malevolent again. The hair rose on my arm, and I turned around, but no one stood out.

When I turned back, I saw Zoey Wilkens waving frantically at me. "Thank goodness I ran into you," she said as she neared. "I've been calling Ve all afternoon and thought I'd just run over to As You Wish to see if she was around." Worry lines creased her forehead. "Is she? I know she's been ill. . . ."

"She's finally feeling better, which is why she's not at home." My worries increased. Ve had mentioned going to the Stove for lunch—apparently she'd never made it there. "Actually, I don't know where she is."

She nodded and wrung her hands.

"Is there something wrong?" I asked.

"It's about the wedding menu," she said nervously. "There's been . . . an issue."

"What kind of issue?"

The feeling of being watched faded, replaced now with a sudden panic that I was about to hear some news I wouldn't like.

Zoey tucked a piece of her blond hair behind her ear and suddenly looked her age. Gone was the confident chef, replaced now with a nervous young woman. "Someone left the fridge and freezer open last night. All the food has spoiled. Everything we had on hand for Ve's wedding is rotten."

I let her news sink in. "The fridge and the freezer were left open?"

"It's very strange. The alarm on the doors didn't work, either. A freak accident, I suppose," she said.

Sounded more like sabotage to me. "Will you be able to order more food in before the wedding?"

"Some, but unfortunately not all. I'm guesstimating at this point we'll be able to do half of the original menu. Do you want to go ahead with that? Or if you'd rather switch vendors, I'd understand."

I thought about those invitations in the trash—and all the people who hadn't received them. Maybe Dorothy's high jinks would end up being a wacky sort of silver lining. "Go ahead with what you'll have on hand."

Zoey clutched her heart. "Oh, thank goodness. I was so scared that you'd cancel on us." Her lip quivered. "Honestly, we need the business right now to stay afloat."

"Because of the food poisonings?"

"You heard about that?"

I nodded.

"It's horrible, Darcy. Just horrible." She let out a breath and said, "I need to get back. I'll see you tonight?"

"We're still having class?"

She nodded. "The dish we're making has mostly dry ingredients. The rest were easily replaced."

"Maybe in light of everything, you should just cancel the class?" I said.

"I wish. But I can't do that. We'd never be able to refund the class fees. See you later?"

My nerves tingled, but her wish hadn't been phrased in a way as to be granted. I wondered if she was a Crafter or if she and Jonathan were Halfcrafters. I'd assumed she was a Foodcrafter with her talents, but I didn't know for sure. And if she were mortal, and married a Foodcrafter, I couldn't be certain they were both now Halfcrafters. If Jonathan didn't tell her about his powers, she would be no wiser.

"I'll be there." I watched her head back to the Sorcerer's Stove. Anger simmered inside me and my jaw clenched.

First the wedding invitations. Then the fire. Then Ve's dress. Now the reception food? Enough was enough. I stomped the rest of the way over to Third Eye to have it out with Dorothy and deflated when I saw the CLOSED sign hanging on the door again.

Okay. Fine. I'd just go see her at her house.

Then I let out a breath and groaned. I had no idea where Dorothy lived. I racked my brain for a quick solution and my gaze snapped to where Starla had been standing on the green.

Except now she was nowhere to be found.

Who else would know? I perked up. I knew just the

pair who could point me in the right direction. Godfrey and Pepe. Either would know.

I spun around, crossed the square, and headed for Bewitching Boutique. Godfrey was helping a customer when I came in, so I snuck into the back room to see if Pepe was around.

He wasn't in the workroom, so I knocked on Pepe's door in the baseboard, but he didn't answer. I realized he was probably out on patrol with Archie. Hopefully, they had already found Ve, safe and sound.

Across the room, I saw Ve's wedding dress hanging on a freestanding rack. I melted a little bit at the sight of it. It was truly lovely, and she was going to look amazing in it. I really hoped she was making the right decision marrying Sylar.

A moment later, Godfrey bustled in and kissed my cheeks. "To what do I owe the surprise of your company?"

"I need your help. I need to talk to Dorothy, but I don't know where she lives. I assume you do?"

"What do you need to talk to her for?" he asked, aghast.

"Well, it's not so much as talk to as it is to see if she hasn't maimed Ve in some way." I explained how Ve was going to see Dorothy and hadn't returned.

He paled. "We must call the police at once!"

I put my hand on his arm. "I don't think it's that drastic." Yet. "Let me just run by and see what I can see. Then we'll call the police if we have to. Where does she live?"

"She's moved since we dated. I think . . ." He scratched at his temple. "I believe she moved to Cauldron Lane. No, Woodland Court." He threw his hands in the air. "My memory, it's not so good." He clapped twice and a little black book appeared.

He had a similar trick for his customer records that never ceased to amaze me.

His finger glided across the page. "Aha! Here it is. Old Forest Lane. Do you know it?"

I knew it well.

It was Nick and Mimi's street.

Chapter Twenty-eight

Opposite ends of the street, it turned out. Dorothy's house, a cute cottage, was the third house on the street, and Nick's was far on the other side — at the dead end.

For some reason, that knowledge gave me some comfort.

But that comfort was short-lived. As I walked up the driveway to Dorothy's house, toward the open garage door, what I saw stopped me in my tracks and made me want to turn around and run all the way home, sore ankle and all.

In fact, I thought that was a splendid idea.

I spun around, hoping they hadn't seen me.

"Darcy!" Nick called out.

Damn, damn, damn.

Slowly, I turned back around and pasted a phony smile on my face. "Hi," I said, giving a little finger wave.

Glinda glared back at me, looking as pretty as pretty could be in a yellow sundress. "I'm surprised to see you here, Darcy," she said.

Suddenly I felt like I should have put more care into my denim capris and white tank top as I approached them in the garage. "I, ah, came to see if Ve was still here."

The two-car garage was spacious and open. On one side, a pair of bikes was parked along with other household riffraff, like the lawnmower and trash cans. The other side of the garage, however, had been fashioned into a woodworking shop. Dozens of chisels sat on a work top, and several pieces of big equipment—planes and lathes and saws—took up most of the space. Along the wall were dozens of handmade wooden items, ranging from brooms to plaques with kitschy sayings, to frames and even baskets. Shelving held freestanding objects, like bowls and statues. All were exquisitely made.

I glanced at Nick. "I'm surprised to see you here."

He was in casual clothes. Jeans and a T-shirt. His hair was rumpled and stubble darkened his cheeks. He looked fairly exquisite himself.

"Just taking a walk," he said, "and saw Glinda in here. Thought I'd see what she was working on."

He had a tone to his voice I couldn't quite place. I studied him closely and was taken aback when he winked at me. A flash of red across the street caught my eye. Archie was sitting on a tree in the neighbor's yard.

Ah. I got it now. Archie had tipped off Nick that I was coming over here and he had come as backup—only he'd beaten me here.

"You're working on something?" I asked her, all sweetness and light, now that I realized Nick didn't hang around here in his free time. Then it dawned on me. If Dorothy was a Broomcrafter, there was a good likelihood Glinda was, too. "Brooms?"

She lifted a perfectly plucked eyebrow. "A bowl." She lifted it up to show me. It was beautiful, and I realized I'd seen one just like it recently.

"Do you know Zoey Wilkens?"

Glinda's eyes widened; then she laughed. "Know her? Of course I do. She's my sister. You didn't know?" She rolled her eyes. "I shouldn't be so surprised you don't know. Zoey doesn't like to remember that she's part of this family, too. She's embarrassed of us. Well, of Mom. Why did you ask about Zoey?"

"She had a bowl like yours and said she made it. It was gorgeous."

"She's very talented. A natural talent, because she's not even a Broomcrafter," Glinda said. Then laughed a little. "She doesn't know about the Craft at all. She's not even a Halfcrafter. Jonathan never shared his Craft secret with her when he married her. Zoey's still a full mortal."

"How is that possible?" I asked, trying to figure out how Zoey was a mortal with Dorothy, a Broomcrafter, as her mother.

Glinda grabbed a broom—a normal one, found at any hardware store—and started sweeping. "Zoey is the lucky one in the family. She was adopted during Mom's second marriage, so she thankfully doesn't share my crazy genetics."

My head was spinning with all this information. And oddly, during this strange, strange conversation, I also realized that I kind of liked Glinda.

I hated admitting that.

"Mom's second husband was a mortal, and Mom wasn't about to lose her powers to tell him about the Craft so he had no idea about our abilities," Glinda said, still sweeping. "And since it was secret from him, it had to be kept a secret from Zoey, too."

Magical subterfuge seemed like such a tangled web.

"Isn't it hard to keep that big of a secret from Zoey?" Nick asked.

"Easier than you think," Glinda said. "As Crafters, we know how to keep a secret. Some of us more than others." She sighed. "With Zoey's talent, she should be woodcrafting as a career, but no. She fell under Jonathan's spell and insists on staying at the restaurant."

Jonathan's spell. Had he really cast one, or was it only a figure of speech? It was something I had to think about. According to everyone, Jonathan and Zoey's relationship had come out of nowhere.... Had magic been involved? Had he made her fall in love with him just like Geer had made Patrice fall in love with him?

"You don't like Jonathan?" Nick asked.

"He's okay." She reached for a dustpan. "But I can't understand what she sees in him. Love is blind, right?"

All I could do was nod. "Sometimes." Which reminded me of why I was here. "Have you seen Ve? Is she still here?"

"I haven't seen her," Glinda said.

"Is your mom home?" I couldn't believe I had the guts to ask. Confronting Dorothy was the last thing I wanted to do. Having the agate ball made me feel a little bit more confident.

"She's working today." She set the dustpan on the ground.

"At Third Eye?" I asked.

She nodded and angled the broom to sweep the debris into the dustpan.

"But it's closed," I said, wandering over to the workbench for a look at the little wooden snowmen on the shelf. They were adorable. "I was just there."

Worry crept into Glinda's eyes. "Are you sure?"

"Very."

"That's strange."

Nick said, "She was there an hour ago when I questioned her about the fire."

Glinda went pale. "You questioned her?"

Nick folded his arms across his chest. "I had to."

"What did she say?" Glinda asked.

"She said I had no proof. And she's right. Unless you know something you want to share."

With a blank look, she said, "No."

She finished sweeping and picked up the dustpan. It was filled with wood shavings. My gaze shot to hers, and she quickly looked away.

"Glinda?" I said.

"Hmm?"

I held up the little snowman. "Did you make this?"

Her cheeks colored. "No."

"Did Zoey?" I ventured.

She shook her head.

"Dorothy?"

After a long second, she nodded.

"And what kind of woodwork is this, exactly?"

When Glinda didn't answer, Nick took hold of the snowman and examined it.

"It's been whittled," he said solemnly.

Whittled. Just like the person who'd been in the woods the night Evan was attacked.

We both turned and looked at Glinda.

She closed her eyes and slowly opened them. "I know what you're thinking."

"What's that?" Nick asked in his official cop voice.

"You're thinking my mom was the one who assaulted Evan in the woods Monday night." She looked into the distance, then focused on us again. "And I think you're right."

I was still reeling from what Glinda had said in her garage as I pushed open the back gate to As You Wish. I glanced at the woods where Dorothy had been Monday night, whittling while she watched what was going on inside the house.

She hadn't been lying in wait for me at all, as Evan and Ve had so kindly suggested.

She'd been watching Ve. According to Glinda, Dorothy had been trying to find some dirt that she could take to Sylar so he wouldn't marry her.

Glinda had dropped even more bombshells during our conversation. Not only had she figured out days ago that her mother must have been the whittler in the woods, but she admitted that she suspected her mom had been the one who stole the wood shavings from her car. Glinda denied knowing anything about the fire, and finally said she really needed to find her mother and talk to her. Very curtly, she had asked me and Nick to leave.

Archie, who'd been waiting for us across the street, then informed us that Ve was back at home, safe and somewhat sound.

Apparently, she had taken ill again.

Had she eaten at the Sorcerer's Stove and Zoey just hadn't seen her? Or was this a recurrence of what she had been battling all week?

Returning to As You Wish, I opened the back door, but only silence greeted me. I kept my bag with me, since Ve had me really freaked out about having the agate sphere on me at all times and the Elder had me paranoid about letting Melina's diary out of my sight.

Stepping into the kitchen, I was about to call out a hello when I heard voices upstairs.

"I wasn't very happy at first, as you know," a woman's voice said. "But I have become accustomed to the idea. It's rather nice to have a Crafter on the police force. Someone who understands both worlds. I just hope he is careful. For Mimi's sake."

It was a voice I recognized, but I didn't know who it belonged to. I assumed a familiar, though Ve refused to admit we had one in the house. And neither Tilda nor Missy would talk to me, so if it was either of them I didn't know why they wouldn't just reveal themselves.

Ve sneezed. "I trust that he will figure out what is going on around here. Which reminds me that I need to cast another protection spell on the house. I didn't have time to do it properly last night."

Why were they talking about Nick? And what did Ve mean she hadn't had time? She was gone for hours. How long did a protection spell take to cast?

"For now you're resting. Cherise warned you not to do too much too soon."

Ve said, "I had some big decisions to make today. I needed to speak to a few people."

"Did you?" the woman asked.

"Some. Not all. I couldn't find Dorothy." She sneezed. "I don't like hurting others."

"Perhaps it will not hurt as much as you think."

Ve said, "I believe you may be right about that."

"You should tell Darcy what is going on."

"I will," Ve said.

"Soon."

"Don't be so bossy," Ve said with a laugh.

"It's my job to be bossy. Now rest."

I backed away from the stairs and headed outside. I sat on the porch steps and tried to make sense of what I'd heard.

Who was that woman? And what was Ve keeping from me?

Chapter Twenty-nine

Later that night, I still didn't have any answers as Harper and I walked into the Sorcerer's Stove. Ve was, in fact, unwell again. Her fever had returned, her head was congested, and she wasn't too happy about it.

I'd called Cherise to see what she had to say. "Darcy, it sounds like a recantation spell to me. Which is alarming for a couple of reasons."

"Like?" I had asked.

"The number one reason being that someone really doesn't want Ve to get well. Number two is that the person had to know I was there, casting a spell to cure her. A recantation spell must be cast within an hour of the original spell. Is it possible anyone has been watching your house?"

I'd laughed and laughed until I had tears in my eyes. And when I said, "It would be easier to figure out who hasn't been watching the house," she promised to sneak by tonight and cast another spell. I had been ordered not to tell another soul about it—not even Ve. The spell would be cast while she slept. I'd readily agreed.

When I left for the cooking class, Ve had been bundled on the couch watching more *Survivor* episodes with Archie. He was in charge of her while I was gone.

The Sorcerer's Stove was eerily quiet, with only a few

customers scattered about the large restaurant. I did see Lazarus and Andreus Woodshall in a far corner having dinner. Thankfully, it was a well-lit corner.

When Andreus saw me, he gave a slight nod. I nodded back.

"Who's that?" Harper asked.

"Andreus."

She craned her neck for a better view. "Mr. Macabre? He doesn't look so scary."

I pushed her along to the classroom. "You'd be surprised."

We passed the bar, waved to the friendly bartender, and saw Jonathan sitting alone in a booth, poring over several ledgers. He didn't look too well, and I wondered if he'd seen Cherise yet. If so, I was going to have to start questioning her abilities.

Even though Harper and I were early, Harmony, Angela, and Colleen were already in the classroom. As was Zoey, who gave me a wan smile.

I couldn't believe she was Dorothy's daughter.

"So it was love at first sight?" Angela said, her eyes twinkling.

Zoey nodded.

Harper pulled out her stool. "What are we talking about?"

"Zoey and Jonathan," Harmony said.

Colleen frowned. "Do you really believe in love at first sight?"

Zoey was scooping flour out of a canister. She said, "I suppose it wasn't first sight. I've lived in the village my whole life and have known him for years. He always flirted with me—he flirts with everyone, as you all probably know—but I never thought anything of it. Then one day, I was in here eating lunch with a friend and I looked at him and he looked at me.... It was as if lightning struck. I was instantly in love."

"Aw," Harmony said.

Harper frowned but didn't say anything.

I was frowning, too. The "instant" part of that story was bothering me. As was what Glinda had said earlier — about Jonathan's "spell" on Zoey.

"We eloped that weekend," Zoey said, smiling, "and have been inseparable ever since. Going on two years now. Sometimes I have to pinch myself to remind myself it's all real. A fairy tale come true."

Two years . . .

Something Yvonne said the day Elodie threw her hissy fit at Patrice's house suddenly came back to me, the part about Elodie's only friend being too busy for her now. "Zoey, who was the friend eating lunch with you the day lightning struck?"

She looked up. "Elodie Keaton. Why?"

My heart sank. "Just wondering."

The conversation continued about love at first sight and whether it existed. My mind was elsewhere. It churned with a suspicion I couldn't let go.

Harper leaned in. "What's wrong?"

I shook my head. It wasn't something I could share. Not yet. I had to talk to Elodie first. If I was right . . . it would change everything with regard to Patrice's murder and how I'd been thinking about it.

"I'll be right back," I said to Harper as I hopped off my stool. I wanted to ask Jonathan some questions.

She gave me a confused look but nodded. "You'll tell me later?"

"Yes."

"Promise?"

I smiled. "Promise."

Marcus was walking into class as I was walking out. I was thrilled to see him wearing glasses. Dark-rimmed rectangles that were a perfect mix of trendy and nerdy. I grabbed him by the arm and said, "Any chance you can meet me at Patrice's house tomorrow morning?"

His face paled, which really highlighted the bruises on his jaw from the bookcase. "I really want you to stop saying her name. It freaks me out. Why do you need me?"

"I'm having a cat problem and need someone with your feline talents."

He laughed. "Nine o'clock?"

"Perfect." I watched as he sat next to Harper, and was pleased by the shy look she was giving him.

The restaurant was still as empty as it had been five minutes ago. Even emptier, I noticed, since Jonathan was no longer sitting in a booth.

I walked over to the bar and asked Ula where he was. "I'm not sure," she said. "Want me to go look?"

"If you could, I'd really appreciate it."

"Can you watch the bar for a second? I don't think anyone will come along, but you never know."

Smiling, I nodded. Once upon a time I'd loved the movie *Cocktail* with Tom Cruise. I had to restrain myself from playing with the martini shakers.

"You should not be without your protection," a voice behind me said.

I spun around and gasped. Andreus was standing in a shadow, looking as frightful as ever. I latched on to his arm and pulled him into the light.

He stared at my hand on his sleeve.

I quickly removed it and dusted the fabric. "Sorry," I said, "but that is so much better."

His head tipped. "What do you mean?"

"You and the shadows ... Never mind. What were you saying?"

"You should not be without your protection."

My protection? Why did I suddenly feel like I was in a bad safe-sex commercial?

"I feel as though you're in grave danger, Darcy. You should not be without your sphere."

Oh! That *protection.* The agate. I could feel my cheeks heating. "I have it. It's in the classroom."

"Keep it with you at all times, Darcy. Walk with it; eat with it; sleep with it. There is a darkness around you. The sphere will protect you."

I swallowed hard as I recalled all the times lately I'd felt something sinister watching me. "You can see darkness? Evil?"

He sidestepped, in and out of the light, his appearance alternating from distinguished to dreadful with each step. "You must remember that things, that people, are not always as they appear."

I didn't know what to say to that, so I simply nodded. Near the exit, I saw Starla standing with Lazarus. They looked to be in deep conversation. Lazarus was talking, and she didn't look too pleased with what he was saying. In fact, her hands were balled into fists.

Andreus must have seen them, too. He sighed deeply. "Another town, another heart broken."

"Is he breaking up with her?"

"He has not yet learned about the power of love. Someday, I hope, he will. Until then, he loves them and leaves them."

"You're leaving?" I asked.

"Soon. I was hoping you would have news for me first. About the Anicula. Have you recovered it?"

"No sign of it," I said truthfully.

"That is a shame."

It really was. If I could find it, then maybe it would lead me to Patrice's killer.

Lazarus finished his speech, and Starla drew her shoulders back, lifted her chin. Vince Paxton came in behind them and circled wide around the pair.

"What's going on with them?" he asked as he approached the bar.

Andreus eyed him. "I don't believe we've met."

I made the introductions and they shook hands. "Lazarus is breaking up with her."

Vince was trying to get his hand out of Andreus's grip, but the older man wouldn't let go. He was inspecting Vince closely, like one would a bug under a microscope.

"You have an interesting air about you," Andreus said.

Vince tugged and finally freed his hand. The motion sent Andreus into the shadows.

"Eee!" Vince said, jumping back. His gaze darted from me to the very creepy Mr. Macabre.

Starla slammed her purse down on the bar top, making us all jump. "That swine!" she cried. Then she sighed. "It wouldn't have lasted anyway."

"Why?" I asked.

"He called Twink a dust ball."

I gasped.

"I know," Starla said. "He doesn't like dogs. I should have cut it off right then and there, but it was nice dating."

"I like dogs," Vince said.

We all stared at him.

He shrugged. "I do."

Starla said, "Sorry to be so dramatic, everyone. I was just caught a little off guard."

Harper came out of the classroom and approached us. "Zoey's ready to get started." She looked at each of us, and when her gaze stopped on Andreus, she let out a scream. "Holy sh—"

Her exclamation was broken by a louder scream. An ear-splitting one, coming from the back of the restaurant.

Harper, Marcus, and the rest of the class came running out of the classroom at the same time Ula flew through the swinging kitchen doors.

"Someone call 911!"

Zoey ran to her. "What's happened?"

Tears streamed in Ula's eyes. "It's Jonathan. Come quick!"

I saw Marcus dialing his cell phone as we all raced through the kitchen and into the back office. Jonathan was lying on the floor behind his desk.

Zoey dropped to her knees. Andreus sank down next to her, completely in the shadows. If anyone noticed how utterly terrifying he looked, they didn't say.

Zoey let out an anguished cry as she cradled Jonathan's face. "What happened?"

Jonathan's eyes slowly blinked open and focused on her. "Fell," he mumbled.

Vince knelt next to them. He manipulated Jonathan's head, and his eyes widened. He drew back his hand and stared at it. It was covered in blood. "He must have hit his head on the corner of the desk."

It was the last thing I heard before I passed out.

"At least it wasn't the sight of your own blood that made you faint this time," Harper said.

"There's that." A half hour later, I sat on a bench in front of the Sorcerer's Stove, breathing in the crisp night air. The last time I'd fainted it was because I'd been shot. Absently, I rubbed the scar on my upper arm.

Harper sat next to me, her elbow linked in mine.

The ambulance had left ten minutes ago, with both Zoey and Jonathan aboard. I had refused treatment. The fresh air made all the difference.

Class had been canceled, the restaurant closed for the night. We were waiting for my wooziness to pass completely before heading home.

"Do you think May-December romances can really work?" Harper asked.

"You're thinking of Jonathan and Zoey?"

She nodded. "Zoey can't be much older than me. And he's ancient. It doesn't seem like it should work. . . ."

"But?"

"Did you see the way she looked at him?"

"Yeah." I'd seen. It had been filled with aching adoration.

"I don't understand how it can work between them."

I didn't want to mention my suspicion about a wish being involved. I'd rather think that love at first sight was possible. "Love is funny that way. You don't really get a say."

"I feel bad for her," Harper said.

"Why?"

"Because he's dying. And she's going to be alone."

Stunned, I stared at her. "It's just a little head wound. I'm sure he'll be fine."

"There's more to it," Harper said. "I can feel it. Do you remember the year I spent volunteering at the nursing home?"

I nodded.

"I've seen death, Darcy," she said softly, completely serious. "And I see it in him. He doesn't have long."

Chapter Thirty

The next morning, I skipped my run and headed for the Gingerbread Shack for my coffee and maybe a cupcake or two. With the week I was having, I felt I deserved it.

Heck, with the week I was having, I deserved the whole case of treats.

The bell on the door jangled as I pulled it open. Evan was whistling as he tidied the beverage center. A large coffee urn beckoned, and I went straight for it. Evan handed me a mug and kissed my cheek. "You look exhausted."

"Long night," I said. "I slept with a ball under my pillow all night and kind of know what the princess from 'The Princess and the Pea' must have felt like the morning after."

Evan smiled. "I hate when that happens."

I playfully shoved him and took the ball out of my bag. "I'm beginning to hate this thing."

"Oh! You were serious about the ball. What is it?"

I laughed and explained.

"Starla told me about that scary Andreus Woodshall. Is he really that creepy?"

"In the wrong lighting."

He winked. "I hate when that happens, too."

"Right. Like you've ever looked bad. Well," I amended, "except for the time with that rash."

He restocked the creamers. "Let's not talk about that."

I fought back a yawn. I didn't mention to him that I'd also been awake in the middle of the night to let Cherise Goodwin into the house under the cover of darkness.

Ve had slept through the entire curing process—and had still been asleep by the time I left this morning. I had high hopes that she was going to wake up as good as new.

"Where are you off to?" Evan asked.

I stirred two packets of sugar into my mug. "Patrice's. I'm going to try and make a dent in the living room today. And Marcus is coming over to do a little cat whispering. How's Starla? Is she okay after last night? With Lazarus?"

"She watched *Beaches* two times in a row last night. I wanted to jump out the window by the time the credits rolled the second time."

"You lie."

He smiled again. "I do. You know how I love myself some Bette Midler." He checked the level on the hot water urn. "Starla seems okay this morning. Time will tell. How's Ve?"

"I have hope that she'll be just fine for the wedding. But . . ."

"What?" he asked.

"Sylar called this morning. He thinks he may have food poisoning. He ate at the Sorcerer's Stove yesterday."

"Oh no. The wedding?"

"As far as I know, it's still on as planned."

Evan let out a relieved breath. "Good. I've been working on Ve's cake all week. Do you want to see it?"

"Are you kidding? I'd love to." I followed him to

the kitchen. Dozens of trays filled with goodies sat on stainless-steel counters. "You have the best job ever."

He walked to the far end of the kitchen, to an over-sized refrigerator. He pulled open the door and said, "I know."

Suddenly, his face lost all color.

I peeked around him into the fridge and said, "Where's the cake?"

"I—I—I," he stammered, pointing. "It was there last night."

"It's missing?" I asked.

Dumbfounded, he nodded. Then he raced around the kitchen, checking all the refrigerators, ovens, cupboards. No matter where he looked, the outcome was the same.

The cake was gone.

He sat on a stool, his shoulders slumped. "Who would steal a wedding cake?"

I had a pretty good idea. Dorothy Hansel. "Can you make another one by Sunday?"

Closing his eyes, he nodded. "I can do it."

I put a hand on his arm. "Before you do," I said, hatching a plan, "do you mind if we set a little bait for our saboteur?"

When I told him my plan, he smiled. "I'm in. Do you think it will work?"

"I certainly hope so." For my peace of mind more than anything. If Ve found out about this latest act, she would be beside herself. Which was the last thing she needed right now.

I walked the block to Patrice's house, thinking about Jonathan. I hadn't heard any updates on his condition.

What would happen to the restaurant with him being so ill? I doubted it could afford to remain open without him. Not with what Zoey had said yesterday about the Stove barely staying afloat financially.

Business was already bad at the restaurant—and I had a feeling it was going to get much, much worse.

As I neared Patrice's house, I saw Yvonne across the street, loading up the trunk of her car. I veered over to her, to see if she had any updates on the break-in.

When I called out a "Good morning," she didn't look up. I tapped her on the shoulder and she jumped.

"Darcy! Oh, I didn't hear you."

Her eyes were red-rimmed. "Have you been crying? Are you okay?"

"I'm fine." She walked to the front porch, grabbed a suitcase and heaved it into the already full trunk.

"Are you going somewhere?"

She slammed the trunk closed. "Not really. Just coming to my senses. I'll be staying at the Pixie Cottage for a few days until I can sort some things out."

I glanced at the house. "And Roger?"

"Who cares?" she asked.

Okay, then. "You're leaving him?"

"It's a long time coming, don't you think?"

I didn't have an answer to that.

"Darcy, thanks for your concern, but I'm all right. I just finally decided that I didn't want to live the rest of my life being second best. I should have realized that years ago. It would have changed a lot of things." She squeezed my arm. "I'm sure I'll see you around."

With that, she got into her car and drove off.

I was left staring after her.

And when I looked at the house, I was taken aback to see Roger standing on the front porch.

He glanced at me with a look of such sadness that it nearly broke my heart, turned, and went into the house.

The front door closed with a soft click behind him.

Chapter Thirty-one

I lay facedown on my belly in the grass. "Do you see her?"

"All I see is your head," Marcus said. "Can you move a little to the left?"

I wiggled left and felt Marcus shift next to me. We were peering under Patrice's back deck.

Marcus made kissy noises, and I glanced at him.

"Respect the process, Darcy."

Smiling, I *respected* while he continued to make the kissing sounds.

"Should I leave the two of you alone?" someone asked from behind us.

I rolled over and saw Elodie watching us with a smirk. Standing, I dusted myself off and nodded to Marcus. "He's cat whispering."

"Oh," Elodie said. "He can do that?"

"It's his true calling."

Marcus levered up on his elbows and peered at me. "Are you mocking me?"

"Never," I said, straight-faced. "I've seen your work."

"You two should take a step back. You're interrupting my mojo."

Grinning, we stepped back.

"Here, kitty, kitty," Marcus crooned.

Nothing.

"She's a stubborn one," he said. "I'm going to have to play my best card. Prepare yourselves."

"Should we be worried?" Elodie asked.

"I'm not sure," I said.

Marcus gave us a withering glare and cleared his throat. He began singing about black and orange stray cats sitting on a fence.

I burst out laughing. "You can't be serious! 'Stray Cat Strut'?"

Marcus ignored me and kept on singing. "'I'm a la-dies' cat, a feline Casanova . . .'"

My eyes were watering from trying so hard to keep my laughter in.

Suddenly, Elodie elbowed me. "Look!"

An orange head had popped out from beneath the deck, followed quickly by another — that of a small kit-ten.

"Awww," Elodie said.

Marcus gave us a triumphant smile as another kitten and another trotted out. It was like he was the Pied Piper of cats. They all circled around him, and the mama cat even climbed into his lap.

He kept up the harmony of his pop song but changed the lyrics to, "Please go get a box. I think they have fleas."

Elodie ran inside and found a box. She brought it out, and Marcus carefully loaded each cat into it. When they were all inside, he closed the top, picked up the box, and said, "My work here is done."

"That was amazing," I said, completely in awe.

"What will you do with them now?" Elodie asked.

"Bring them to a vet friend of mine for a checkup. Then find them all homes."

I couldn't wait to tell Harper about this. If this didn't seal the deal on a date between the two of them, there was something seriously wrong with my sister. "Can you tell if the cat is a familiar?" I asked. I'd been harboring the notion that the cat might be the spirit of Patrice. . . .

"It's not," Marcus said.

"How do you know?" I didn't think there was a way of telling by looking.

"Familiars can't procreate," he said simply.

Ah. I hadn't known that.

Elodie and I saw Marcus off, and I pulled hand sanitizer out of my tote bag and lathered up with it. Inside the house, I said, "I'm surprised to see you here today."

"I'm going stir crazy at home. I thought I could help. And . . . ," she said.

"What?"

"I got a call from Zoey Wilkens this morning."

"Oh?"

"I haven't heard from her in forever, but she said she thought of me last night—because of a conversation your cooking class was having about love at first sight. She mentioned that she could use a friend right now."

I imagined so, what with Jonathan being so ill and all. I folded a shirt that still had its tags and looked at her. I had a feeling I knew where this conversation was going. "Do you believe in it?" I asked. "Love at first sight?"

"No."

"No?"

"Love is hard work. It doesn't happen instantaneously. It has to be babied and nurtured."

I added the shirt to a pile of clothes in a "Yard Sale" box. Once we were done sorting Patrice's house, we were going to have the biggest yard sale the village had ever seen. "Then how do you explain what happened with Zoey and Jonathan?"

Softly, she said, "I think you already know the answer to that question."

I picked up a dress—it also still had its tags. "I think I do, but I'd like to hear it from you."

She let out a deep breath and leaned against the wall next to the shadowbox holding her baby footprints, rattle, and hat. "Did you ever think you were doing something so right only to find out how terribly wrong you were?"

Once I'd tried to keep Harper's (slightly) criminal past from the people of the village. That had been a mistake that had almost cost me my relationship with Nick. "Haven't we all at one time or another?"

"Did you know my mother dated Jonathan for a while?"

I nodded.

"What she didn't know—or didn't want to realize—was how much of a womanizer he was. He cheated on her left and right. It made me sick. I had to do something. So one day while she was in the shower, I snuck into the bathroom and borrowed the Anicula. It was the only time she ever took it off. I made a wish that Jonathan and Zoey would fall madly in love with each other."

"You were the one who stole the Anicula?"

"Not me! I borrowed it. I returned it before she even knew it was gone."

I wasn't sure I believed her. "I understand why you chose Jonathan—you wanted him permanently out of your mom's life—but why Zoey?"

She sighed. "Honestly, I thought I was doing her a favor. She grew up in Glinda's shadow. Can you imagine what that was like?"

I shook my head. I couldn't quite imagine growing up as Dorothy's daughter, either.

"Zoey was never pretty enough, talented enough, smart enough. It really shook her confidence. She'd never even had a boyfriend before Jonathan. I—I was trying to help her. Plus, I thought it would make their lives easier if they were together."

"How?"

"Before she and Jonathan were married, she over-heard him having a huge argument with my mom. Mom had gone to see him, to beg him to come back to her. When he wouldn't, she accused him of using her for the Anicula's powers. They discussed the Craft openly and Zoey overheard. Later, when Zoey asked him what he had been talking about, he admitted he had tricked my mom into using a wish to get rid of those rats."

It sounded to me like the biggest rat around might have been Jonathan.

"The Elder summoned both of them immediately. Jonathan lost his powers and Zoey's memory was cleansed of everything she overheard about the Craft."

"Jonathan lost his powers?"

She nodded sadly. "It's why the restaurant is failing. Zoey's a good chef, but not good enough to keep the place going. It's lost its magic. Plus, whenever Jonathan cooks now, he tends to give people food poisoning."

Oh. My. That explained a few things. "But I'm confused. It sounds like Jonathan hadn't intentionally told her everything about the Craft. The Elder said in cases like that, a Crafter wouldn't lose his power."

"Well, I don't know what to tell you. He lost his." Tears pooled in her eyes. "I've made a mess of everything. My wish helped no one. It only ruined people's lives. Don't you see, Darcy? My mother wasn't the one who was cursed. It's me. *I'm* cursed."

Putting the dress in the box, I said, "Why do you think that?"

"It turned out that my mother didn't just like Jonathan; she loved him. It nearly killed her when he broke up with her. And when I confessed it was my fault, that I'd made a wish, we had a huge argument and didn't talk for months. I don't think she ever really forgave me." She paced in what little space she could find. "And then Jonathan lost his powers and started poisoning people because he can't get it through his thick head that he can't cook anymore. Then stuff started happening with my wedding. Venues canceling. Lost orders. The date kept getting postponed. Then my mom went missing." She burst into tears. "It's my fault my mom was murdered."

I crossed over to her and gave her a hug. "You aren't to blame."

"I am. It's my fault. I know it."

"You didn't kill her."

"Maybe not literally. But I might as well have. And now"—she sniffled—"I've doomed Zoey to a life of loneliness."

"Why? She's happy with Jonathan."

"True enough. But when she called me, she admitted that Jonathan is really sick. He has ALS, Lou Gehrig's Disease, and he's in its final stages. If only I knew where that Anicula was—I could wish him back to health." She shook her head. "No! I'm done trying to change destiny. I hate that Anicula. If you find it, it's yours. I don't want it. In fact, I never want to see it again."

Chapter Thirty-two

I spent the whole day at Patrice's house, sorting and organizing, and even though the living room was still a mess, at least every box had a contents label. There were dozens of garbage bags to be put out to the trash next week.

I'd found soup from years ago, a box of Waterford crystal, a purse stuffed with one-dollar bills. What I hadn't found was the Anicula. I'd tested each and every stone I came across. None yielded my wish of a hot fudge sundae.

When I came home, I was happy to see Mrs. P and Mimi visiting with Ve, who looked remarkably better. I had come home at lunchtime to find her fully recovered, and I couldn't have been happier.

They were playing a game of poker with peanut M&M's as ante. By the looks of it, Mimi was cleaning house. But she didn't look too happy about it.

"You look like someone stole your magic wand, Mimi." It was a phrase Harper had introduced to the family.

She dropped her head in her hand and ate some of her winnings. "I'm fine. I'm going to take Missy for a walk. Is that okay?"

"As long as you stay on the green," I said. Where it

was well lit. Technically, there was still a Peeper on the loose.

As soon as she went out the back door, Ve said, "She's been like that since she got here. I don't know what's wrong."

Mrs. P said, "She was fine earlier."

I went to the back door and looked out. Mimi was just crossing the street. Missy trotted along happily next to her. "Maybe Nick's hours are getting to her."

"Maybe," Ve said.

I spotted the wedding file on the counter. "Is Sylar doing any better?"

"Still can't keep anything down," Ve said, *tsk*ing. "But I'm sure he'll be just fine for the wedding."

I wasn't sure that was a good thing, so I said, "I'm going to run upstairs and change. I have decades of dust covering me."

I took a quick shower and gathered up my towels to throw into the wash. "I'm going to do a towel load," I called down the stairs. "Do you want me to wash yours, too?"

"Sure," Ve said.

I went into her bathroom and grabbed her towels. Still hanging from the bar was the handkerchief I'd seen the other day, the paisley one.

I tipped my head and stared at it, feeling like I'd seen it somewhere before. It was an unusual pattern. . . . I waited and waited for it to come to me, kind of an aha moment.

Nothing.

Try as I might, I couldn't place it. As I went about tossing the laundry in the wash, making dinner, and trying to cheer up a still-moping Mimi, I couldn't get that pattern out of my mind.

Or keep the notion that it was *very important* that I remember at bay.

*   *   *

"Are you sure this is going to work?" Harper asked later that night.

"I've been thinking," Mrs. P said absently, "that I should get a Taser. I heard about how Glinda took down Roger with one zap. A Taser might be handy if I come across that Peeper."

Until that statement, I'd been having trouble keeping my eyes open. Now, I was wide awake. It was a little past eleven and the three of us sat on the bakery floor, waiting for Dorothy Hansel to make an appearance. Evan and I had made sure the whole village knew he'd "re-created" Ve's wedding cake today—and that it was a showpiece worthy of such a lovely couple.

Now, while Evan was at the cast party, all we had to do was lie in wait. And confront her when she showed up to steal another cake.

"You don't need a Taser," I said.

"What if the Peeper attacks me?" Mrs. P asked.

"Yeah," Harper said.

I eyed her in the dim glow of the security lights. "The Peeper is looking for the Anicula. I think you're safe. Unless either of you has something you want to tell me?"

"Trust me." Harper stretched her legs. "If I had that Anicula, I'd wish I was home with my new kitten."

"New kitten?" I asked, eyebrows raised.

"Marcus gave him to me," she said bashfully.

"I like that Marcus," Mrs. P said. "He's a good boy." She nudged Harper with her elbow. "Do you like him?"

"He's nice," Harper murmured.

I held back a smile. "What's the kitten's name?" Marcus was a genius for giving her one.

"Pie."

"Pie?" I repeated.

"Pumpkin Pie," she said, "because his fur is the same color."

Mrs. P glanced around. "I could go for some pie. Do you think Evan has any around here?"

I ignored her. So did Harper, who said, "But Pumpkin Pie is a mouthful. Then I thought I'll call him by his initials."

"PP?" I said, giggling.

Mrs. P threw her head back and laughed her famous cackle. She clamped a hand over her mouth. "Sorry."

Harper smiled. "Exactly. So now he's Pie."

"Cute," I said.

"He is!" Harper gushed. "Want to see a picture?"

"Sure," I said. Why not? There was no telling when Dorothy would show up.

Harper whipped out her smart phone and scrolled through dozens of kitten pictures. By the time she was done, I was "awwwed" out.

Mrs. P poked me with her elbow. "If you don't mind me asking, Darcy, did you grow a third boob when I wasn't looking?"

"Darcy!" Harper whispered as she looked my chest. Her eyes widened in horror.

I reached into my shirt and pulled out the agate ball. I shrugged. "I was tired of carrying it around in my tote bag."

The diary was tucked into a plastic bag and hidden in the big box of Tide in the laundry room at As You Wish. It was a temporary hiding spot—until I could find something a little more permanent. Like a bank deposit box.

Harper peered at my shirt. "How is it staying in there?"

"Sports bra."

"Those things have stretch. Stretch is good when you're keeping a rock in your bra," Mrs. P said as if she knew from experience.

"Do you think that rock ball really works?" Harper asked.

"I've been warned by two people to keep it with me at all times. I'm not taking any risks. Besides, so far so good."

Mrs. P yawned. "If anyone can pull off a third boob, it's you."

"Thank you, Mrs. P."

"You're wel—"

We fell silent as noises came from the back door.

"She's here," Harper whispered.

"Take your places," I said as quietly as I could.

We spread out.

The back door creaked open. The intruder had on a Crafter cape with the hood up. She crossed to the refrigerator and pulled open the double doors. When the light didn't come on (we'd emptied and unplugged the fridge in advance), she reached up. That's when Harper jumped up and stiff-armed her from behind. The intruder went stumbling into the empty fridge. At that point, Mrs. P and I slammed the doors closed.

Evan assured us that Dorothy would be okay in there for at least an hour—and what we had planned wouldn't take nearly that long.

"We can call Nick now," I said, flipping on the light.

"Darcy Ann Merriweather, is that you?" the voice said from within.

"That doesn't sound like Dorothy," Mrs. P said.

"Mrs. Pennywhistle, open this door at once!" the voice demanded.

"Sounds a little bit like . . ." Harper glanced at me.

"Harper! Open this door!"

". . . Aunt Ve."

We swung the doors open. Ve stood inside, having the good grace to look embarrassed. Slowly, she strolled out, patted her hair, and looked at the three of us. "I bet you're wondering why I'm here."

We all nodded.

"I, ah ... heard the cake was beautiful. I wanted to see it."

"You lie," I said, putting pieces together and coming up with a picture I couldn't quite believe.

Harper and Mrs. P nodded.

"Velma Devany," I said. (I figured if she could use my full name, I could use hers.) "Have you been sabotaging your own wedding?"

She held up two fingers, about an inch apart. "A little."

"The invitations?" I asked.

"Well, actually, that was Dorothy. I figured out a week ago what she must have done when those RSVPs didn't come in. It gave me the idea to take it a step further."

I gasped. "You stole your own dress?"

"Spoiled all that food at the Sorcerer's Stove?" Harper added.

"Made off with the cake Evan made?" Mrs. P asked.

Ve's head bobbed. "Guilty, guilty, and guilty."

"Why would you sabotage your own wedding?" Harper asked.

Ve glanced at the floor and didn't answer.

"You don't want to get married?" Mrs. P suggested.

Looking up, Ve said, "I don't love him. I love —"

"Oh. My. Goodness," I cried. "I just realized what that handkerchief was in your bathroom. It's not a hankie. It's a pocket square!"

Ve's cheeks reddened.

I babbled on. "Not only is it a man's pocket square; it's Terry Goodwin's pocket square!" That's where I'd seen it before — the night he put out the fire. He'd had an identical one in his dinner jacket's pocket.

Harper's mouth dropped open. "You and Terry?"

Mrs. P threw her head back and laughed. "Hot diggety! This is the best news I've heard in an eon."

My brain was whirring, thinking about the morning I'd found that pocket square in Ve's bathroom. And how it had been right after the "intruder" had broken out through the kitchen window.

I recalled how loud Archie had been that morning, too.

I pointed at her accusingly. "It was Terry in the house Tuesday morning. You and he . . . he and you . . . in the tub! Archie was your lookout." That's what was up with his loud trilling. When I got my hands on that macaw . . .

Harper stuck her fingers in her ears. "Lalalalala."

"Oh, to be young again," Mrs. P said dreamily.

"Guilty?" Ve winced.

"Why didn't you just call off the wedding?" Harper asked. "Wouldn't it have been easier?"

"I didn't want to hurt Sylar's feelings. I thought the sabotage would postpone things for a while until I could figure out how to talk to him."

"Were you making yourself sick, too?" I asked. How far would she go in this little scheme of hers?

"*Not* guilty," Ve said fiercely. "I was truly ill."

I bit my lip. "Were you going to let Dorothy take the blame for the sabotage?"

Ve smiled. "It would have been a perk, don't you think?"

Mrs. P cackled.

I sighed. "Did Dorothy set the fire or was that you, too?"

Ve's eyes darkened. "That, my dear, was all Dorothy, and I've yet to have it out with her."

"Can we go home now?" Harper asked.

"Good idea, Harper dear," Ve said, taking our arms and heading for the door.

Mrs. P turned out the lights. "I still think a Taser would be a good idea."

"No," Harper and I said.

As I locked the door behind us, Ve said, "Darcy dear, I hate to be the bearer of bad news, but did you know you have a third boob?"

Chapter Thirty-three

When we got home, I pleaded a headache and went straight up to bed. I was tired. So tired. Ve had taken Missy for a quick walk before turning in herself. I wondered if she was going to stop at Terry's on the way back.

I still couldn't belicve the two of them, sneaking around.

A rooster crowed outside my window. I pulled down the shade. I was mad at Archie and didn't really want to talk to him right now.

I kicked off my shoes and walked into the bathroom to take out my contacts and brush my teeth. When I flipped on the light, I came face-to-face with ... the Peeper, ski mask and all.

In my bathroom.

At midnight.

I screamed.

The Peeper grabbed my arm and shook me. "Be quiet. I don't want to hurt you, but I will if I have to." The voice was garbled, but I could understand every word. Gloved hands held a gun. "We're going to take a walk," the Peeper said.

"We are?" I asked.

The Peeper nodded.

"Where?"

The Peeper didn't answer, but waited patiently as I put my shoes on. As I was escorted down the staircase and out the front door, I could feel the agate ball nestled against my chest. Would it really protect me?

I wondered how the Peeper had gotten inside As You Wish with the protection spell being in place.... Then I recalled what I'd overheard earlier. Ve had said she needed to recast the spell because she hadn't had enough time to do it properly.

Because she'd been out stealing her wedding cake.

Great.

We skirted the house and went through the back gate, over a small bridge, and then onto the Enchanted Trail. It was empty this time of night. As we walked, with the gun pressed into the small of my back, I was trying to think of some way to escape.

The Peeper wasn't very big. Maybe a little taller than I was. I frowned. Clearly, the Peeper wasn't Jonathan or Andreus or Lazarus. Not tall enough.

Maybe if I could get the Peeper talking again, I would recognize the voice. "My aunt Ve is sure to notice me missing and call the police."

"I'm sure she will," the Peeper said, seemingly undisturbed by my pronouncement.

I tried to place the voice. It was a medium tone, and I realized I couldn't tell if it was a man or a woman.

"They'll look for me," I added.

"I'm sure they will."

"They'll find me," I said bravely.

"Maybe."

I could probably make a run for it—I'd been getting pretty fast. But then I realized no one was fast enough to outrun a bullet.

So I started wishing with all my might that Ve would discover my absence. Despite what I'd said, I wasn't sure she would. She might just assume I'd gone to bed for the night and not notice I was missing until the morning.

That thought turned my stomach inside out.

Finally, the Peeper said, "Up here, turn right."

It was the trail's exit onto Incantation Circle's cul-de-sac. The path right next to Patrice's house. The Peeper walked us around to the back door. The boards I'd put up earlier that day were lying on the deck.

Suddenly, a rooster crowed from nearby.

I almost cried in relief. Archie was near. I immediately forgave him for keeping me in the dark about Ve and Terry. The crowing was his way of letting me know help was on the way. I just had to hang on.

The Peeper pushed the door open and motioned me within.

"Why are we here?" I asked.

"I want the Anicula."

My eyes went wide. "I don't know where it is."

The gun came up to my nose. "I suggest you find it. Right now."

I looked at the Peeper helplessly and shrugged. "I don't know where it is."

Suddenly, the front doorknob turned. Elodie stuck her head in. "Hello?"

"In here," the Peeper said.

My pulse pounded. Elodie was in on this?

She came into the light and her eyes grew wide with alarm. "What's going here? Darcy, are you okay?"

"Just fine," I said, as though we were chatting in the grocery aisle. "You?"

"I got a call that there was an emergency here. I came right over."

I glanced at the gun. I'd say this was kind of an emergency. "Who called you?"

"I did," the Peeper said, "so don't get your hopes up

that your knight in shining armor is going to rescue you. Either of you." The gun pointed at Elodie. "I want the Anicula, and I want it now."

Elodie tipped her head and stared at the Peeper. "I don't know where it is. Someone stole it before my mother died."

"I don't believe you," the Peeper said. "You have ten seconds; then I start shooting. I am not bluffing."

The voice, I realized, leaned more toward the feminine. I racked my brain trying to figure out who it could be.

"Ten," the Peeper said. "Nine. Eight."

Elodie grabbed my hands.

"Seven. Six."

The front door swung open and a big grizzly filled the doorway. "What's going on in here?" Roger boomed.

The Peeper didn't seem the least bit fazed. "Time is up." The Peeper leveled the gun at Elodie, took aim, and reached for the trigger.

Roger charged forward. "No!"

He dove in front of her as the gun went off. The bullet hit him square in the chest. He fell backward with a howl.

The Peeper said, "One down. Now, am I going to get that Anicula or not?"

Roger moaned. Elodie's face was frozen in terror.

"Okay," the Peeper said. "The choice is yours."

The choice is yours. . . .

The Peeper took aim at Elodie and deliberately placed a finger on the trigger.

"Wait!" I cried. "I know where the Anicula is."

"Where?" the Peeper asked.

My mind churned. *The choice is yours.* I knew that phrase. I knew that voice. I knew who the Peeper was. And I knew why she was doing what she was doing.

I walked over to a box in the corner, rummaged inside, and came out with a beautiful amulet that Patrice had stashed away among the clutter. In the center of a sturdy intricate platinum filigree hung a round black opal. "Here," I said, handing it over.

Elodie stared at me. I winked at her as the Peeper snatched the amulet out of my hands.

Roger moaned and Elodie went over to him. She fell to her knees and took his hand in hers. "Hang in there," she said. "Hold on. We'll get help as soon as we can."

"Not so fast," the Peeper said. "How do I know this is the real Anicula?"

"Make a wish," Elodie said, catching on. "Something simple maybe, since the Anicula hasn't been used in a while."

The Peeper curved a hand around the amulet. "I wish I had a . . . pizzelle."

My skin tingled as I covered my mouth and whispered the words. "Wish I might, wish I may, grant this wish without delay."

I was counting on my hunch about the Peeper's identity being true. The only way this plan would possibly work was if my kidnapper was a mortal and the Elder didn't have to get involved.

A pizzelle appeared in the Peeper's hand. She stared at the cookie in wonder and let out a cry of triumph.

"Take the amulet and go, Zoey."

Elodie gasped. "*Zoey?*"

Zoey tugged the mask off her head. Her hair stuck in a mass to her head, and her eyes were wild. "How did you know it was me?"

"'The choice is yours.' You said the same thing last night during class."

Elodie stood up. "*You're* the Peeper Creeper?"

"I had no choice," Zoey said. "I need the Anicula. I have to heal Jonathan. I have to make him better."

How did she still know about the Anicula if her memory was cleansed? Then I recalled what Elodie had said about charms being for Crafters and mortals alike. The Elder must have cleansed Zoey's memory only of the Craft references she'd heard.

"I've been looking for this amulet for a year and a half, ever since Jonathan was first diagnosed." Her crazed gaze shot to mine. "I can't tell you how many times I've broken into this house looking for this charm." She cradled it in her hands. "I can't believe I finally have it. I wish Jonathan were here."

I covered my mouth so she couldn't see my lips moving and cast the wish.

My thoughts were spinning. Jonathan had been diagnosed with ALS eighteen months ago? Was it a coincidence that it was the same time frame Patrice went missing?

Zoey's eyes gleamed as she grasped the amulet. They held a spark of insanity—of recklessness. She'd been breaking into homes around town to find the Anicula. The sicker Jonathan became, the more desperate she had acted.

But what about eighteen months ago? How desperate had she been then to cure her ailing husband?

A chill swept down my spine. "Was it you?" I asked softly. "Did you kill Patrice?"

Zoey waved the gun. Her hand was shaking. "She wouldn't grant Jonathan another wish! How could she not grant him a wish that would save his life? She tried to tell me the Anicula had been stolen. Does she think I'm stupid? I knew she wanted him to suffer. She was jealous because he chose me over her."

Elodie let out a sharp cry and barreled forward. Zoey ducked and missed the blow, but Elodie locked onto her legs. They toppled forward and into me. I fell backward into the wall behind me and shadowboxes rained down around me, crashing to the floor. Glass shattered and burst out like shrapnel, slicing into my skin.

"How could you?" Elodie cried.

"I have to save him," Zoey shouted. "He's all I have. He's all I have, El."

"That's enough!" a voice boomed. "Zoey, stop." Jonathan stood in the doorway. There were tears in his eyes. "What have you done?"

She burst into tears, but continued to wave the gun around crazily. "They're going to tell. We have to get rid of them."

"No, Zoey, no," he said.

"I'm sorry," she said, taking aim at Elodie.

I had to do something. *Anything*. If only I hadn't cleaned up the clutter in here. I could have easily reached something to throw at her.

And then I remembered I had a secret weapon. I reached into my shirt and pulled out the agate ball. Without thinking twice, I threw it at her just as she pulled the trigger. Zoey cried out and doubled over as the ball hit her in the head. The bullet hit the ceiling.

Jonathan rushed over to her. He wrapped his arms around her and held her close while taking the gun from her and tossing it across the room. Rocking her, he kept saying, "What have you done? What have you done?"

I tried not to look at my arms, which were dripping blood from the shattered glass (I didn't want to faint again), as I rested my head against the wall. I saw the crushed pizzelle on the floor and said, "*I* really wish the police were here."

"Me, too," Elodie said, crawling over to Roger.

"I wish for an ambulance, too," I added. "That would be nice right about now." Roger didn't look too well. His face was the color of chalk.

Suddenly, sirens split the air.

For a second, I thought my mind was playing tricks on me. But within moments, Nick rushed into the house, gun drawn. He crouched down next to me. "Don't move, okay? The ambulance is right behind me. I'm not sure how they got here so fast, but I'm glad they did."

"Roger's been shot—he needs help first."

Other officers filed in, including Glinda. She spotted Zoey in the costume and raw emotion flooded her face. She reached a hand out to her sister, then slowly curved her hand into a fist and withdrew it. A beat later, she turned and walked out of the house.

Zoey had said that Jonathan was all she had.

Maybe she'd been right.

Chapter Thirty-four

I was sitting on the porch swing the next afternoon, lazily swinging away when Evan came strolling up the walkway. I closed Melina's diary and smiled at him.

"You look good in white," he said.

"You're such a flatterer." He was referring to the white bandages that wrapped both my arms—the cuts were minor, all flesh wounds.

"I've come bearing bad news," he said, shifting uneasily on his feet.

How much worse could it be after the week I'd had? "Lay it on me."

"Sylar lied about being sick yesterday."

"Oh?"

"Turns out he and Dorothy ran off and eloped last night."

I smiled. "They did?"

"You're smiling? Why? That's bad news. Isn't it?"

"Long story," I said. "But no, it's not."

"Incoming!" Archie called from above.

I glanced up, squinting against the sun. Archie circled overhead, a colorful flash against the summer sky. Pepe clung to Archie's neck feathers for dear life as they came in for a landing on the porch railing. Pepe slid down Archie's tail like a slide.

"Are you telling Evan of my bravery?" Archie asked, spreading his wings and taking a bow.

Pepe elbowed him. "*Our* bravery."

"Our bravery," Archie said reluctantly.

They had heard my scream the night before and followed Zoey and me to Patrice's house. Then they'd gone for help, but strangely, Nick had already been on his way.

"Yes, you're both very brave," I said. "Thank you."

"Has there been any word about what will happen to Zoey now?" Evan asked.

"Not yet," I said. "Do you think Dorothy knows what happened?"

Evan nodded. The goose egg on his head was all but gone. "Apparently Glinda called her last night and told her."

"Is Dorothy coming home?"

"Not until after her honeymoon."

Poor Zoey. Her family life didn't excuse what she had done—not by a long shot—but it hadn't helped, either.

I had thought Dorothy warned me away from the Keaton job because she possibly had something to do with Patrice's disappearance. . . . But what if it had been because she knew Zoey had something to do with it and had been, in her own way, trying to protect her daughter?

I doubted that there was any way to find out, unless Dorothy was willing to confess all she knew.

And that was never going to happen.

But that wasn't to say she was going to get off scot-free. As soon as she returned from her elopement she was going to have to face charges of her own—for the assault on Evan. There hadn't been enough evidence to charge her with the fire, though Glinda all but confirmed her mother had set it.

"What are you reading there?" Archie asked, hopping over.

I ran my hand over the diary. I'd been reading the page on spells, over and over. "Something illuminating, as Starla might say."

"Care to share?" Evan asked.

I smiled. "A girl has to keep some secrets."

"Does this have anything to do with why Godfrey was over here so early this morning?" Pepe asked, being inquisitive.

I shrugged. "Maybe."

The fewer people who knew what I planned, the better.

"Well, I need to get back to the bakery," Evan said. "Do you need anything?"

"I'm fine," I said. "Really. Just a little scratched up. In fact, I'm planning to go to Patrice's house this afternoon to get some more work done."

I wasn't telling the whole truth. I had another hunch I wanted to check out. After that, I had a date ... with Mimi.

"Alone?" Archie asked.

I raised my eyebrow. "Maybe you can sit outside and be my lookout?"

Archie fell backward onto the porch and covered his chest with his wings. " 'A blow with a word strikes deeper than a blow with a sword.' " He flopped around as if dying.

"Didn't I tell you he was dramatic?" Evan asked. He waved and trotted off.

Archie was still on the porch floor. "Dramatic? Me?"

I smiled. "Was that a movie quote?"

"*Non*, it's from an old English vicar," Pepe said.

Archie sat up. "Pepe might have known him personally, he's so old."

"He's amusing, is he not?" Pepe asked sarcastically.

They sat with me awhile longer, then went on their way. I picked up the diary again, said the spell Godfrey had taught me, threw the book into the air, and watched it disappear.

I smiled. I had searched deeper within and finally realized what the Elder had been telling me.

I was a Crafter.

A witch.

I had spells at my fingertips. Literally.

But as I thought about the conversation I had to have with Mimi later, I knew that there was so much about my legacy that I still had to learn.

Patrice's house was eerily quiet.

I walked around, looking at the mess the scuffle the night before had left behind. Glass littered the floor. Blood stains had turned a rusty color. My neat boxes had been overturned.

There was so much work still to be done.

But I wasn't there to do it.

I was there about that hunch I had. About a wish I'd made—that the police and the ambulance would arrive—that had been granted immediately. And I thought about how Yvonne's wish to find Patrice's body, Zoey's wishes for the pizzelle and Jonathan's appearance last night might not have been granted by my spells at all.

But by the Anicula.

I recalled how Elodie had said the Anicula only had to be in close proximity of the person making the wish for the wish to be granted, and looked around.

I cleared the spot on the floor where I'd sat last night, and realized it happened to be almost identical to the spot Yvonne had stood when she made her wish to find Patrice's body all those days ago. I looked around, a foot in all directions.

I was knocking on the wall, looking for a hollow spot, when the front door opened. I was more than a little surprised to see Jonathan walk in.

He looked worse than usual. I didn't know how much of that had to do with his disease — or if it was a result of the trouble Zoey was in.

I tried to pretend I sat on a glass-littered floor all the time. "What are you doing here?"

"I came to see you," he said, clearing a spot and sitting next to me. "I had a feeling you'd come back here."

"Why?"

"Because your wish for the police and an ambulance to appear was granted last night." He bent his knees and rested his elbows atop them. "Because I figured by now you'd suspect that the Anicula is here."

I hadn't been scared when he came in, but now I was getting a little nervous. Had Zoey acted alone in killing Patrice?

"Do you know about my past with the Anicula?" he asked.

"Some. What Elodie told me. That you used Patrice to get rid of the rats."

"What else did she say?"

I saw no reason to lie. "That you were a womanizer and cheated on her mother. That you and Patrice had a huge argument that Zoey overheard, and the Elder had to do a memory cleanse on Zoey and you lost your powers as a result. . . ."

He smiled a humorless smile. "There she is wrong. I didn't lose my powers because of what Zoey overheard."

"No?"

"I lost my powers because Patrice wished for me to lose them. She was angry about the breakup. Very angry."

I drew in a breath. "She wished your powers away?"

"Not only that, but she wished that whatever I cooked from that point on would taste terrible and make people sick. I mentioned she was angry, right?"

A woman scorned. "Yet you still cook? Why?"

Sighing, he said, "Sometimes I forget. I jump into the kitchen fray and help out when there's a crush. My customers pay the price."

"You had no recourse? Through the Elder?"

"None. The wishes of the Anicula are binding. So when Patrice threatened to wish that Zoey and I would break up, I knew I had to do something. I couldn't let that happen. I love Zoey. It's such an incredible feeling to be in love. Even if it was wished upon me without my consent, I couldn't lose it."

"You know about that?" I asked softly.

"Patrice told me what Elodie had done. She hoped it would somehow change my mind. It didn't. That's when she threatened to wish Zoey and I would divorce."

"What did you do?"

He grinned. "I stole the Anicula."

"But . . . but . . . if you have the Anicula, why not wish you can cook again? Why not wish yourself well?"

"I made a decision the day I stole it to never use it. It's dangerous. Evil, even. Life needs to be led the way it was meant to be."

"Like the way you and Zoey fell in love?"

With a quirk of his eyebrow, he said, "Touché. But I stand by my decision. The kind of power the Anicula holds—it's all-consuming. Devastating." He took a deep breath. "It breaks my heart that Zoey has been looking for it all this time. I blame myself for what's happened. For what she did to Patrice."

Ah, so she had acted alone.

"For the break-ins. For what happened to you."

"The argument I heard at the Dumpster the other day—you suspected Zoey, didn't you?" It explained the police comment.

"I begged her to stop looking for the Anicula, that if she stopped the police would never figure out it was her.

I never dreamed how far she'd taken her obsession. I hadn't realized what she had done to Patrice." He held my gaze. "I wanted to let you know that I'm turning myself in to the police this afternoon."

"Turning yourself in?" I didn't understand.

"For the murder of Patrice. I'll sign a full confession. Admit to the break-ins. Everything. I obviously can't lie about what happened last night, but I hope the judge will be lenient on Zoey for what happened."

"But you didn't do any of those things. . . . Why take the blame?"

"I'm dying, Darcy," he said simply. "And Zoey has her whole life ahead of her. She deserves to live it."

I wasn't sure I agreed with that. We sat in silence for a moment before I said, "Why are you telling me all this, Jonathan? Why track me down here today?"

"The Anicula can't fall into the wrong hands. It needs to go to someone who appreciates its power and can protect it. You, Darcy."

"Me? What makes you think you can trust me with it?"

"I've been watching you," he said. "I see the way you are with your sister. With your aunt. With Mimi Sawyer. The Elder verified that you're the right person to trust. You will figure out what to do with it."

I was honored and at the same time horrified. What was I going to do with the Anicula? Could I cast a spell on it like I had Melina's diary?

"When I stole the Anicula," Jonathan said solemnly, "I hid it in the one place she'd never think to look. Under her nose." He reached into a smashed shadow-box on the floor next to me and pulled out Elodie's baby rattle. He shook it and it made a clunky thunking noise. He passed the rattle to me. "Good luck to you, Darcy."

He rose and made his way out the front door.

I watched him go, then worked the rattle apart. Inside was a small teardrop opal.

The Anicula is shaped as a small teardrop. Because, my father said, it had brought so much pain to those who abused it.

I wrapped my hand around the stone and thought of Patrice and how she'd taken revenge on Jonathan, of Elodie and how her good deed of wanting to protect her mother from Jonathan's womanizing and help her friend at the same time had gone horribly wrong by indirectly causing Patrice's death. Of Zoey, who would do anything for love, and of Jonathan, who finally learned that love meant making the ultimate sacrifice. And of Roger, who would have given his life to save his enemy's daughter—because she was, in a way, his daughter too. And even of Andreus and his strange wisdom. His words floated back to me.

You must remember that things, that people, are not always as they appear.

As I stood up, the stone warm in my hand, I knew what I had to do with it.

I just didn't know how.

Chapter Thirty-five

"What gave me away?" Mimi asked, her big, dark eyes troubled.

I clapped my hands twice (the trick Godfrey taught me), and the diary appeared in my palms. "Watch," I said. I dropped the book on the table and it automatically fell open to the spell page. The page that had the instructions for a recantation spell.

Mimi sighed.

"Plus, Cherise mentioned how a recantation spell had to be cast within an hour of her spell. There were very few people who knew when she was going to be here."

Mimi scrunched her nose.

"But I didn't really know for certain until yesterday, when you were so distraught and went storming off over the green with the dog. You were upset that Ve was well. But what I want to know is why you did it. Why did you cast those recantation spells that kept Ve ill?"

In a small voice, she said, "I didn't want her to marry Sylar."

"Why?"

"Do you ever watch them when they're together?" she asked. "Really watch them?"

"I . . . I think so."

"They laugh. They smile. But they don't really look at each other. They don't look at each other the way . . ."

"What?" I prodded.

"The way you and my dad look at each other. They don't look at each other like they're in love," she went on quickly. "And I don't think anyone should get married if they're not in love."

I let out a slow breath, not quite knowing where to start. I decided to bypass the whole part about me and Nick and said, "But that's not for you to decide."

She slumped on the swing. "So I heard."

"Ah. So that's what the Elder was talking about." I recalled what she had said to Mimi in the meadow.

You cannot always control what is going on around you. Nor should you, even if you believe you're doing the right thing.

I added, "She knew what you were up to."

Mimi threw her hands in the air. "How does she know? I still don't understand."

I put my arm around her and drew her close. "Maybe it's not for us to understand, but for us to just accept."

"I don't have to like it."

I laughed. "No. You don't."

"Are you going to tell my dad?" she asked.

"Nope," I said. "You are."

She looked aghast. "Why would I do that?"

"Remember that whole responsibility thing the Elder was talking about? Taking responsibility for your actions is part of that."

Her lower lip jutted. "I think I'm going to go watch *Survivor* with Ve and Archie." She stomped off, and I smiled. Sometimes she reminded me a lot of a teenaged Harper.

Missy lifted her head, and I patted it. "Want to go for a walk?"

She jumped up and wagged her tail.

I grabbed her leash from the mudroom and set off around the village green. The Roving Stones tents still flapped, but for some reason it didn't feel so ominous anymore. I circled around and waved to Mrs. P and Vince inside Lotions and Potions.

Tourists laughed and window-shopped.

A tiny orange kitten sat in the window of Spellbound Books. I peeked in and saw Marcus moving another large bookcase while Harper supervised. What would happen with them, I wasn't sure, but I hoped it would work out.

As I neared the Charmory, I was surprised to see the lights on, and even more so when I saw Elodie in the window, taking down the crystals that hung there.

When she saw me, she waved me inside. Missy bounded ahead as we went in, and I blinked at the store's transformation. Gone was the magical, colorful wonderland, replaced now with cardboard boxes that reminded me a lot of Patrice's house.

"What's going on?" I asked.

Elodie set a crystal into tissue paper and carefully rolled it. "Andreus Woodshall made me an offer I couldn't refuse."

"What kind of offer?"

"He wants Connor and me to join the Roving Stones. We accepted. It's time for a change."

"Wow," I said as Missy sniffed around.

"It's a good time," she said. "Roger's out of the hospital and doing well. Thankfully, the gunshot missed all vital organs. Things here have been settled," she said quietly. "I trust you to take care of my mom's place and to have that yard sale. It's time to start living my life. Our lives. Mine and Connor's. We've been in limbo for so long. It's time to move on."

"When will you leave?"

"After my mother's funeral next week we'll meet the

Roving Stones in Portland, Maine." She wrapped another crystal. "I think Andreus asked us to join only because he thinks I have the Anicula, but that's okay. I'm going to embrace the opportunity. Connor and I always wanted to travel."

"What you said yesterday about not wanting the Anicula if I found it . . . is that still true?" I just wanted to be sure.

She nodded. "I'm not going to even ask if you did find it. I don't want to know. If you did, do with it what you will. Just be careful."

The tear-shaped stone was burning a hole in my pocket. "Will there be a wedding soon?" I asked.

"I hope so, Darcy. But I'm not sure. The curse . . ." She pressed her lips together, and I could tell she was trying not to cry.

"I'm not sure you are cursed," I said softly.

"Why do you say that? Look at all the things that have happened. That's not just bad luck."

Okay, maybe she was a little cursed, but she hadn't been responsible for her mother's death, and she needed to know that to truly move on. "Jonathan's powers as a Foodcrafter weren't taken away by the Elder."

Her hands stilled. "What are you talking about?"

"Your mother wished them away. And also wished that whatever food he made would make people ill."

Confusion played across her face. "Who told you that?"

"Jonathan. Apparently, it was in retaliation for the breakup."

She sighed. "Which was my fault."

I couldn't argue with that, but it was likely Jonathan's relationship with her mother wouldn't have lasted anyway. "But don't you see? She misused the Anicula, too."

Holding my gaze, she said, "We were both cursed."

Again, I couldn't argue. "Curses are made to be broken, Elodie. Maybe you can change your fate."

Closing her eyes, she said, "I can't change the past, as much as I'd like to." She pulled her shoulders back, lifted her chin. "I bet you regret taking on this job."

Laughing, I said, "I can't say you didn't warn me."

She sighed. "Maybe you're right, Darcy, about my fate. I can't change what I've done or what's happened, but I can move on. Try to put this behind me. Start with a clean slate."

"I think that's a good plan." I happened to have one of my own. "But are you ready to put it into action?"

"Do you have something in mind?" she asked.

I smiled. "What are you doing on Sunday?"

"Why?"

"There is a wedding all planned—it just doesn't have a bride and groom anymore. I think it's the perfect day for you and Connor to get married, don't you?"

Darkness was falling as Missy and I headed home. I had a lot to do before Sunday, since Elodie had readily agreed to what I had in mind.

A loud bark had me turning around. I screamed as Higgins rose up and put his paws on my shoulders. He licked my face.

"I think he likes you," Nick said, tugging the dog off. Missy pranced around Nick's ankles and he bent down to pat her head. "Oh, are you talking to me again?"

She licked his hand. I wasn't quite sure what had gotten into her where he was concerned, but she seemed to be over it. I wiped drool from my cheek with my sleeve. "Ew. Dog slime."

Nick laughed and stepped closer to me. "He's not the only one who likes you, you know."

I suddenly noticed he was holding something. It was a daisy. He handed it to me. I closed my hand around its stem and tried to find my voice. It was hiding.

"Mimi mentioned you liked daisies," he said. "And

peppermint patties. And old movies. And cartoon-themed T-shirts. She's not very subtle."

"No," I finally said, rubbing delicate petals with my fingertips. "This is very sweet," I said, holding up the flower. "Thank you."

Missy and Higgins were tussling in the grass. It looked like Missy was winning.

"Mimi insisted I bring the flower to you," he said.

"Oh." I was disappointed. I didn't want it because Mimi had nagged him to give it to me. I wanted him to *want* to give it to me.

"It's not what I wanted to give you," he said quietly.

He touched the tip of my chin, nudging it upward so I would look him in the eye. What I saw there in the shadowy depths stole my breath. My heart.

"Oh?"

He took a step toward me. He was close. So close. Our chests touched. Our noses. Our foreheads. My heart beat a crazy rhythm. Or maybe that was his heartbeat. I couldn't tell.

His hands skimmed up my arms, along my neck, and settled on my jaw line. His touch was light, delicate. It sent waves of heat spiraling through me.

In a whisper, he said, "I wanted to give you this."

As if in slow motion, he leaned in, pressing his lips to mine. I melted into him. Into the kiss. I wrapped my arms around his neck, wanting to lose myself in the kiss. In him. If only for one glorious moment.

Somewhere down the block a car honked. Higgins barked. Missy yapped and chased him. Suddenly, I was falling. I landed atop Nick, and he let out a whoosh of air, then started laughing.

I wasn't sure what had happened until I saw the dog leashes tangled around our legs. I glanced at Nick and started laughing, too.

We spent the next few minutes untangling each other.

A car cruising by caught my attention. It was a pink village police cruiser. Glinda met my gaze with a blank expression and slowly drove off.

Nick hadn't noticed her at all as he unraveled the leashes. Finally freed, he said, "Darcy?"

I focused on Nick. "Yeah?"

"What do you think about a date?"

My heart was doing that drunken leprechaun thing again. "I'd love to." *Please not coffee. Please not coffee.*

"Maybe you could come over for dinner? We can watch a movie? Even an old one," he said with a smile. He helped me stand up as he navigated the leashes.

I thought about being snuggled up with him on the couch, eating popcorn. I didn't even care what we watched—as long as it wasn't *Survivor*—but I kind of hoped that Mimi would be around to watch an Elvis movie. I tucked my hands into my pockets and felt the Anicula there. I bit my lip. "I'd really love to, but first . . . maybe we could do something else together. Something a little dirtier."

His eyes flared, then narrowed. "Why do I have the feeling we're not thinking about the same definition of dirty?"

Laughing, I told him how I'd found the Anicula. "I want to return it to where it belongs."

His brows snapped together. "And where's that?"

"With Andreus Woodshall's grandmother."

"Isn't she dead?"

I nodded.

"Maybe you should tell me what you have in mind. And please don't tell me you're planning to dig up a grave."

"Technically, it's a crypt. I thought we could break in and—"

He pressed a finger to my lips. "You have the Anicula?"

I nodded.

"Why not just *wish* it back inside that crypt?"

I gazed at him, moved his finger aside, and said, "That would be easier, wouldn't it?"

"I really don't want to have to arrest you for grave robbing."

"Technically, it's not robbing. It's returning."

He kissed me again, and I think I forgot to breathe. He pulled back and said, "Make the wish, Darcy."

Chapter Thirty-six

Technically, two nights ago with Nick I made two wishes, the second of which sent the Anicula back to its rightful place alongside Grandma Woodshall—a wish that included an addendum that the Anicula never see the light of day again. Better to be safe than sorry.

But my first wish? It was also about being better safe than sorry.

Because even though I'd optimistically told Elodie that curses were made to be broken, I had ensured with a wish that hers would be. Whatever happened to her from here on out was of her—and destiny's—own making.

It was a true fresh start.

And as I sat here on the village green in a white wooden folding chair, I watched the very beginning of that fresh start.

Next to me, Mrs. P snuffled and wiped her eyes. "I just love weddings."

"Me, too," Mimi whispered, sitting on my other side. Her eyes were wide with wonder as she watched Elodie and Connor exchange vows.

It was a glorious Sunday evening. The sun hung low in the sky, getting ready to set, birds chirped, and a gentle breeze kept the temperature from being too hot.

Nick looked over his daughter's head at me and smiled. His arm was draped across Mimi's chair, which allowed his fingers to rest softly on my shoulder.

Ve sat in the row in front of me next to Harper, who, I noticed, held hands with Marcus.

My PI license had arrived in the mail yesterday.

I smiled as I saw all the orange cat hair on the back of Harper's pink dress—she was so in love with that kitten, I wouldn't have been surprised if she'd brought it with her to the ceremony, tucked away in her purse.

Ve had come alone—Terry still refused to come out during daylight hours. She said they were taking their relationship slowly. But I knew Ve, and she wasn't one for patience. How soon before she started planning her next wedding? Or...how soon before Terry became an ex again? Ve wasn't one for long-term commitments, either.

I studied her profile. If she had any ill will because this should have been *her* wedding, she didn't show it. In fact, I'd never seen her looking happier.

In the front row, I was glad to see Roger and Yvonne sitting together. He had his furry arm curved around her, and their heads were bent close. It looked like all had been forgiven.

I stole a surreptitious glance to the left of Mrs. P. Starla was wiping tears as Elodie and Connor placed gold bands on each other's fingers. She was still pouting over Lazarus's love-'em-and-leave-'em attitude and had sworn off men for the foreseeable future.

I glanced over at Evan, who stood in the reception tent near a banquet table with a lovely three-tiered wedding cake on it. He was smiling ear to ear as he looked on. No one loved a wedding more than him.

There was a painful ache in my chest as I watched the exchanging of vows. I couldn't help thinking back to another wedding, years ago, when I'd stood in front of family and friends and repeated vows that would eventually be broken by someone I loved.

Biting my lip, I also thought about how on that day I'd missed my mother something fierce yet somehow still felt her presence around me. It had been comforting.

I hoped right now Elodie felt the same—that her mother was there with her, wishing her nothing but happiness. It was, I figured, what all parents wanted for their children.

Nick's fingertips skimmed my shoulder, and I turned to look at him. He met my gaze, held it, and slowly smiled.

My heart ached again—but this time because it was so full. I was taking a risk falling for Nick, but like Ve, I believed in second chances.

Even if it was a second chance I was giving to myself.

A clean slate. A fresh start. A heart that has finally healed.

I smiled back at Nick as the officiate boomed, "You may now kiss your bride!"

We all clapped when Elodie and Connor kissed, and I had to blink away tears. I was thrilled all this had worked out. Elodie had already had a dress, Ve had returned the cake to Evan, the venue was already set.... The only thing that had changed from Ve's planning was that the Sorcerer's Stove wasn't catering the event. In fact, it had closed completely.

It took some last-minute finagling, but everyone pulled together to have a pot-luck reception. Every guest had brought a dish. It wasn't the fanciest affair, but it was certainly full of love for the happy couple.

As everyone rushed forward to congratulate the bride and groom, I made my way toward Yvonne. She put her arm around me. "I couldn't have wished for anything more lovely."

"I don't think any of us could." I nodded toward Roger. "You two look happy."

"I've moved back home."

"What changed?"

"Roger," she said. "And that gunshot. He said while he was lying there bleeding and thinking he wasn't going to make it, all he could think about was me. And how he wasn't going to be able to tell me how sorry he was. Or show me how much he truly loves me. That's all I've ever wanted to hear, Darcy. I better go—he's motioning me over." She gave me a squeeze and hurried off to her husband.

I watched as he wrapped an arm around her and grinned, looking less like a grizzly and more like a teddy. A happy teddy.

I turned to look for Nick, and in the distance, I saw a man standing under the tree near Mrs. P's bench. I recognized the silhouette—it was the same man who'd been watching the house earlier in the week—and it wasn't Vince.

I walked over to him. "I thought you'd left." The Roving Stones had packed up earlier that afternoon.

"Without saying good-bye?" Andreus said. "Never. It was a lovely ceremony."

I nodded.

"And you look lovely as well. You're glowing with white light—the darkness is gone."

"I'm glad to hear that."

"However, I thought you might want to keep this, just in case." He held out the agate sphere. "It served you well, and will continue to protect you as long as you keep it in your possession."

The last time I'd seen it was when I'd thrown it in Patrice's house. I took it from him and gave him a hard stare. "I thought you couldn't go into Patrice's house."

He smiled slyly. "I may have been lying about that."

"And about breaking into Patrice's?" In light of the agate ball, I suspected that Zoey hadn't been the only one doing so over the past year and a half.

"That, too, from time to time when I'm in town."

"And following me around?"

He conceded his guilt with a nod. "I thought you'd be the one to finally find the Anicula. I had to keep a careful eye on you in case you found it."

"And if I had?"

"I would hope you'd return it to me."

"And if I refused?"

"I would take it from you."

His eyes narrowed and the hairs rose on the back of my neck—it was the feeling I'd been having all week. After she kidnapped me, I thought it might have been coming from Zoey—but it had been Andreus all along.

I was glad my instincts were right that I couldn't trust him to return the Anicula to its rightful place. He had lied about everything else—I had no doubt that he would have kept the Anicula. Used it for himself.

"Well," I said brightly, "it's a good thing I don't have it."

"Yes. A very good thing."

As I held the agate sphere tightly, I thought again of big bad wolves in disguise and regular old sheep. And how sometimes it was nearly impossible to tell them apart.

"I must be going," he said, bowing slightly. "Until next time, my dear."

"Next time?"

"The Roving Stones will be back in a few months. I look forward to seeing you again." He smiled and strode away.

Funny, but I wasn't looking forward to that at all.

"Is everything okay over here?" Nick asked from behind.

I turned and smiled. "Better now."

He put an arm around me and led me back to the reception tent. "What's that?" he asked, nodding to the sphere.

"My third boob."

He stopped dead in his tracks. "What?"

I laughed and laughed. "Long story."

"I have time, Darcy Merriweather. All the time in the world for you."

I leaned in close to him and smiled. I confess, I'd thought about making a third wish on the Anicula. One that would guarantee things with Nick and me would work out.

But in the end, I hadn't. I'd given myself that second chance and decided to trust that I wasn't going to end up with a broken heart again.

I glanced up at him.

So far, so good.

Read on for a sneak peek at the next
Wishcraft Mystery,

The Good, the Bad, and the Witchy

Coming in Spring 2013 from Obsidian.

The longer I lived in the Enchanted Village, the more I realized that not only did magic live here but also the truly eccentric.

There were some strange, strange people in this neighborhood.

Including eighty-year-old gothic maven Harriette Harkette, who was throwing herself a girls-only birthday party to celebrate the big day. She had hired As You Wish, my aunt Ve's personal concierge service, to plan the black-and-white-themed party—which was taking place tonight.

Ve shouted to be heard above the thumping music. "Are you sure you hired a stripper, Darcy?" She adjusted the black rose flower arrangement on the refreshment table.

The flowers, named Witching Hour roses, were quite stunning. They were a midnight black—Harriette's favorite color—and had recently won international awards and acclaim from elite rose societies for being the first naturally black flower ever cultivated. However, the roses still felt a little morbid to me—the dark color reminded me more of a funeral than a celebration.

Trying to ignore Ve's question, I checked the food platters. There were plenty of hors d'oeuvres, but the birthday cake, the centerpiece, hadn't yet arrived.... I pulled out my cell phone and sent a quick text message to my good friend Evan Sullivan, owner of the Gingerbread Shack, the local bakery, asking how soon till delivery of the beautiful three-tiered cake he'd made.

The deejay played a dramatic drumroll, and I looked up as the door to the party room slowly opened.

All smiles, Harriette slinked in. The women went wild.

I'd never seen anyone who slinked before, but Harriette did. One long stride after another—she looked ready to launch into a tango at any moment. She threw her arms in the air. "Let the party begin!"

"Staying Alive" started playing, which I thought was the deejay's form of retribution for all the glares he received during "I Will Survive" earlier and Harriette speared him with a glowering look.

He pretended to ignore her. Wise man.

In my opinion, Harriette possessed a Dr. Jekyll and Mr. Hyde complex. One minute, she was happy as could be, the life of the party, and the next minute . . . a viper. I hoped tonight her fangs would stay sheathed.

"Velma! The place looks glorious!" Harriette kissed both of Ve's cheeks—and then both of mine.

She cast a dubious glance at my dog Missy, who growled low in her throat.

Harriette leaned down and growled right back.

Missy bared her teeth, and I scooped her up before she could take a nip out of Harriette's bony ankle.

Harriette screamed money. Tall, lithe, with gaunt cheeks, a long nose, and a pointed chin. Razor-sharp blue eyes, crisp white hair pulled back into a fancy hairdo. Diamonds dripped from her earlobes, her neck. A long black gown hugged her thin frame, and its cuffs and hem were edged in white feathers. A diamond-crusted belt cinched her tiny waist. Sparkling silver peep-toed heels showed off crimson toenails, completing the outrageous outfit.

An enormous yellow diamond glittered on her ring finger, and for the millionth time since learning she was engaged, I wondered about her supposed fiancé.

Louis.

Harriette never revealed his surname, so unless he was of the Cher or Prince mindset, she was probably keeping it mum on purpose. As far as anyone knew, Louis wasn't from the village, and Harriette revealed frustratingly little about the relationship.

My cell phone buzzed.

"Excuse me," I said, stepping aside to check the message. I shifted Missy to the crook of my left arm and opened my phone. The display revealed: *Michael left an hour and a half ago.*

The message was from Evan, responding to the text I sent him a few minutes ago. I frowned. Where was Michael Healey, the bakery's deliveryman, then? The Gingerbread Shack was just across the square—it shouldn't have taken him but five minutes to drop off the cake.

I texted back (not easy when holding an irritated Schnoodle): *No sign of him. Or the cake.*

"The Wickeds have packed their five-dollar bills, Velma," Harriette said loudly, eyebrows high, "so I hope the stripper is outstanding. Young, hot, sexy." She wiggled her hips.

I wondered what constituted "young" to an eighty-year-old. Because it was true I'd hired a stripper, but according to his bio, he was pushing seventy. I suddenly had the feeling the joke wouldn't go over as well as I'd hoped. If I didn't fix this soon, I was sure to see Harriette's fangs tonight.

I bit my lip and shuddered at the thought.

"Is your fiancé young, Harriette?" Ve asked oh-so-casually.

I had to give it to my aunt—she had no qualms about prying into other people's affairs.

Harriette pursed fire-engine red lips. "Louis is a bit younger than I am, it's true."

"How much so?" Ve pressed.

My phone buzzed.

Evan: *I can see van in lot.*

Me: *How? Superhuman vision?*

Him: *Binoculars.*

I didn't even want to know why Evan had binoculars at the bakery.

"Enough to make me feel young again," Harriette said with a long, drawn-out sigh. She glanced around, and her snake eyes narrowed on the empty spot on the dessert table reserved for the cake. "Has the cake not yet arrived?"

I smelled venom in the air and said quickly, "I'm going to go check on it. I'll be right back."

Stepping out would also give me time to walk Missy and make a phone call. I wondered how expensive a last-minute exotic dancer would be. . . .

I pushed my way through the pub-goers and out onto the sidewalk facing the village green. I clipped on Missy's leash, set her down, and looked around. The village looked nothing short of incredible. The Harvest Festival was in full swing. A huge bonfire lit one end of the green, and a Ferris wheel anchored the other. In between were booths and carnival rides and even a mock haunted house — all attractions to lure in tourists. But underneath it all, below the surface, something crackled in the air. Magic.

It made me smile. This time of year was special to Crafters. Halloween, which was next weekend, was our biggest holiday celebration.

The square was packed with tourists and villagers alike. The moon, a waxing crescent, hung high in the sky, the night was mild, the fall foliage glorious, and I wished I could enjoy it fully.

Unfortunately, I couldn't grant my own wishes (one of the Wishcraft Laws), which meant I had to find a young, hot, sexy stripper ASAP.

I nibbled a fingernail and thought about the "entertainment" Web site that had been recommended to me by Evan. I didn't remember seeing a phone number, but as it was the only local place to hire strippers, once I was done out here I would borrow Ve's smartphone to access the site and see if I could reach someone in charge to change my order.

Missy and I dodged a gaggle of window-shoppers as we made our way toward the public parking lot adjacent to the pub. During our walk, I couldn't help thinking about single dad Nick Sawyer, and how young (okay, he was thirty-five, but still), hot, and sexy he was. Alas, he wasn't a stripper (I could dream), but the village's police chief. We'd been dating since the end of the summer.

I turned the corner, and sure enough, the Gingerbread Shack's delivery van was parked at the back of the lot, near the path leading to the Enchanted Trail, a paved walkway that looped behind the square.

The Ghoulousel's (a ghost-themed carousel) calliope piped a happy, perky tune amid the backdrop of all the other sounds. Bells, whistles. Murmured voices. Squeals from small children. Laughter.

I was enjoying the ambience until Missy suddenly stopped short.

"What?" I asked her, looking around for anyone hiding in the shadows along the pub's stone exterior.

She growled.

Not a warning growl, but something primal. Almost fearful.

Goose bumps raised on my arms. I picked her up. "You're freaking me out, Missy."

It didn't help that she was trembling.

The calliope suddenly sounded ominous as I doubled

my pace and made it across the parking lot in record time. Cupping my hands around my eyes, I peered into the delivery van's window. On the driver's seat were a cell phone and sunglasses; an empty lemon-lime sports drink sat in the cup holder, and a fast-food take-out bag rested on the passenger seat. There was no sign of Michael.

Try as I might, I couldn't see into the rear part of the van.

Pinpricks of fear poked my spine as I walked around the van to the rear doors. The wind kicked up, rustling leaves and bringing a chill to the air. Missy started growling again. I held her more tightly and told myself I was being silly, that Michael was just fine, the cake was fine, that everything was fine, fine, fine.

But . . . lately, the village hadn't been so idyllic. There had been murders here—cases that I'd helped solve.

Maybe that's why I was being so paranoid. I had murder on my mind—never a good thing when creeping around in the dark.

Michael probably just went over to the festival—it *was* hard to resist its lure. There were caramel apples over there, after all. Lots of them. They certainly tempted me.

In fact, after Harriette's party ended, Nick and I had a date that involved one of those apples. We also planned to ride the silly rides, and play the outrageously priced games. I really couldn't wait.

Swallowing hard, I pulled the door handle and jumped out of the way as though I expected the bogeyman to leap out.

Fortunately, for my sanity, he didn't.

Inside the back of the van, Harriette's cake sat proudly, looking beautiful with its black-and-white motif.

There was still no sign of Michael.

My ponytail slashed across my face from a sudden gust of wind. I tucked it into the collar of my turtleneck as I tried to figure out how to carry the cake into the pub myself. Missy continued to shake, and I startled when I heard voices on the Enchanted Trail. Old-fashioned gaslights and white twinkling lights strung in the trees illuminated the shortcut path that led from the parking lot to the paved trail. A couple emerged, holding hands and snuggling against each other.

I relaxed a little, trying not to let my anxiety get the better of me, but as they passed by, Missy growled and wriggled. I set her down and she took off toward the trampled dirt path, stretching her leash to its limits.

She beelined for something lying in the brush. Something that suddenly brought back those pinpricks.

A shoe.

A large sneaker.

So out of place that it made me nervous.

Glancing around, I advanced slowly. Wind whistled through the trees, echoing eerily above my head. The faint noise carrying from the carousel's calliope suddenly sounded keening instead of peppy. "Wh-what did you find, Missy?"

Missy half-growled, half-cried.

My heart beat so hard I could feel it in my throat.

Fine, fine, fine, I sang in my head.

The shoe lay on the edge of the path, upside down in the long grass. I held up my cell phone, using its glow as a flashlight as I looked around the shrubby area.

Missy pulled me deeper into the tall brush, her nose to the ground. Suddenly she let out a loud *yap* and then started whimpering.

My hand shook as I aimed my cell phone her way. The wind stopped, and the night was deafeningly quiet as the light fell upon my worst nightmare.

A bloody sock-covered foot stuck out from beneath a mound of branches.

ALSO AVAILABLE

FROM

Heather Blake

It Takes a Witch
A Wishcraft Mystery

Darcy Merriweather has just discovered she hails from a
long line of Wishcrafters—witches with the power to
grant wishes using spells. She's come to Enchanted Village
to learn her trade but soon finds herself knee-deep
in murder...

"Blending magic, romance, and mystery,
this is a charming story."
—New York Times bestselling author Denise Swanson

"Magic and murder...what could be better?
It's exactly the book you've been wishing for!"
—Casey Daniels, author of Wild Wild Death

Available wherever books are sold or at
penguin.com
facebook.com/TheCrimeSceneBooks

Juliet Blackwell

Hexes and Hemlines
A Witchcraft Mystery

Lily gets called away from her vintage clothing store to give the police a witch's take on how the leader of a rationalist society could be murdered, surrounded by superstitions he discredited.

Evidence points to dark witchcraft. Lily's determined to use magic of her own to find the murderer, before everyone's luck runs out.

"As delectable as the previous two…A cleverly written, top-notch cozy mystery." —4 Stars, *Romantic Times*

Also available in the series
A Cast Off Coven
Secondhand Spirits

Available wherever books are sold or at
penguin.com

facebook.com/TheCrimeSceneBooks

VICTORIA LAURIE

The Psychic Eye Mysteries

Abby Cooper is a psychic intuitive.
And trying to help the police solve crimes
seems like a good enough idea—but it could
land her in more trouble than even she could
see coming.

Available wherever books are sold or at
penguin.com

OM0014